For A, A and A

PART ONE

CHAPTER I
GLASS

9.11.1938

Picture this. Two SA men in tan uniforms, wearing swastika armbands, black riding boots and matching holsters, their faces glowing with artificial warmth, drops of perspiration on their unwrinkled brows. They stand, thumbs in their belts, fixated on the scene before them – pleased with what they see. One of them wears round eyeglasses which reflect the flames raging through the synagogue in front of him. The two men stand in awe of the ferocity of the fire. They have been tasked with 'protecting' the synagogue from the organised mob; members of their own SA unit, dressed in mufti, who had earlier ransacked the ornate eighteenth-century building. Laughing, shouting, throwing Torah scrolls onto the pavement, setting them ablaze – *smells a bit like roast lamb, don't you think?* – or smearing pig shit on them.

Everywhere, the sound of fire-fractured roof beams crashing, explosions of glass, some of it showering onto the street below. The Berlin fire department hoses down adjacent buildings, but does not direct water at the fire itself, which is now spurting ferociously from every window and doorway. Aside from the hiss and growl of the conflagration and the shouts between firemen, there isn't much noise. Sometimes a fireman's boot crunches broken glass. Onlookers stare and marvel. Some smile.

SA-man Jürgen Meißner turns to his companion. He tells him an old joke.

'An old Jewish tailor told me this. For a Jew, he's a decent enough fellow…'

'No such thing,' his companion interjects mechanically, not averting his eyes from the blaze.

'Well, this was before. And he is a good enough tailor. Anyway, this old Jew tells me this story. It seems that some other old Jew is crossing the street and is hit by a car. The driver gets out, is very sorry and tries to comfort the man, who is groaning on the pavement. He puts a folded-up blanket from the back seat under the man's head. The victim then opens his eyes and gives a small smile of thanks. The driver asks him, "Are you comfortable?" The old Jew shrugs, "I don't know about comfortable, but I make a living." Jews are good at jokes, I think.'

Jürgen's companion doesn't share in the laughter.

'That miserable little Jew-swine spoke the truth, at least. For them, it's all about money.'

Jürgen nods, continuing to stare at the burning synagogue.

Kristalnacht had begun.

—<o>—

Max was alone, sipping a beer at the counter of the Roxy Bar, known by some as 'the missing persons' bureau'. If someone were late coming home, their wife would ring the Roxy before contacting the police. Six years ago, before Hitler, almost all of Berlin's artists, actors, dancers, writers, movie directors and musicians could be found there, perched on stools or lounging within incongruous easy chairs, arguing, laughing, drinking and flirting into the late hours. By now most had disappeared; into exile – to the United States, France, England, even Hungary. Jews mostly, a communist or two. Definitely quieter now – a missing persons' bureau of a different, darker hue. New faces, with Aryan features and uncontroversial notions had begun to appear, but most of the clientele hadn't yet lurched with the country to the Nazis, or if they had, managed to cover their party badges before arriving. Anyway, at the Roxy people rarely discussed politics. 'It makes too much stress. Better to gossip.'

This evening was an exception. The conversation had been about Ernst vom Rath, whose death a few hours before was in all the late editions. This harmless looking man, a nondescript bureaucrat in the Paris embassy, had been shot by a seventeen-year-old Jewish boy.

The Roxy's owner, Willi Bauer, was absently drying a beer glass. He leaned across the bar towards Max. 'But why would anyone, especially a Jew, do such a thing, Schmeling? For what purpose? It only can bring out worse.'

Max shrugged. 'At that age people sometimes do crazy things.'

The telephone rang.

'It's for you, Max'.

'Who can it be this late?'

'He didn't say, but that it's urgent.'

It was David Lewin, Max's tailor.

'Hallo, Lewin. Are you alright?'

'Yes, Max, so far we're fine, but I can tell you, we are very worried. Especially the boys. They're really frightened.'

'I've been hearing about it. Bad business. Listen, why don't you send them to me at the Excelsior. They can stay in my suite for a while. I'll be there in twenty minutes. Use the back streets. They'll be OK.'

'Won't this make trouble for you?'

'Let me worry about that, Lewin.'

'Maybe I should send them in a taxi?'

'It's not that far, and you'll never find one at this time of night. Just tell the boys to stay on the back streets and put caps on to cover their hair. They'll be fine.'

CHAPTER 2

TURNING BACK THE CLOCK

The boy was trying to enjoy a small glass of kosher wine. 'You only get to have one Bar-Mitzvah, son,' his father said, 'so you can live a little. But only a little.' No one thought to laugh.

He stroked the blue velvet bag. On it a silver hand-stitched star of David, inside a new prayer shawl, *yarmulke,* and prayer book, as well as leather *tefillin* in its own smaller velvet bag. The house smelled of cakes, flowers and furniture polish, and there were newly fluffed cushions on the chairs.

He could smell rosewater when his mother leaned over to kiss him. She was wearing her new blue frock; a family present for her last birthday.

'Use these every single day without fail, Herschel, his mother said, 'and thank God for your loving family, and especially for your wonderful father who made this for you.'

He put on the shawl, his father straightening it at the back. He then tried the black silk yarmulke.

'It keeps slipping off. Why won't this stay on?'

'That's because your hair is too long,' his sister Esther smirked.

'You are beginning to look like a girl with all that hair,' his brother Mordechai added.

He stuck out his tongue in response. 'Maybe I can borrow a hairpin, *Momme*, to keep it on.'

'Even better, Herschel,' Mordechai laughed, 'take some lipstick too.'

He made a move towards Mordechai, but was restrained by his mother.

'We don't fight in this house,' she admonished.

The moment subsided. 'I'll love showing off the tallis and *yarmulke* in *shul*,' he announced. 'It's the only place I feel at home, I feel safe. Except here, of course.'

—◂o▸—

Before Hitler came to power, the boy had idolised Max Schmeling and rejoiced when his German compatriot won the heavyweight championship of the entire world in 1930, although he won it on a disqualification.

'He was beating Sharkey throughout, not so?'

They were standing with him in the corner of the schoolyard unofficially reserved for Jews. There was Wolf Weiss, who would delight his friends by bringing small cakes from his father's bakery, Schmuel Rapaport, whose mother had been married once before to a man who died on the Somme, and Joseph Rosenstein, who was good with numbers. They formed a circle around the boy.

'Everyone knew Schmeling was way ahead.'

No one argued with him – though small, his fists had a reputation of their own.

'And that low blow that stopped the fight, Sharkey did

this because he knew he couldn't win.' His peers nodded sagely.

'And then after that, didn't Max beat that Stripling, even knocking him out in the fifteenth round?'

'Why did he wait so long to finish him? Answer me that, Herschel,' asked Rosenstein, who was the tallest of the four.

Almost everyone was taller than he was.

'He was just playing around with him, cat and mouse, to show who is boss. That's how a proper champion behaves. Everyone knows that, even you, Rosenstein.'

When Schmeling faced Sharkey again in 1932 and lost on points, he shared in the general German outrage.

'How could they give it to that loser Sharkey??! Our Max was miles ahead. No contest. It's those biased American judges who cheated us.'

But his brother wasn't interested. 'Boxing is for gentiles,' he said.

◄o►

After Hitler became Chancellor, the boundaries of the boy's world began to close around him, as if on casters. The changes were gradual but relentless. The first official restrictions against Jews seemed inconsequential, perversely beneficial.

Zindel put things into perspective.

'Is it not actually a blessing for you, Herschel, that Jews are now excluded from military service? This isn't for you a disappointment, is it?'

As each new regulation slid gradually into place, his father continued to offer optimistic consolations.

'For you, at least, it's no misfortune that Jews are now prevented from sitting examinations in medicine or dentistry. You hate the sight of blood, not to mention that your mother and I have to keep reminding you to brush your teeth, and when was the last time you passed an examination?'

Home was the boy's refuge; he was fearful of leaving the house alone, even of walking to school. He tried to stay alert when outdoors, avoiding any groups of young men in the street, hiding from the government lorries which ambled noisily, loudspeakers blaring. *Anyone who doesn't belong in our country, leave! And soon! If you don't, we'll make it bad for you.*

His thoughts screamed: *but I was born here, idiots!* But he kept *shtumm.*

'It's so unfair! I have to watch myself every minute when I go outside. Even at school. They all look at me. Always. As if I'm some sort of monster, or some sort of... I don't even know what. I can feel people's eyes following me. It's all so unfair!'

'But what can we do?' his father asked. 'We can't push back the clock, Herschel. Who knows, perhaps things will change back again. Maybe people will soon see what that man is and kick him out. We must trust in God, Herschel.'

'But why doesn't God listen?'

'We should leave Germany for good, Zindel,' his mother said. 'We should all go to Palestine.'

The children agreed.

'Rivka, you know how hard it is to get in. The British have locked all the doors.'

'We should keep trying,' she said.

When the family's welfare payments, meagre as they were, stopped abruptly, Zindel could offer no consolations.

'But without a letter, without a warning, just stopped,' Rivka said.

'Pointless to enquire,' Zindel said. No one argued.

The Grynszpans instantly became much poorer.

Over time, new thoughts continued to jab at the boy's mind, photographs in the newspapers showing his champion at one of those Party Day celebrations. *Why is Schmeling so friendly with those Nazi bigwigs? How can he let himself be a Hitler pin-up? Is Max a Jew-hater too?*

His support of the German champion waned quickly; his pugilistic allegiance soon shifted to the Californian, Max Baer.

'This other Max, this better Max, a breath of fresh air,' he proclaimed to his mother. 'He's an antidote, that's what he is, an antidote. With his curly hair, and always smiling, and very witty, and what a suave boxer! And he's a Jew! He even wears a large white star-of-David on his boxing shorts!'

But Rivka wasn't so sure. 'He's not even properly Jewish, Herschel. Not by his mother, only by his father. And maybe not even by him. Who can say with gentile women, who they go with? But I agree, it's nice of him to remember Jews on his boxing trunks.'

CHAPTER 3
CAN YOU SHOOT A GUN?

'What are we going to do with you, Herschel?' Zindel asked, during the short walk to the school. The boy didn't reply. It was a mild spring day, a gentle breeze promising warmth, extravagant birdsong filling the air. But as they walked down the Burgstrasße, the Grynszpans were enveloped in wintry thoughts, as if the spring blessings were denied to them alone.

'When your mother and I tell you something, you ignore us, just standing there like a statue, biting your nails, looking who knows where.'

He didn't respond.

'I know it's been hard for you, Herschel. This is natural at your age, but you must make a special effort, particularly now, with all this craziness going on. An effort at home, an effort at school…'

'I'm not staying on at school. I told you before. The others treat me like dirt, they stare at me, they pick on me. I fight back, but always get blamed for everything.'

—◆—

Dr Berger rose as they entered his office. He offered his fleshy hand to Zindel and Rivka, then pointed to the three chairs in front of his desk. All sat, the boy in the centre. On the wall behind the Principal, the ubiquitous portrait of Hitler. Three-quarter view. Unsmiling.

However, Dr Berger did smile.

'So, Herschel, young man, today a decision, yes?'

'I have decided, Herr Principal, that I want to leave school now, as I am of the legal age to do this. You know that I have not been happy here. I have been picked on, just for being a Jew, and this has affected everything.'

Dr Berger opened a yellow folder.

'Truthfully, Herschel, I think we can say that you were never a good student, even before. Hardly ever doing your homework, arguing all the time, getting into fights. But here it also shows that your grades have actually improved a bit since 1933, which given what you say, is surprising. And since repeating the sixth grade, you have shown some slow progress. But this is not surprising, as you are quite intelligent, a trait shared by many Jews, as my long experience can attest to.'

He smiled knowingly at the Grynszpans.

'I understand what you say about bullying. I must admit that it occurs. Regrettable. I try to stamp it out. But one can't be everywhere. It is of course natural that students from your folk community tend to band together, as in fact they have some reason to feel apart from the others, since this is a German school, and you are not German.'

'I was born German.'

'Well, it may be true that you were born *in* Germany, but the definition of German-ness is more complicated, as we now know.'

'At least the Jews don't pick on me.'

'But the teachers, they have all been considerate?'

'Mostly. Except for that Frau Rausch, who last week made me stand up in front of the whole class, next to that giant imbecile Wolf Martins, so that she could show the differences between a Jew and an Aryan.'

He looked to his silent parents for some sign of support, or even mild outrage, but each stared down, as if they too were being chastised. Dr Berger closed the file.

'This is all of little importance now, I think, given your decision. I understand that the government is soon planning to restrict German schools only to Germans, so perhaps you have decided to leave at the right time.'

Dr Berger smiled warmly and rose. 'Let me take this opportunity to wish you and your family all good wishes for the future.' The three Grynszpans went home.

―◦―

'This is not a good situation for you, Herschel. You have no diploma, your Principal's report says that you are 'mean-spirited, sullen, taciturn, sly...'

'They hate all Jews. What can you expect? Do you believe that Nazi?'

'Maybe you forget that you were even kicked out of the Jewish Day Centre. They asked for you to leave, again for arguing, for fighting. Your mother and I pleaded with them, so they let you stay, but only a few weeks later you were expelled. Because if you came up with any crazy idea, you'd tell everyone, and then if they disagreed, you'd punch them. Even at home I've seen this anger in you.

The veins in your forehead and neck sometimes stand out with rage. Over little things, trifles.

'So what now to do? No diploma, no skills, you remain argumentative, sullen. In such a situation as this, what are you good for?'

He stood there biting his fingernails until his mother pushed his hand away.

'Maybe I can be a fighter for Jews. At the Maccabee Sports Club, some of my friends are now applying to emigrate to Palestine. They say that even the Nazis will help them. So maybe that. Maybe the whole family can go.'

'But you left the Maccabees.'

'They wanted everything to be so military! Everything organised. Just like the Hitler Youth.'

'And you'd know all about the Hitler Youth, yes?' Rivka asked.

The boy glowered.

—◄○►—

The following week, the boy and his parents, dressed in their finest High Holiday clothes, arrived at the offices of Hanotea Ltd.

'Let me straighten your tie,' his mother said, pushing his hands away. 'First impressions are very important.'

He scowled. 'In photographs from Palestine no one wears ties. I should take it off. That will make an even better impression.'

'In Germany, we still wear ties,' his father said, ending the discussion.

They climbed the stairs, opened the glass panelled door. They were greeted by a stout, middle-aged man, sitting behind a small desk. Behind him stood acres of shelves, rising to the high ceiling, filled with box-files. Noisy traffic could be heard through the window. A small portrait of Theodore Herzl, the founder of Zionism, was fixed to the wall behind. On the desk, two smaller signed photographs, in silver frames, of Haim Weizmann and David Ben-Gurion, current leaders of the Zionist movement.

'Levy,' the man announced. He stared at them. 'You are?'

Zindel introduced himself and his family in Yiddish.

'Let me stop you there, Grynszpan,' Levy said, holding out his arm like a traffic policeman. 'In Palestine, in the Land of Israel, we do not speak Yiddish. Understand? It is the language of the *shtetl,* a bastardised amalgam of Hebrew and German. In Palestine we are building a new land out of the barren dust and ashes of the old, and so you will understand that Yiddish has no place. We need a new kind of Jew as well; therefore only Hebrew. But as I see from your faces that you don't speak the language, today we can do our business in German. I assume you are here about emigrating.'

The Grynszpans nodded in synchrony.

'I am a Jew and I want to help build Palestine.'

'Good lad,' Levy said, while writing their names in the large book. He then looked benevolently in their direction. He leaned back in his padded armchair.

'The official name of this company is Hanotea, which

means 'the planters'. It is actually a citrus fruit company now importing German agricultural goods into Palestine. But it is also aligned with the Jewish Agency, which is where I come into the picture.'

His visitors nodded politely.

'Emigrating is definitely a good idea, especially now. So to the whole world's surprise, we have managed to make a deal with both the Nazis and the British. The deal is called *Ha'avarah*. This is how it works. First, you put your money into a blocked account – it is frozen until you arrive in Palestine. Then, when you arrive, the Jewish Agency takes about a third of it, in order to help more people emigrate and settle. The German government also gets a third. The rest of the money you can keep, but only in the form of German goods which are sent to Palestine and bought by Hanotea, then sold on. You get the proceeds.'

Their silence surprised Levy.

'So something is better than nothing, yes? And let me tell you, that when you get off the ship, probably they will first put you in a nice apartment in Tel-Aviv, maybe Haifa. Forget about a kibbutz – we don't send German Jews there, mainly Americans. And then you're safe, you're finally free, and then you can start a new life.'

Zindel asked, 'What about the British? I thought they were strict about anyone coming to Palestine.'

'That's the beauty part of the agreement. The funds are managed by the Anglo-Palestine Bank. It's all completely kosher. Now, tell me, how much money can you put into the account? Once the money is deposited, the British Government will issue you an entry permit and the

German Government will let you out. So tell me, how much money are we talking about? The normal amount is at least £1,000.'

The Grynszpans exhaled in unison.

Zindel said, 'We could maybe find a tenth of that, with help from relatives, but we have very little money ourselves. And the government has even stopped our welfare payments. No reasons, just stopped.'

Levy closed his book.

The boy rose, his fists clenched. 'But I want to fight for Jews. I want to fight the Arabs and the British anti-Semites. I can work, I can do whatever is required. Don't you ever take Jews with no money?'

'Rarely. We are not organised for such purposes. We're a business. It is true that sometimes we help organise passage for orphan children, sometimes young people with exceptional skills, but it's difficult. Do you speak Hebrew?'

'I have attended Hebrew school in the afternoons, and regularly go to the synagogue, three times on the Sabbath!'

'That doesn't count. Synagogue Hebrew is not the modern, living Hebrew, no comparison. Can you shoot a gun?'

'I've never tried.'

'Well, it might have been possible if you had some useful practical skills, or some kind of agrarian training, but as it stands...'

'I was a member of the Maccabees, but I left...'

Zindel and Rivka had already risen. 'Thank you for your time, Herr Levy,' Zindel said.

'Don't mention it.'

The Grynszpans closed the door quietly as they descended into the bright spring day.

CHAPTER 4
WATCHING A FILM

They were sitting on a green leather sofa, staring at a screen. June sunlight was held in check by heavy red curtains, through which only a single brilliant shaft sliced into the room. Blue-grey smoke danced upwards, illuminated by the projector. Joe Jacobs puffed on his cigar. People usually called this little man Yussel – Yussel the Muscle.

The film finished, clackering on its spool. Yussel leant forward, turned off the projector and stared at the much larger man sitting next to him.

'You see that, Max?'

'I see what I saw at ringside. He punches harder than anyone I ever saw before, maybe even harder than Dempsey.'

'Yes. Goes without saying. Louis really gave that big wop lunk Carnera a shellacking. But he still has a lot to learn, and you can teach him, Max. They all think you're a bum, Max, winning the championship on a foul, then losing it on points by not finishing Sharkey off. You were miles ahead on points, of course, but they stole it, the bastards.'

Max grinned. 'You were a picture, Joe. Running around the ring, waving your arms like a windmill, shouting,

"We wuz robbed! We wuz robbed!" over and over.'

'I shouted till I was blue in the gills, but of course they wouldn't listen. Now they think you're washed up. They're underestimating you, Max, so that's good for us.'

Yussel re-spooled the film and switched the projector back on. They stared again at the black-and-white images, ignoring the projector's noise; the silent scene of a bleached-out ring, where two men, one black, the other scared, circled each other jerkily.

'Do you see now, Max?' Joe bit heavily on his sodden cigar.

'You mean after the jab?'

'Now you got it! He drops his left after every jab. He's just asking for a right cross.' Yussel mimicked the moves.

'Maybe someone else thought of that before.'

'Well if they did, they didn't last long enough to try it out. He's just too fast for them. And anyway, they were mostly kids, or clowns, or has-beens, or no-hopers. Bums with glass jaws.'

'But Louis can take a punch. Do you really think I can beat him, Joe?'

'Certainly, or I wouldn't be sitting here looking at this cockamamie silent movie on such a nice day. Listen', he took another long pull at his stogie, 'Louis makes amateurish mistakes which he can't afford to make against you. But he'll keep making them anyway, since everyone is telling him he's so great and that no one can beat him.'

'So if I just keep moving to my left and wait for the arm to fall, I can get him?'

'It's simple ring intelligence. That's the most important

thing, a good right and an even better brain. Just keep into your crouch and make him reach out for you, make him find you, then spring up with your big right. That's all you need. We'll train for that. Anyway, the crowd will be right behind you, even in New York. They're only hoping that some white man will knock the bejesus out of that *schwartzer*. They still haven't forgotten Jack Johnson, and how he spoiled things for all their white hopefuls, and how he ran around with white women, and teased all them palookas in the ring before flattening them. OK, Louis is more polite, but he's still a nigger, isn't he? So they'll be behind you even though you're a German, because they're desperate for Louis to lose. Of course, in Harlem people will root for their own, but only on the radio, since they can't afford to come to Yankee Stadium, can they?'

'Joe Louis is a good fighter, though.'

'Not a good fighter, Max, a *great* fighter. Strong and young. Smooth and fast. But inexperienced. And maybe a little bit stupid. That will change, but not yet. The main thing is, he's black. And you're not. Let's look at the film again.'

CHAPTER 5
THE YESHIVA

'Let us look at the facts,' Zindel said. 'The facts are as follows. You have no qualifications. You have no job. Or any prospect of one. Your thoughtful brother Mordechai has already asked his employer if you could come and join him as a plumber's apprentice, even though he already knew what the answer would be. "One Jew, even a decent one like you, is enough, I think." That's what Herr Dollman told him. And now Mordechai is worrying about his own job.

'More facts. We don't have enough money. The welfare is gone. My few tailoring jobs are flowing away like rainwater in the gutter. So you'll need to find something to do to help us. But what?'

'I've been thinking about this, *Poppe*. I've been thinking about what I could do to help the family, to help us emigrate to Palestine. But how? Especially after our meeting at Hanotea. So, I've been thinking that perhaps they don't only need muscles in Palestine, but maybe they need rabbis, too. After all, with all those Jews living together, in a new place. And also, you know that I have always been very observant. I go to *shul* every day, I celebrate all the holidays and observances, and I think I could be a good rabbi. So maybe I could train to be a rabbi and emigrate that way. Afterwards the whole family can come.'

'You mean to go to a Yeshiva?'

'I guess so, if some way could be found to send me.'

Zindel and Rivka regarded him silently. Then Rivka rose and walked to the kitchen. 'Tea is good when decisions need to be made.'

'Better schnapps,' Zindel said.

'We can't afford it, and anyway, he has enough time to be a drunkard on his own. We don't need to help him.'

Zindel turned to his son, offered him a half-smile. 'This might not be such a stupid idea. In any event, it would keep you somewhere more-or-less secure instead of roaming the streets of Hanover, so easy for them to pick you up and send you who knows where. But this also involves expense, this Yeshiva.'

Rivka returned with three glasses of lemon tea, but without any lemon. 'Lemons are too expensive nowadays,' she announced, as if this were news.

The boy became more animated. 'I was talking to Michael Solomons the other day. You know him. His father was the other kosher butcher, the one on the Johanstraße, the one that was just closed down. He said that the Jewish Community Centre is willing to support someone who wants to go to a Yeshiva. And they'd pay. And there's a particular Yeshiva in Frankfurt, not the big famous one, but a small one in the old ghetto, that might be a good place. And I could live and study there, and you wouldn't have to give me any money.'

'They would do that? Even with things as they are?'

'Absolutely,' he guessed.

He sent letters.

—◁◦▷—

He almost tore the letter in his haste to open the envelope.

'They've accepted me! *Momme, Poppe,* they write that I can come right after Rosh Hashanah. And last week, the JCC said that if I was accepted, they would send 15RM a month for support.'

'We must prepare for this,' Rivka said. 'Zindel, maybe make him a new suit? He'll need a new coat too, by the way.'

—◁◦▷—

They took an early train to Frankfurt, and the brisk morning walk from the station to Ostendstraße filled him with wonder. *It's so big! So many theatres, cinemas and cafes!* As usual, most had signs stating: 'Jews are unwelcome here'. *The same Nazi flags and banners, and the same SA thugs walking in pairs.*

'Remember, Herschel, as we walk, never look anyone in the face, and get into the gutter if any SA or police come along. And move quickly, like you're going somewhere official.'

'I know this, father. It's the same at home.'

'It doesn't hurt to remind ourselves.'

It was an old building in an even older street. They were greeted at the door by Rabbi Lippmann Rachow, the headmaster.

He looks so old, with a genuine rabbi beard. A kindly face, though, through all those whiskers.

Reb Rachow smiled warmly at them, took the boy's small suitcase and ushered them into his office.

It was a small, austere space. Four straight-backed chairs and an old wooden table, piled with papers and open books, filled most of the room. All available wall space was covered with shelves, on which heavy volumes groaned, their spines written in Hebrew, in German, a few in Russian.

Reb Rachow spoke to the Grynszpans in Yiddish.

Not like that fat Levy at Hanoteah, the boy thought.

'It's wonderful that you have brought to us your son to begin his studies,' he said. 'Nowadays, not so many young people are interested, and as a result, we don't have that many scholars with us. Still, we have just enough.' He looked at the boy and smiled with his eyes.

'Herschel, I tell this to all the boys, so why not you, eh? The word "Yeshiva" comes from the root of the Hebrew verb *lashevet,* which means "to sit", *sitzen.* And sitting in the classroom, or at your desk in the dormitory, studying the wonderful holy books, that is what you will do most of the time. And you will enjoy it so much, that you won't even notice the time going by! But to do this you will need to develop the bottom-flesh, *sitzfleisch,* so that you can concentrate all your attention on your learning. It goes without saying that we also have other activities; young men need to get exercise, to stretch out and smell the air.'

Rachow paused to gauge his response. The boy smiled.

'Let me show you the classroom and your dormitory.'

The Rabbi led them down a musty corridor to the

31

classroom, a teaching space which doubled as a small synagogue.

'You'll sit here.' He pointed to a place on one of the wooden benches set up as school-desks, in three rows, facing the ark where Torah was kept.

Maybe there are cushions, the boy wondered.

'This is where you will develop your *sitzfleisch*. After a year or so, you will sometimes sit in another room, around a large table, where you young scholars can discuss the things you have learned, especially the book of laws, the *Mishna,* and the fascinating commentaries that great scholars have made upon those laws. This is called the *Gemara.*'

I know about these things already, so I can make a good start.

The three then walked over to the dormitory, once a capacious room, now cramped. It smelled of old shoes, books and tears. He first noticed the four triple bunks, constructed of rough wood on which rested horse-hair mattresses covered with striped sheets. There were four wardrobes and four sets of drawers, constructed from the same wood as the bunks. Along the length of the far wall, a long table, over which shelves of books loomed. A small black stove on a flagstone plinth occupied the centre of the room. Four small windows threw sunless light onto the floor.

'Soon, the other boys will come and show you around, and they will make space for your clothes in the wardrobes.'

Zindel left soon afterwards, satisfied about the accommodation, and pleased by the Rabbi's affable gravitas. He looked forward to telling Rivka, Mordechai and Esther all about the place, about the relief of speaking

Yiddish, and how at home Herschel seemed, even on his first day. He was just able to catch the early afternoon train back to Hanover.

Alone in the dormitory, he sat on a bottom bunk, his suitcase at his feet, as if he were waiting for a train. For the first time in months, he felt optimistic.

Such a relief. I'm sure I will fit in here. Maybe even make some friends. And I'm really looking forward to my studies. Who knows, in five years, I might become a rabbi! And then we can all go to Palestine.

◄o►

His first visit home was to be a joyous occasion. The family had been planning it for days.

'But why, Rivka, do we have to get our meat at Mendel's? So expensive.'

'Because there's nowhere else. I told you before. They closed down Solomon's shop. And when I asked Mendel why his meat is so expensive, do you know what he said?' She tried to imitate butcher Mendel's sing-song voice. *Do you think, Mrs Grynszpan, that it's easy to get kosher meat nowadays? Now that kosher slaughtering is banned in Germany? And by the time I get the meat from Denmark, and it meets the approval of the rabbis, for how long do you think it keeps? If only people bought more kosher meat, the price would go down, but so many are now eating mostly fish, even God forbid, vegetables.'*

Zindel relaxed. 'Well, I suppose for such a special occasion, a bit of flanken is not such an extravagance. So long as there's plenty of potatoes and vegetables.'

'Thank God,' Rivka said, 'the outdoor vegetable market is still Jew-blind.'

—◦—

From the soup course onwards, the boy couldn't stop talking, his napkin tucked into his shirt-front.

'I didn't think I'd like it at first, but getting up early and praying three times every day I now find very satisfying. The regularity of it all, the daily study in the morning and afternoons, all this routine calms me.

'And I've definitely learned something about sitting, that's for certain. But it's easy because the studies are wonderful. You know how I love the Torah, all those stories about Abraham, Moses, Joshua, Kings Saul, David and Solomon, back in the days when the Israelites were heroes and warriors. We have also started on the *Mishna*, the book of laws derived from the Torah.'

Mordechai looked across at his younger brother. 'We *all* know what the *Mishna* is, little *pischer*. You're telling us something new?'

He ignored Mordechai. 'The *Mishna* is now my favourite study. In it, an observant Jew can find all he needs to know about everything. Everything has a law; everything has a place. Eating, working, property, marrying – everything is covered. With these laws, we are no longer rudderless, and when we have our own land, we can put them into practice!'

'This may take some time, Herschel,' his father said.

'I asked Reb Rachow how can we fight against what the Nazis are doing to us. He answered, "We must have

34

faith, Herschel. And we must be patient. He alone has the power to save us. As He has done before, in the Sinai, by parting the sea, and giving us manna for food, and when He acted through Esther against the murderous Haman. He will save us again." I told him, I'm young, I can wait. And when I am a rabbi in Palestine, I can help build a home for our people.'

◄o►

His next visit was at Chanukah.

As the meal began, his sister, Esther, asked, 'So, Herschel, how are the studies going? Have you developed more *sitzfleisch*? Turn around and let me see.'

Mordechai tittered.

He ignored them. 'I am still enjoying my studies and have even made a few friends. Minshkin is my best friend; he shares my desk. He's from Berlin, by the way. We sometimes go out for walks together – don't worry, we are very careful – and even sometimes we have some tea in the Jewish Café not far from the Yeshiva.' He looked down at his plate, a solitary dumpling floating amongst thin noodles and a lone carrot in a pale-yellow liquid.

'But, I have to admit that I'm having trouble with the *Gemara*, the books of commentaries on the laws. In the *Mishna* everything is clear, the laws are straightforward, and everyone knows how he should behave in order to be a good Jew. But the *Gemara*, that's another matter. There are too many different opinions. We read that Rabbi Elazar says one thing, Rabbi Yehoshua says another, and Rabbi Gamaliel another thing entirely. For example, we spent four entire days discussing what should happen if a farmer's bull strays into a neighbouring field and gores a pregnant cow to death. Does the farmer pay damages just for the cow, or for both the cow and the calf? For four whole days we discussed this, reading all the opinions from those old scholars, who all lived in Babylon hundreds of years ago. And at the end I was no wiser. I got into trouble for suggesting that maybe the story was there to tell us to build better fences. So I don't really know what to think.'

But what were you expecting, Herschel?' his father asked. 'It's a Yeshiva. In a Yeshiva you study such things.'

'I know, but I thought that they would be also teaching me all about how to be a good rabbi, how to help other Jews out with their problems. Not to be a lawyer. But maybe I'll see the point of the *Gemara* later.'

—◄o►—

He came home again in April, in time for Passover. He had always loved this festival, especially the *Seder* meals, the glasses of wine, the reading of the story of the Israelites escape from Egypt, not to mention the food, now somewhat less copious than in previous years – all this followed by wonderful songs. However, on this visit he was more subdued. He took part in the ritual, but went to bed immediately after the *Seder*. The next day, he handed his parents a letter from Reb Rachow.

My Dear Mr and Mrs Grynszpan

Your son Herschel is a boy of average intelligence. But he is lively, curious, and good-hearted. From the beginning, he was not the most dedicated student, but, especially at first, he seemed to settle in with the life here, with his studies and with the other students.

However, it has daily become clearer that, sadly, your son doesn't have the diligence or the commitment for this life. He's too interested in the outside world. He is interested in clothes, in popular music, even in Cafés, where he sometimes goes out at night, or so I have been informed.

However, the main problem which prevents him from continuing with us is his anger, especially if people don't agree with him. He had a violent argument about some obscure section of the Gemara which resulted in fighting. Another student was injured. Nothing serious, but this we cannot tolerate.

Don't be too hard on him. He is seeking his way, as most of his age do, but is everywhere blocked.

Generally, however, he is a most sympathetic and delightful person, and I'm certain that he will do well in the future. I pray that he and your family will soon find yourselves in our Holy land of Palestine.

I wish for him and for you all good things, and blessings from the Almighty,

Rabbi Lippman Rachow

CHAPTER 6
THE MURDER OF WILHELM GUSTLOFF

David Frankfurter, born in Croatia and the son of a rabbi, was a twenty-three-year-old medical student when the Nazis came to power. He immediately left Frankfurt and moved to Bern, Switzerland, where he continued his studies. He was a small young man, full faced, brown haired, and well dressed for a student. Outwardly composed, there was a rage seething within him. His soul paced angrily. He felt he must do something, anything, some large dramatic act which would call attention to the suffering of his people.

Frankfurter bought a short-barrelled Browning revolver with the intention of travelling back to Germany and killing Hitler, or Goering, or Goebbels, or whoever was most convenient. But on reflection he thought his odds of approaching any of them, still less succeeding in an assassination, stood close to zero. However, the need to kill someone in order to avenge his people's plight was festering in his mind. He decided to act nearer to home.

Wilhelm Gustloff was the perfect target. He was head of the Nazi Party organisation for Germans living in Switzerland. An infamous anti-Semite, he had recently organised the Swiss publication of the notoriously fabricated *Protocols of the Meetings of the Learned Elders of Zion.*

On the evening of 3 February, David Frankfurter had a meal of sausages, kraut, potato salad and beer in the Rathaus, then slept soundly, the Browning revolver under his pillow.

The next morning, after a croissant and coffee, he made his way to his target. On arrival, he was greeted by Gustloff's wife, Hedwig, who had once been Hitler's secretary.

'I need to see Herr Gustloff on important business.'

Frau Gustloff ushered him into the house.

'My husband is very busy. He's on the telephone at the moment. He will see you soon, but you mustn't keep him for long. Can I tell him your name?'

'It won't mean anything to him.'

'Please make yourself comfortable in his study.'

It was a large room, a Persian carpet obscuring most of the parquet flooring. An ornate desk dominated the room. Several photographs and certificates filled the wall above Gustloff's desk. One of them was a large photograph of Hitler in his SA uniform, thumbs in belt, unshakable will set into his face. The photograph was conspicuously signed: *To ever faithful Party member Gustloff, with cordial wishes, A. Hitler.* An SA honour dagger dangled on a cord attached to the corner of the black frame.

Gustloff could be heard on the landing above, talking loudly, laughing, then closing his conversation with the customary *Heil Hitler.* The sound of his footsteps preceded him.

He stopped at the doorway, stared pointedly at his guest. He was in his SA uniform, replete with boots, armband, leather belt and swastika tie pin. This pleased David Frankfurter. *A proper Nazi. And an SA Stormtrooper as well!*

'So here I am. As my wife told you, I am very busy at the moment. What could possibly be the purpose of your visit?'

Without speaking, Frankfurter took two steps toward Gustloff. He removed the Browning from his jacket pocket, pointed at Gustloff and fired four shots. Noise filled the room and echoed throughout the house. All bullets found their target, and Gustloff fell to the floor, blood gushing from his head and torso onto the Persian carpet. Frau Gustloff rushed into the room shrieking. David Frankfurter pushed past her and calmly left the house, gun in hand. He made directly for a police station, where he turned himself in. *Escape is probably impossible,* he thought, *and in any event, what function would it serve?*

'Do you not regret what you have done?' the police inspector asked.

'Not in the slightest. By killing this pig, I have sent a message to the entire world.'

In Berlin, Propaganda Minister Josef Goebbels immediately put the press into action:

The criminal bloodlust of the Jews finds another victim!

A World-wide Jewish Conspiracy uncovered!

Jews living in Germany must take responsibility for this outrage!

And so on.

That evening, Goebbels wrote in his diary: 'This Jewish pestilence must be eradicated. Totally. None of it should remain.'

Hitler agreed. 'The whole of Jewry is responsible for this. This gang of criminals.'

But there was some delay. Two hours after the assassination, the Winter Olympics began in Garmisch-Partenkirchen. Hitler's call for a 'spontaneous demonstration against the Jews' would have to wait. In fact, an order was soon issued to all SA, SS and police. *Throughout the winter and summer Olympic Games, all anti-Jewish actions are prohibited.* As a result, signs forbidding Jews from entering shops, cinemas, restaurants and theatres were removed, although few Jews were brave enough to test the change. 'Jews only' carriages on streetcars and trams were trundled into sidings. Yellow park benches were repainted dark green. This state of affairs lasted until late August.

The week following the Olympics' closing ceremony, things returned to normal. Aryan-only signs re-appeared, dingy streetcar carriages rattled through streets, and casual, daily insults were resumed.

Rigorous medical and psychiatric tests had confirmed that David Frankfurter was healthy in body, and remarkably free from any mental illness. He was speedily brought to trial. Hitler dispatched one of his best attorneys, Friedrich Grimm, to represent the German government's interests in court.

Frankfurter pleaded guilty and was sentenced to eighteen years in prison at hard labour. At his trial, he explained his motives. 'If you ask me why I made the decision to kill Gustloff, I can tell you the following: a wave of hate against everything that was connected to the Brown Shirts or Nazis overcame me.'

Attorney Friedrich Grimm voiced the German government's outrage. 'Cold blooded murder is a capital crime and deserves the death penalty!' The court was not persuaded. Luckily for Frankfurter, Germany was never to gain jurisdiction in Switzerland.

Grimm reported back to Goebbels. *I'm convinced that this young straying Jewish student could not have committed this crime on his own initiative. It bears all the hallmarks of International Jewry, who have always been pulling such strings.*

Gustloff's lavish state funeral was attended by Hitler, Goebbels, Goering, Himmler and other luminaries of the regime. Thousands of Hitler Youth lined the route in the rain as the flag-covered and flower-strewn catafalque was pulled through the town. Hitler delivered the funeral oration.

The international Jewish conspiracy is behind this degenerate act, and if any further act of armed hooliganism against the iron will of the German Reich is encountered, the consequences will be severe and thorough. We understand this challenge, and we accept it.

After the service Hitler took the widow's hand in both of his, looked into her eyes and said, 'Germany will ever honour your brave and loyal husband. On my honour and on the honour of the German people, I promise that those who are responsible will be made to pay dearly.'

CHAPTER 7
UNCLES

He met old Katz the watchmaker on the steps of the synagogue.

'Do I not know you, young man? Aren't you that Grynszpan lad? I remember you from when you were little. Tell me, how are your parents?'

'Why not visit? They'd be happy to see a friendly face again. Then you could ask them yourself.'

The next evening Katz arrived, carrying a small brown box tied with string. There were six shortbread biscuits inside.

'I brought something else as well.'

The old man removed a cloth bag from his jacket pocket and handed it to Zindel, who looked inside, then up at Rivka. 'Coffee beans. Real coffee! I could smell them before you took them out of your pocket. Rivka, smell.'

Katz smiled at their pleasure. 'Almost impossible to get, especially for us Jews, but as you know, I have my contacts.'

'Come, sit,' Zindel said as he pointed to the only stuffed chair in the room.

Katz moved slowly to the chair and sat down with a grateful sigh.

'Have you injured yourself, Herr Katz?'

'My limp? Nothing serious. Shrapnel wound from the Somme. Weather aggravates it. But one good thing comes from this. I still get my invalidity benefit. The Nazis have agreed not to remove it, not even from Jews, but only if they were front-line soldiers in the war. So I suppose I am lucky. So where is Herschel?'

'He's still at the synagogue. He takes his observance very seriously nowadays.'

'Maybe it is better we are on our own. You see, Herr and Frau Grynszpan, it is essential for all of us Jews, especially the young ones, to escape Germany as soon as possible. Zindel, I spoke to the boy. He has a crazy idea that they will take him in Palestine. I didn't want to tell him that this is nonsense, but only mentioned that he might have a better chance getting there from France than he would from Germany. Anyway, who can tell? It's possible. The main thing, he leaves Germany. A boy like Herschel cannot stay here under such conditions, where a Jew is not treated as a person, but lower than any animal.'

'This is not news, Herr Katz,' Zindel said. 'So why now especially?'

'Did you not hear about this Gustloff business in Davos? Believe me, the Nazis will use any excuse to make things worse and worse for us. The Nuremberg Laws are just a beginning. Of this, you can be certain. Take my advice, just ship him away somewhere. Do you have relatives in other countries? Best would be in America or Canada.'

◄o►

The Grynszpan family were dispersed across several European countries. Zindel's mother, Gika, had remained in Poland. But her five sons had settled westward, Zindel in Hanover, Isaac in Essen, Wolf in Brussels, Solomon and Abraham in Paris. 'An impoverished version of the Rothschilds,' they would tell themselves.

They were family, but they didn't get along. It all centred on money. Their mother wrote letters.

Dear child.

I write you letters and you are silent. I am after all your mother. Why do you treat me this way? Every day I await some answer from you, you may not wish to know anything about me, but I, your mother, wish to know about how you are doing, what you are doing, how your health is doing, how your wife and my grandchildren are doing. Also, as you know times are very hard for us here. Any small amount of money you could send would be a great kindness, a Godsend.

Believe me, I am crying as I write this letter. My dear son, I don't know how I have offended you. Please write and send money. All our hopes here are placed in you.

Each letter was identically worded. The five brothers ignored their mother, her letters, and each other, each believing that the others were holding out.

'But family is family, Herschel, even if we don't get along so well. And families will always help each other – if absolutely necessary. I think the best thing is for you to go to France, on the condition, of course, that my brother Abraham will take you in. I can even send him a little money for your upkeep, but you'll need to find work there, or maybe help him in his shop. I'll write to him.'

Two days later, an answer arrived from Abraham, agreeing to take the boy, perhaps even to adopt him, which would allow the boy to remain in France, and to become eligible for French citizenship.

Zindel was livid. 'Straight away, even before Herschel arrives, he offers to adopt him and take him away from us for good.'

'Abraham is just trying to make things smoother,' Rivka said. 'No one wants to take him from us.'

Zindel showed the letter to the boy. 'You can stay with Abraham and Chava in Paris. They say they are happy to take you in. I will send him some money for your upkeep, a little I put away before the welfare stopped.'

'I don't even know them. And now they want to adopt me?'

'Don't pay attention to that nonsense. No one is going to adopt you.'

'I can't even remember what they look like.'

'You met them when you were little. Before all this craziness.'

'I hope Uncle Abraham is not so sour as you are.'

Zindel looked up at his son. 'Show me a Grynszpan who smiles.'

◄o►

Exit visas were required. He arrived at the central Hanover police station three days later. Perched on a high stool at

46

a long wooden bench, he completed the documents in his neatest hand, then handed them to the desk sergeant, who looked seriously at the papers, then at him. Sergeant Stöffel then clarified the situation.

'If you are to be allowed to exit Germany, you are under the legal obligation to return within nine months' time. After that date, you will be forbidden ever to return. But somehow, I believe that we won't be seeing you again, not so?'

The sergeant stamped the papers forcefully, then handed them back to him.

'Have a good journey. Try not to come back.'

'It might be easier, Herschel,' Zindel said, 'for you to get into France by way of Belgium. That's what Katz said. So last week I wrote to your uncle Wolf and aunt Leah in Brussels. They wrote back agreeing to take you in for a few weeks. You can stay with them until you can get papers for France. Of course, later, once you arrive in Paris with Abraham and Chava, you might have to remain there for some time. By then, things may have changed, and a visa for Palestine might even be possible. Because the main thing is to get you to Palestine. We don't want you to turn into yet another wandering Jew.'

◄o►

The platform was crowded. As they waited for the train he said, '*Poppe, Momme,* I'm still so worried. I know no one in Paris, not even uncle Abraham and Aunt Chava. I don't speak the language, so I'll be a prisoner with them.'

'They'll look after you,' Zindel said, 'and you'll soon

learn French, it's not so hard. Or so I'm told. You can even start learning while you are in Brussels.'

'But what will I do there, *Poppe?* I'm only fifteen?'

'It will be fine, Herschel, you'll see.'

Rivka said, 'You may be only fifteen, but see how grown up you look in that new suit and coat your father made.'

'You'll be shaving before you know it,' Mordechai teased. 'Certainly by the time you're thirty. Unless you grow a rabbi beard.' He was rewarded with an ironic smile.

Rivka had crammed his small suitcase with his *tallis* bag, four pairs of underwear, two shirts, a second pair of trousers, five pairs of socks, and five handkerchiefs. She also packed a family photograph from 1932, when he was eleven and the family was as reasonably happy as Grynszpans could be.

As he boarded the train, his mother began to weep softly. Mordechai and Esther smiled solemnly. He shouted to them through the din of the station, leaning out of the train window.

'You're sad because you'll miss making fun of me, that's what.'

'Absolutely. Without you, who will we pick on? Mordechai said.

'We'll have to take turns with each other,' Esther added. They tried to grin.

The train pulled away. The journey took eight hours.

◄o►

Uncle Wolf was waiting for him at the railway station, holding a small sign on which the word 'Grynszpan' was written in an uneven hand.

Who needs a sign? I would recognise him anywhere. Small like Poppe, same nose, same beard, same forehead, same sour face. He even stands like him, one foot in front of the other, ready to run away at any moment.

Hands were shaken solemnly, then the two walked quickly away from the station. They boarded a tram.

No special trams for Jews?

'Everything is in French,' the boy said, gazing out of the window.

'So what do you expect, Chinese?'

'I've never left Germany before. Everything is strange, but also it's nice without swastikas and SA everywhere.'

As he entered the flat, he received two kisses from Aunt Lea. Then the three sat down for tea. *With lemon!*

'Did your father not send you with any money to help with your upkeep?'

'It would have been impossible to bring it out of Germany, even if he had.'

'He's a tailor. He could have sewn something into your jacket. It's not unknown.'

'There's no extra money to send. He thought that you would help me.'

'Does he think that we have so much? That it's easier here to make a living? You think we eat lemons every day?'

'At least you don't have the Nazis breathing down your neck every minute.'

'That's true, but even so, times are hard. Especially for little people, especially for Jews. You think Germany has the only anti-Semites?

'Listen, Herschel, this is how it is. We can feed you,

but there's nowhere for you to sleep, as you can see well enough. There's only our bedroom, and this room which has to be our kitchen, dining room as well as living room. During the day, I do my tailoring in here, sometimes into the evening. So where would you sleep?'

He surveyed the room. *Did Poppe know about this?*

'But where *will* I sleep?' He could feel tears beginning to form.

'You mustn't upset yourself,' Aunt Leah said, reaching over to touch his arm. 'It's all arranged. We have a neighbour who has a spare bed. Zaslawsky. Nearby. Only a street or two. He has offered to put you up. You can sleep there and have your meals here.'

So now I have to sleep in the house of a complete stranger? Tears pushed at his eyes, but he suppressed them.

Wolf said, 'The main thing is that you need to get an entry visa to France as soon as possible. You can stay in Belgium a few weeks. Maximum. In Paris, your Uncle Abraham and Aunt Chava will have more room for you.'

The next day he went with Uncle Wolf to the French Embassy.

'They're unlikely to speak to you in German, even if they can. This is because of the war. So only French. I can translate for you.'

Wolf helped him fill in the forms, which were detailed and complicated. They had to wait for two hours before being called to the visa desk. He tried to talk to his uncle, but Wolf seemed preoccupied, only offering monosyllabic replies.

Then Wolf said, 'Herschel, no one likes the sound of Yiddish here. Keep quiet.'

He let his thoughts wander as he waited – remembering the Yeshiva, passages from the *Mishna,* that terrible Passover *Seder*, his old friends at school, missing his family, and missing his synagogue.

They were finally called to the desk, their surname mispronounced.

The officer was brusque but friendly. Wolf translated.

'How much currency will you be bringing into France?'

'I am only allowed to take 10RM out from Germany. That's the new law. At least for Jews.'

'That's not nearly enough. French law prohibits the importation of indigent refugees. Without financial backing, I can't see what we can do. Perhaps you can somehow obtain proof of economic independence.'

'But sir, I am only fifteen years old and the Nazis treat me like a dog. I have an uncle in Paris who will look after me. I have brought his letter with me as proof of this. And I want to work. Not to be a drain on France.'

'I'm truly sorry, messieurs, but that is the law.'

On the way back, Wolf said, 'Look Herschel, don't worry. We will find a way. Maybe you can get a permit for Palestine.'

'No. It will be the same business all over again. The Zionists only take Jews with money.'

'We'll think of something. Some way to get you out. If not to Palestine, then into France at least.'

CHAPTER 8
KNOCK HIM OUT!

The boy meets Zaslawsky in the hallway.

'An old man and his bladder make frequent nocturnal excursions together. That's my excuse. But why are you up, Herschel? It's late, maybe 3am.'

'Do you remember? You said that I could listen to the Schmeling-Louis fight.'

'So late?'

'It's in America. It's earlier there. Do you know, Mr Zaslawsky, I hope that this Joe Louis, he knocks that Nazi's block off! Who better than a negro to teach this *shlump* a good lesson? Some *schwartzer* giving him a real beating. That would really get to those Hitler bastards. Almost as good as being beaten by a Jew!'

Zaslawsky shrugs, yawns. 'About boxing I know nothing, and care less. Jews don't box, so I have no opinion about who should win. But, Herschel, listen quietly, yes?'

The boy nods to Zaslawsky's back as the old man shuffles back into his bedroom. He walks into the kitchen and cuts a slice of day-old pumpernickel, spreads margarine on it and returns to the living room. Cross-legged in his underwear, he sits in front of a large brown radio, its calibrated dial glowing with a low mustardy light.

Just before the fight begins, he squints his eyes shut. *Knock him out, Joe!*

The German announcer is ebullient with confidence. 'Now is the showdown, ladies and gentlemen, now the world will see the power of the German folk, through the will and strength of its own champion.'

—◦—

Max hardly notices the screaming crowd as he walks, accompanied by ring officials and policemen, from the far edge of Yankee Stadium, that colossus of baseball dominating the Bronx. *So big. How can everyone see? A hot night. That might help Louis. Negroes are used to heat, I think. People cheer me as I pass, so many people. A good feeling.* He walks through a crescendo of light towards the klieg brilliance of the ring, then through the ropes, his ring-men holding them apart. He walks to his stool, where Yussel waits. He begins to speak the instant Max sits down.

'This is *your* night, Max. Louis hasn't trained enough. *Your* night. Just keep away and wait for that left to fall. And it will.'

Max nods, but only faintly notices Yussel, or the ring announcements; the introduction of movie stars and past champions. As they parade around the ring, arms aloft, waving and smiling at the multitude, Max stares blankly ahead. Jack Dempsey comes over to his corner, waving and smiling at the crowd. His face becomes serious as he leans forward to talk into Max's ear, as if whispering a secret.

'Flatten that nigger, Max.'

Then the former champion stands upright, resumes his grin, bows and gracefully passes through the ropes.

Dempsey does look like me, just as they say. Max thinks.

The boxers and their managers are called to the centre of the ring. The referee's instructions float into the Bronx night, as Joe Louis stares at Max with nonchalant menace. Max smiles back amiably. They touch gloves and return to their corners. Then the bell.

Louis hasn't trained much, Yussel says. But he looks strong enough to me anyway. Maybe he's underrated me. Let's see.

They move to the centre of the ring. They paw the air.

Keep moving, Max. Find your range. There's his jab, light this time. Louis seems completely unfazed, just workmanlike, just doing his job. His eyes have no emotion, only concentration. There's another jab. Hard. Felt it. Crouch down. Make him reach for me. Now I throw a sharp right. But it glances off him. The pattern starts early. It's like a piece of music. Jab. The themes are announced, his left jab, my right cross. We will develop these themes later. There's the bell. Not bad, not too bad at all.

Seated again in his corner, Max hears Yussel shouting at him, but he can't really respond. His mind is too full. Anyway, Yussel is always shouting at him.

━◅◦▻━

A good start, the boy thinks. *Take your time, Joe, find that Nazi's range. Find his ugly face. He's no match for you, Joe.*

━◅◦▻━

Max rises quickly from his stool as the bell sounds.

Here he comes again, leading with the hard jab. He's pretty, and fast, and quiet and smooth. Left jab, left jab. I am studying his jab from inside the ring this time, before I could only see it from outside. The angle is different. Left hook! Good punch. It hurts. I must avoid these. Move to the left. Keep the low crouch, make him reach with his jab. He telegraphs when he sets himself for a punch, so I must step back when I see it. I'll need to take more of his jabs in order to counter. My mouth is bleeding, my face is swelling. He certainly can hit. The jab, and he's dropped his left. Now comes my right cross. He felt that, I think.

─◄○►─

The German announcer's voice rises a few tones. 'What a wonderful right cross, listeners, I can see the nigger's legs shake.'

Half standing, the boy shouts in despair, then stifles the noise, listening to see if heard. Silence from the bedroom. *Don't worry, Joe, just keep at him. Shove that jab into his face. Hit him hard, Joe, teach that superman a lesson.*

─◄○►─

The bell. There's the jab. Drops his left again. Now! Another right cross, a good one. Louis certainly felt that one. I can see it in his eyes. Blurry for a moment. His concentration falters. But now he comes at me as hard as he can, but I can block him. Keep the pattern going, work the themes, make them flow. Concentrate!

─◄○►─

A two-note siren passes by outside. The boy stiffens. *Be calm, we're not in Germany anymore.* The German announcer warms to his role, his voice modulating into the hubris of certainty which he only partially feels. 'So now we see it, *meine Damen und Herren,* our Aryan champion is giving this primitive a good lesson in boxing, and with every round he becomes stronger and the nigger shrinks.'

The boy clenches his fists, staring at the radio dial, which seems now to glow more brightly. *Enough playing with him, Joe. Don't let him get to you. Take control. Show him who's the boss! Knock him out!* The round ends. He walks into the kitchen for a glass of water, almost spilling it in his rush to return.

◄○►

The bell. Back to work. He's still very dangerous. Keep away, let him jab air. Now, another right. Now he staggers and shakes. He does that little dance on his heels, but he feels that last right cross down to his feet, I think. I can just hear the crowd. Everything seems to be in slow-motion. I give him a right, and now another with all my shoulder behind it. He goes down, his legs under him. But immediately he springs up again. Foolish. An experienced fighter stays down longer. He tries to get the jab pattern going again. I give him two more rights. And now he really looks hurt and bewildered. And there's the bell.

'It's alright, Yussel, I think I have the measure of him.'

'Don't get cocky, Max. Keep away from his right. Also his left.'

Max sits, calmly noticing the canvas. *So many patches. You'd think they'd get a new one.* He looks across at his opponent.

He's slumped on his stool. His corner-men are beside themselves, hovering about him like flies on a dead horse. Shouting at him. His eyes tell me he has a muddy brain now. I too have felt this, before. His cheeks are swollen, as if he has eaten golf balls. Yes, that's good. He really likes golf. Perhaps he golfed more than he trained. Yussel is screaming at me again, saying nothing, but very loud. I feel that I have Louis in my pocket now, but just be careful, Max, he's still dangerous.

Now the bell for the fifth. But I can tell the fight is really over. This black superman has legs of rubber. How long will it go on? But I can do this all night, I feel so strong. He's like a punching bag, strung up from the lights overhead. He offers me very little, and still I hammer him with my right cross. Pop, pop, pop, every time I hit him I hear this, like water bags bursting.

—◦—

The boy is in despair, tears of anger and frustration beginning to form behind his tired eyes. Moving nearer the radio, he pleads, 'Don't let him get you, Joe. Fight back. Not just for yourself, but also for me, and for all us Jews, not to mention all the negroes.'

—◦—

Sitting on the stool in his corner, Max smiles at Yussel, who whispers calmly into his ear, 'You got him, Max. I think you really got him.'

57

I feel full of energy, full of fire. I wonder if Anny is listening? She'll be so proud. I can see Dempsey at ringside, smiling at me. I'll smile back. They look worried in Louis' corner. How can he last so long? There's the bell for the twelfth. Up, Max, finish the job. Surely, he can't take any more. He puts out a left to me, but it's only a push. He knows what is happening. I smash over it and he holds on. The referee breaks us and I follow him to the ropes. Another right. Another. Now he goes down. He won't get up. He hangs on the ropes, blinking, shaking his head. But it's over, and everyone is screaming. So am I, I think. I wonder if Anny heard it on the radio. I hope he's not badly hurt.

Max rushes over to help Joe Louis to his stool.

—◦—

The boy turns down the volume as the German announcer nearly shouts himself hoarse.

'As the negro is counted out, our Max Schmeling dances with delight, arms raised. A victory-dance. Now he moves over to the stricken Louis, offering help, but he is pulled away. A glorious moment for Germany and our Führer!'

The boy switches off the radio and goes to bed, his fists still clenched.

—◦—

The commotion in Max's dressing room continued for some time, longer than it took Yankee Stadium to empty, longer than it took for the thousands of fight fans to flow up to the elevated subway trains and begin their sweaty judder downtown. Max's small dressing-room was overflowing with a noisy cluster of newsmen and hangers-on, pushing forward, shuffling for position, shouting questions. Max sat in the centre of the room, on the rub-down table, smilingly dazed, his face swollen, his purpling left eye almost closed, his body collapsing gratefully under the multi-patterned dressing gown which had been thrown over his sweaty shoulders. Standing beside him, Yussel was discharging chimneys of energetic cigar smoke, shouting answers to the laughing, back-slapping crush, while gently placing Max's right hand into a tin bucket of iced-water.

'Didn't I tell you?' His voice could easily be heard over the din. 'Didn't I always say so? I told you we could lick Louis. See, that *schwartzer's* not so great. No one is invincible, no matter what you morons in the papers say. I told everyone that, but nobody believed me. So now all you newspaper bums know it, and now you know it real good.'

Max smiled broadly at his bustling, beaming manager. Max said, 'I even told them on the boat when I arrived, when they asked me in front of all the newsreel cameras. I told them, "I see something." And I did. I saw something.'

'We both saw something, Max. But Louis didn't see it, that's the main thing.'

A man in a brown suit and tatty fedora had been pushing his way through the noise and cameras. His large shoes crushed the discarded flashbulbs as he walked. He elbowed his way towards the boxer and his mentor.

'Herr Schmeling?' the man asked, as if the boxer's

identity was in doubt. 'May I offer you my most sincere congratulations.' He said this in German. 'But I also come at the behest of the German-American Bund.' He nodded seriously, reflecting on the weight and significance of his mission. 'They have asked me to congratulate you for re-establishing the racial order!'

Max looked up at the flush-faced man, while moving his hand lazily in the ice-water. 'Better to speak in English. I can't really understand your German very well.'

Disappointment travelled along the man's face, coming to rest on his freckled forehead. 'It's true. My German isn't really so good. I'm still learning. My father was of course fluent. You know, he came here from South-West Africa, but I didn't really bother to learn our language when I was young, and then after the war, since we lost that whole African paradise to the British… But now I think there's a real reason to speak German, is that not so, Herr Schmeling?'

'What, just to talk to me?'

'Of course, yes, but also I mean because of all those wonderful things that are happening in Germany today. But of course, you know all about this. Anyway, the Bund asked me to see if you'd speak at our next meeting in Yonkers. Everyone will be so excited if you could. In six weeks.'

Joe gave Max a small elbow in the ribs. 'Impossible,' he said quickly, clamping his cigar more aggressively between his teeth. 'Max is going back home on the *Hindenburg* before that.'

'What an honour, Herr Schmeling! To fly in this wonderful German airship. How I would love to fly in it. What a privilege! Still, you certainly deserve it after tonight. But perhaps you'll speak to us next time you come.'

Joe ushered the man through the crowd. 'Yeah, you never know, kid, you never know. And by the way, if you really want to fly in the *Hindenburg*, I can set up a fight for you with Joe Louis, that's all it takes, just beat Louis.' Joe pushed the Bundist through the door and closed it resolutely behind him.

'That's all we need,' he said, 'a Nazi fan club in America.'

—◆—

In Joe Louis' dressing room the atmosphere was altogether different, quieter, cooler. A pedestal fan was whirring metallically in the corner. Louis' face was swollen, a brown mirror of Schmeling's. He was slumped like a burlap sack of coffee beans.

The fight's promoter, Mike – also called Jacobs, but no relation, as he pointed out to everyone, whether or not they may have noticed the coincidence – busied himself with pointless activity; moving a duffel bag from one bench to another, straightening a towel. Joe's trainer, John Roxborough, a small light-skinned negro, a round-faced man with a thin moustache, told the few pressmen who had gathered for the wake. 'I had him in tip-top shape, and I know he wasn't doped, so no crazy stories about that.'

A reporter asked, 'What happened, Joe?'

'I just forgot to duck,' said Joe, staring blankly ahead. Then he looked up at them. 'I thought I could beat Smellin'. Starkey beat him, Baer beat him, even Steve Hamas beat him. And he's old. So I thought I could beat him. But I didn't know nuthin' after the fourth round, after his big right cross. After that everythin' was a fog. I went just as far as I could. I couldn't go no further.'

'Are you going to watch the film of the fight, Joe?'

'No sir. I saw all of that fight I want to in the ring.'

After the reporters left, Roxborough wagged his finger at Joe. 'I told you, didn't I? How many times did I tell you about dropping your left? He suckered you, that's what happened.'

'I know you told me, I know it.'

'But you didn't listen. That was the problem, you just didn't listen. So next time, maybe you'll listen to me. Anyway, you should spend some time out of the limelight for a while. Take the car with Marva to the country for the air and a rest. After that, we can work on your lazy left.'

'You know, I owe everything to you, John. You brought me up from nuthin' and got me this far. Don't you worry,' Joe looked up at his manager with sad determination, 'next time will be different. Smellin' won't know what hit him. But I'll tell him later if he asks.'

'If you ask me,' John said, rubbing liniment onto Louis' tired shoulders, 'it's the best thing that could have happened. You were getting too cocky. Even telling *me* what to do instead of taking my advice. But this will make you a better fighter. All the best of them suffered knockouts and then became even greater.'

'That's right,' Mike Jacobs added. 'Maybe you'll listen to us from now on.'

In Harlem that night, many store-front windows were shattered by angry black fight fans, who were in turn chased and beaten by white policemen. Downtown, newspaper editors dusted off their racist metaphors.

—◄o►—

Back at the hotel, a message was waiting for Max.

The desk-clerk beamed as he handed him the envelope.

'That's the ticket, Max. You flattened that Palooka good!'

Maybe it's from Anny. But it was a telegram from Hitler: 'Most Cordial Felicitations on your Splendid Victory!'

CHAPTER 9
A FLIGHT ON THE 'HINDENBURG'

Max had planned to spend a fortnight in New York after the fight, meeting old friends, and shopping for presents for his mother and especially for Anny. But the day after the fight he received a cable from Reichsminister Goebbels urging him to return as quickly as possible.

Yussel was not impressed. 'I just arranged dinner for you with Babe Ruth next week. He's dying to meet you. Do you mean to tell me that this pompous pipsqueak Goebbels is more important than the bambino? Well, OK. I guess it's a good thing for your country to honour you and all that, but just be careful with those Nazis. Bad business.'

'You should come to Germany with me, Joe. I accomplished this victory only with your help. If I ask them, maybe they could find you a berth on the *Hindenburg* too.'

'Are you crazy? Did Joe Louis scramble your brain with one of his stiff jabs? Look, Max, in the first place – I don't know if you've noticed – they have two giant swastikas painted on the tail of the ship – I've seen the pictures – so I don't think that I'd be a welcome flyer, if you follow my reasoning. Second of all, if, for argument's sake, I was dumb enough, and the *Hindenburg* crew were blind enough, so that I actually came with you, the second I am on the ground in Germany, they would put me on a quick train to some prison camp. Who knows? Maybe even worse. So all I'm saying to you is good luck. And take care of yourself. I'll stay here and set up the fight with Braddock while you go and make nice with them Nazis.'

Two days after his famous victory over Joe Louis, Max Schmeling and Yussel arrived at the airship mooring in New Jersey, smiling and waving to a large agglomeration of newspaper photographers.

'Look at the size of that, Joe. Like a floating steamship.'

'It's big alright,' Yussel said, 'just like the Nazis. And full of hot air.'

The silver-blue airship's tight mooring ropes creaked with strain as it tried to escape upwards into the ocean of sky.

Leaving Yussel with a hug at the gate, Max ascended the steps and was met by the Captain, whose close-cropped hair and white goatee reflected the happier times of his Wilhemine past.

'We are honoured to have you on board with us, Herr Schmeling.'

'I am grateful you could find a space for me at such short notice, Dr Eckener.'

'That would never have been a problem. We could always find room for you.'

The senior steward stiffly and nervously escorted Max to his cabin, past the large observation area with its enormous downward facing windows, its chrome framed furniture and its incongruous aluminium Blüthner baby-grand piano – 'the only one ever made, just for us,' the steward proudly informed him – past the dining room with its plush red chairs, and through a corridor of bedrooms. He opened the door to Max's room, bowed smartly and said, 'It is a great honour for me that you will take my berth. I am happy to sleep with the technical crew.'

While reading some of the material left in his room, brochures laboriously extolling the virtues and glories of the airship, others inviting passengers to motor-coach tours of Germany, Max fell asleep on the divan which would later be transformed into his bed. He awoke to the sound of activity outside. He looked out of the window. The ship's mooring ropes, held tightly by squads of running men, were suddenly dropped as other men jumped from the holding rails which might have taken them aloft. Then the *Hindenburg* rose slowly and comfortably into the cloudless sky.

Look how it glides upwards, so effortlessly, so smoothly, reaching out to its home in the clouds, Max thought.

He made his way to the observation area. Entering the large salon, several passengers turned to him, began to applaud. 'Bravo, Schmeling. *Gut Gemacht. Prima.*' Max bowed, then made his way to the windows to watch Lower Manhattan sliding gently below them.

'I thought we'd be going east,' he said to a short man next to him, who was wearing a Nazi party badge on his jacket lapel. He had a florid face and thin ginger hair. The man shook Max's hand energetically. Max pulled it away, grimacing in feigned pain, as his companion chuckled.

'Gärtner. That's me. Helmut Gärtner. Industrial temperature gauges. Supply Krupps, Siemens, lots of others – so it follows that business is good nowadays. Very pleased and honoured to meet you. Not so many heroes walking around these days, especially on airships, so it's a pleasure. Yes, we are going north for a while. They always go this way at first, just for us to have this view of Manhattan, and especially on a day when the weather is fine, such as it is today, as I'm sure you will agree, Herr Schmeling. But of course, nothing can beat a German summer's day, is that not so?'

Max nodded absently. *One of those men,* he thought, *who before Hitler were merely boring. Now they're boring for the Reich. Officially.* He decided to avoid Helmut Gärtner, if at all possible, for the rest of the flight. He knew several such Germans, rich beyond justification, corrupt in the officially sanctioned way, and unable to comprehend why most people's faces glazed over after speaking to them for only a few seconds.

Max was tired; elated but overwhelmed by his victory. He was longing to see Anny, to see her loving face. For most of the fifty-hour flight Max was able to sit peacefully in his cabin, reading an American crime novel he bought in New York, *The Postman Always Rings Twice,* alternating this with several issues of *The Ring* magazine, the most recent of which had a profile of his 'upcoming' fight with Joe Louis, and the inevitability of his defeat. Yussel had promised to send him the next issue as soon it appeared.

'It will be great seeing these know-all bums eat crow.'

The meals were excellent, the cabin comfortable despite its size. In the lounge, someone insisted on playing Lehar on the aluminium Blüthner, but only on the first day. Max occasionally wandered about the ship, sometimes sat at the windows, marvelling at the sea. Flying at 200 metres he could see ships passing below, some of which tooted their foghorns. There was much waving in both directions. Later he stood entranced as the lush green meadows and farmland of Ireland, then England, passed below.

As they were being tethered to their moorings at Frankfurt, Max leaned out of the window and waved to the large surging crowd, a sea of heads and hats and shouts. *There she is!* He could spot Anny almost immediately, standing on the back seat of a large open Mercedes, waving frantically, her white floral frock rustling in the summer breeze, her face radiant with delight and relief, her small mouth broadened into a giant smile. When she saw that Max recognised her, she blew him a garland of kisses, which he returned without embarrassment. Anny ran from the car and met him at the bottom of the metal stairs. His hug lifted her off the ground. They beamed at each other while the crowd cheered.

After being helped through the agreeably boisterous crowd by a cordon of smiling police, Max and Anny finally reached the car. The Mercedes door was held open by an SS driver. An army officer standing next to the car shook Max's hand.

'Major Sauer, Herr Schmeling. A great pleasure. I have been telling your charming and illustrious wife how much your victory means to us all. By the way, I shall be with you throughout the flight to Berlin. But now we drive to the other side of the airport, where a plane is waiting for you.'

Max looked puzzled. 'The flight? What flight? I have just been flying for fifty hours.'

'Well, this is something arranged at the last minute. The Führer himself sent his own plane to collect you to Berlin. He hopes to see you there.'

Max turned to Anny, who was still beaming at him. 'Did you know about this?'

'I was just today told about it. They telephoned early in the morning and then twenty minutes later they fetched me. A nuisance, really. You know I don't much care about all this rigmarole. I've been so excited at the thought of having you back. I'm longing to be snug in our little home together. But I suppose we'll have to see Hitler first.'

Max leaned back into the plush seat and held Anny's hand as the Mercedes threaded its way through the police cordon, the noisy onlookers leaning out as far as they could, that they might glimpse their boxing hero and his movie star wife. Some children, held aloft on parental shoulders, waved small swastika flags.

They were driven to the edge of the taxi-strip where a Junkers JU52 was waiting, its three engines throbbing. Anny gripped his hand tightly during the noisy take-off.

'Look down, Anny,' he shouted over the din of the engines, 'there's the *Hindenburg*. You see, those men are walking it to its hangar, like they are taking a cloud for a walk.'

The plane lifted itself up through the broken clouds, flying east. Anny relaxed when the engines stopped straining. Max kissed Anny on the cheek, rose and walked down the aisle to Major Sauer. He had questions.

'How do I address him?'

'*Mein Führer* is the most usual.'

Max thought about that. *Is Hitler my leader? Do I even need a leader? Was there something else, another title, Herr Reichskanzler, perhaps? That might be a good compromise. A difficult decision. I'll wait and see what happens. I'll ask Anny.*

The Major anticipated Max's next question. 'And as for the Hitler salute, this is appropriate only when you are first introduced to him, or whenever there are cameras in the room. It will be in all the papers and the newsreel, so you can enjoy the added celebrity.'

'What happens then, after we've been introduced?'

'You will probably be invited to sit around a large table, and then some very nice cakes and pastries will be offered. The two Frau Schmelings, your charming wife and your equally charming mother, will sit on either side of their host. It is all really quite informal. Not a state banquet, you know. Then, after all this tea, chit-chat and cakes, when the Führer rises, it will be time to go.'

Max returned to his seat next to Anny, who was staring dreamily at the summer clouds.

'I won't call him Mein Führer, I have decided.'

'Good. Do you know, Max? The morning after your fight I received a telegram and flowers, which I thought were from you, but they were from Hitler. There was a message attached.'

'What did it say?'

'They were surprisingly beautiful flowers, all roses of different colours. I wonder who selected them. And the message said, I remember it exactly, 'most cordial felicitations on your husband's splendid victory.' Very formal and quaintly old world, don't you think?'

'I also received such a telegram, just after the fight. But no flowers. It was exactly the same words as yours, but without the word "husband".'

They sat arm in arm, full of relief and anticipation. She leaned over to him, her small round face exuding love and concern as she gently touched his swollen cheeks.

Max closed his eyes and glowed with a smile which lit them both. They dozed together, her head on his shoulder.

The crowd lining the road from the airport seemed to Max almost identical to the one which had met the *Hindenburg* in Frankfurt. It was as if this one crowd had been sent ahead and resumed their places, primed to wave, shout and raise children onto shoulders who would wave their own little flags on cue.

'I need to change clothes after the flight,' Max said. 'Can we stop first at the Excelsior?'

'We need to go straight to the Chancellery.' Major Sauer said. 'The Führer awaits you with tea and cakes. For a hero, he will forgive a few wrinkles. Also, your mother will be there. And the Reichsminister Goebbels. Perhaps a few other people.'

CHAPTER 10
TEA IN THE OLD CHANCELLERY

Max and Anny were ushered through the Old Chancellery, the Wilhelmstraße office of every German chancellor since Bismarck, its rococo façade contrasting sharply with stark recent extensions. SS guards flanked every entrance, every doorway. Uniformly tall, uniformly erect, staring straight ahead, rigid, as if in neck braces.

Anny whispered to Max as they walked down the long corridors. 'The guards look so impressive, but also fake, Max, like everything else. Like extras from a fluffy UFA film. But you need to be careful with them, Max.'

'Anny, I know who they are and what they represent. Trust me that I will be careful. But without their approval, we have nothing. Maybe less. So what would we do then?'

Anny shrugged.

As the illustrious pair followed Major Hauptmann through the corridors, the guards snapped to attention as the couple passed. Aside from their footsteps, the building seemed silent, no noises percolated from other rooms, nor from the sparse traffic outside. No birds sang in the courtyard.

Hermann Goering was waiting for them in an anteroom. Max had often seen him in newsreels, but was still surprised at the girth of the man, not to mention the extravagance of his uniform, which was festooned with medals from the war as well as other gaudy insignia. Beaming, Goering strode over to the couple, bowed to Anny, kissed her hand, then slapped Max on the back, hard.

'That's exactly what we want in the new Germany, real heroes, real champions for the Reich! For such people, for people like you, anything is possible. The so-called experts gave you no chance. But I knew that you could do it. Tell me later how you defeated the Brown Blockhead. Tell me everything, blow by blow. Ring my office. Both of you should of course come out to visit me in Carinhall, also to meet my wife, Emmy. Anny and Emmy, yes? That will be a fine pair. And Emmy especially wants to meet the beautiful and talented Mrs Schmeling, so she can talk about acting. Of course, she now wishes to go back to the stage, but I have put my foot down!'

Anny suppressed a frown. Goering didn't seem to notice. 'Sadly, I can't stay for the tea and cakes, a meeting – also, bad for my waistline – but I just wanted to meet you and offer my hearty congratulations. Ring my office.' Max nodded at Goering's expansive back – the Reichstag President was already moving swiftly out the room.

'He certainly moves fast for a man of such size. Good footwork,' Max whispered. 'Maybe once he boxed.'

'I don't envy Emmy Goering; I can't imagine his bulk on top of anyone smaller than a hippopotamus. I wonder if she has to polish his medals afterwards.'

Before they could develop this strand, they were ushered into a large reception hall, where a round table had been set and placed in a corner of the room, plump easy chairs alternating with straight backed seats. Surrounding the table were standing lamps, on the walls innocuous but expensive landscape paintings and tapestries; below them a Persian carpet. That corner of the otherwise sparse room seemed to the couple – as they later agreed, giggling in their bed – furnished in upper-middle class kitsch, rather than as the reception area for the most powerful man in Germany.

Adolf Hitler walked towards them, his hands clasped behind his back. He was wearing a neat blue suit, a gold party badge prominent on his lapel. He seemed relaxed. Josef Goebbels followed in his master's wake. The Minister for Propaganda and Popular Enlightenment seemed to move surreptitiously, as if carried in his Führer's slipstream. This slight, beak-faced man had grown in political stature over the last few months, his own self-importance expanding and filling the space around him like a perfumed toxic gas. His many enemies, especially within the regime, referred to him as the 'poison dwarf'.

The Führer took Anny's hand in both of his and said, 'How very nice to meet you.' His voice was low pitched and softly resonant, with only a faint trace of the guttural harshness which emerged fully during his public appearances. His blue eyes stared directly into Anny's, making her feel slightly uncomfortable by the frankness of the gaze.

'I am delighted that you have been able to convince your brave husband to accept my invitation for tea, and especially to bring you with him.'

Turning to Max he said, 'Wonderful, just wonderful. It's simply magnificent that you were able to defeat that subhuman. I wish I could have been there to see it myself.'

'There is a film of the fight, Mein Führer. Unedited, of course.'

'You brought it back from America with you?'

'Yes, but it's still at the airport. We were brought here in such a hurry…'

Hitler turned to an attendant. 'Get it.'

The attendant stiff-arm saluted, then walked briskly to the door. Hitler returned his gaze to Max.

'I have followed all your fights, you know. Pity you let that Jew Baer trick you into defeat. I'm told that he fights unfairly. You must now have another fight with him and put him in his place.'

'Yes, Mein Führer, gladly, but first I need to regain the championship that has been stolen from me…'

'Yes. Everybody knows about this cheating, how the judges were paid by the Rothschilds to turn the decision against you.'

'About this, I do not know, Mein Führer, but I am anxious to regain the crown. I now have a date to fight the new champion, Jimmy Braddock. My manager is working out the details in New York.'

'Yes,' Hitler said, his face darkening, 'I think we need to speak another time about this manager problem of yours. But now I must greet your mother.'

Max's mother had just been escorted into the room. She beamed at Max, started to walk towards him, but was distracted by Hitler's approach. Anny whispered to

Max, 'I thought you said that you wouldn't call him *Mein Führer*.'

'You are right, but everyone does it, so it feels more natural than I expected.'

Hitler now greeted Max's mother, staring into her eyes after kissing her hand. 'You must be very proud of your son,' Hitler said, 'very proud.'

The flustered woman blushed, and made a move between a bow and curtsey. 'Yes, I am indeed. I am very proud, Mein Führer.'

Hitler smiled. 'All of Germany is.'

Goebbels glided into the space vacated by his Führer. He kissed Anny's hand. Twice. 'Good to see you again, Frau Schmeling. You looked wonderful when we met at the premiere of *The Young Count*. Dreadful film, but you were radiant.' A precise smile. He then turned slowly to Max, his smile thinning, still holding Anny's hand. She removed it gently as he spoke.

Goebbels pointed at Max's facial bruises. 'That jungle-man certainly roughed you up a bit, didn't he? Does it hurt?'

'Not very much, not even when I was being hit. And I can tell you that he hits very hard. But it's something you get used to. One doesn't really feel much pain during a fight, thank goodness, and besides, like my manager Joe says, "You should see the udder guy".'

Goebbels didn't reciprocate Max's grin. 'You should appreciate, Herr Schmeling, that you have been chosen by the Führer and the entire nation as a symbol of German excellence and honour. How can you thus continue to associate with a sworn enemy of the German people? Not to mention the insult he gave all Germans last year, when you beat the American Hamas in Hamburg, and at the end this Jew crawled into the ring with the officials. Imagine this *drecksau* giving the German salute, and worse, holding a cigar! And a photograph of this affront, it should be remembered, was in all the foreign papers. A laughing stock! So I ask you, was he *trying* to be insulting? Probably not, his sort don't really have to try to be insulting, do they? Their very presence in Germany is in itself an insult to all true Germans.'

'He's a great manager, Dr Goebbels, and has helped me like no other in the States. And he's a honourable man.'

Goebbels turned back to Anny. 'Maybe you will convince your stubborn husband,' he said, smiling archly at her.

At that moment, a beaming young attendant announced:

'*Mein Führer, Damen und Herren*, tea is served.'

They sat down at the round table, white uniformed staff holding chairs for the women, Goebbels making a point of holding Anny's chair. Anny sat at Hitler's right, Max's mother at his left. Hitler poured tea into Max's mother's cup, then Anny's. Slices of thinly sliced lemon were offered, accepted. Hitler expounded on one of his favourite subjects.

'Of course, tea with lemon is a much better drink than coffee, healthier as well, but it shouldn't be too strong. That's the secret. The English, who have many fine qualities, and who must be credited for bringing tea to

Europe, nevertheless insist on ruining good tea with milk. But Ribbentrop tells me that all their food is terrible, so I suppose they don't notice.' Polite laughter. He asked Anny to choose a cake from a large platter which had been wheeled over to them.

'Is that Guglhupf?' Anny asked.

'You know, I think it is. Imagine. I haven't heard that word for such long time. Guglhupf. You are right.' He served her a slice. She beamed as she tasted it, her eyes closed and eyebrows arched in pleasure.

'Just as I remember from home. Rosewater, almonds, poppy seeds, it brings back memories.'

Hitler chose for himself a chocolate éclair and bit gingerly into its end, while Goebbels nibbled at a small piece of apple Danish. Later, Hitler leaned back in his easy chair and read aloud from press clippings, all of them extolling Max's exploits. The Führer tapped the paper with the back of his fingers, for emphasis. Turning to Goebbels, he said, 'This is an opportunity we must exploit, Reichsminister.'

'Absolutely,' Goebbels replied, nodding enthusiastically, 'absolutely.'

Throughout the tea, Goebbels would look frequently in Anny's direction, smiling. She returned his gaze with a demure look which she hoped would not betray her disgust.

'You know, Frau Schmeling, Anny, if I may, Ucicky is making a new film with Emil Jannings soon. *The Broken Jug*. I've seen the script. Wonderful comedy! I think the part of Marthe would be perfect for you. I could speak with him.'

'Oh, that is so kind of you to think of me, Herr Reichsminister, but you know I already have contracts for so many films next year.' Goebbels smiled thinly, then returned to speak to Hitler. Max and Anny shared a glance, well known to intimates, one which contained elements of mirth, repugnance and relief – a tiny glint in the eye, minutely raised eyebrows and slight tilt of the head.

Max turned to his host. 'This is a wonderful building, Mein Führer, so much history.'

Hitler waved his hand dismissively. As he spoke his voice became gradually louder, his customary guttural inflections, so recognisable from his radio addresses, now became prominent.

'This building is only fit for a soap factory, nothing more. Not remotely appropriate for the headquarters of the Greater German Reich. Soon I will make plans for a new one. Far better. But first, we need to strengthen the Reich so that it is deserving of this new building. We have, of course, regained the Saarland, and this achievement without even a shot being fired! I told the frightened generals, who did not believe I could accomplish this. And now they will listen to me without question, as we widen our borders to include all racial Germans. And this will happen. Not today, but soon.'

He lowered his voice from the podium to the tea table. 'So, you can understand, Herr Schmeling, just how important you are as a symbol of this new, proud and invigorated Reich. And especially, coming from Pomerania as you do, even at the very edge of that open sewer which is Poland, you remind our folk brothers and sisters that no matter where you come from, no matter where you live, as a Racial German, you have a home in our National Socialist Reich.'

'There is still much to do to make this happen, but it will,' Goebbels added, looking for and receiving a slight nod from his master.

'Of course, Herr Schmeling,' Hitler continued, 'you have done your folk community a great service, not only by beating that subhuman, but by being a genuine ambassador for German sport, especially in America. I am told that you were influential in persuading the American Olympic committee to reject the shameless proposal from those Jews who run Roosevelt, that the USA should boycott the Olympics. Your success there is very much appreciated.'

Max smiled modestly. Hitler continued. 'These games are very important for Germany. This is also why we did nothing about that pig-Jew Frankfurter who murdered our old party faithful Gustloff in Davos last winter. We took no action against the Jews, much as it was deserved, to prevent those American Semites from bellowing and spoiling the winter Olympics.

'But rest assured, Herr Schmeling, we will not forget this murderous outrage, I can guarantee you that. But for now, our main undertaking is to make certain that the Olympics are a great success. These games are a providence-given opportunity for us to show the world what our new Germany can achieve. In every sporting event, we intend to beat all comers, especially the Americans.'

His voice rose again in pitch and intensity. 'And afterwards, of course, every future Olympics will be held in Berlin. Wait until you see the plans we are working out for the new Capital of the Reich! The world will hold its breath!' He then reclined back into his chair.

For the next half hour, the guests chatted amongst themselves, their host speaking occasionally and inconsequentially to Anny on his right, then to Max's mother on his left, then reclining again to re-read Max's press clippings as the two women chatted happily to each other about domestic things, Anny having moved from her chair next to Hitler to one beside her mother-in-law.

An SS officer approached Hitler and whispered into his ear. Hitler looked up at his guests.

'I am told that the film of Max Schmeling's great victory is now here and we can watch it next door. So, ladies and gentlemen, if you will please follow me.'

They all rose and trailed behind their host through doors leading to a screening room, furnished with deep curtains, a large screen and plush settees. Hitler gestured for Max and Anny to sit on either side of him. Goebbels and Max's mother sat immediately behind. The film started. It was silent, and Hitler talked throughout, laughing and slapping his thigh whenever Max scored a right cross on Louis' chin.

'That was very clever of you, Herr Schmeling, crouching so low and making the animal reach out for you, then bang with the right hand. Very clever.'

It was really Yussel's idea, Max wanted to say, but thought better of it.

In the fourth round, when Max decked Louis with a hard right, Hitler couldn't contain himself, clapping his hands and almost rising from his armchair.

'*Prima*! I suppose by now you knew that you would beat him, didn't you, Herr Schmeling?'

'He was always dangerous. But I think that he underestimated me. Still, he's very strong, stronger than anyone I've ever fought.'

Hitler waved the statement off. 'Merely animal strength. But incapable of beating anyone who embodies the highest German ideal and racial purity, and especially someone who has the unshakable will to win.' He half-turned to Goebbels. 'I don't want this film material released just as a newsreel. Make it into a feature film. Show both boxers training. But leave Schmeling's Jew manager out of it. Call it, *Max Schmeling's Victory: A German Victory*, something like that. Release it in all the cinemas.'

'It will be a phenomenal success!' Goebbels answered, looking in Anny's direction.

Forty minutes later, just after everyone cheered the final knockdown, an attendant walked up to Hitler and handed him a slip of paper. Hitler rose and turned to his guests, shielding his eyes from the bright projector light. The projector was turned off, and the screen gradually disappeared behind heavy curtains, which closed noiselessly from two directions.

'Oberstleutnant Stahlmann reminds me that the Austrian Ambassador has been waiting for over an hour to speak to me. Perhaps an hour is long enough to wait.

This time.' All rose. Hitler shook hands again with Max, his mother and Anny, then left the room. The guests made their way to the doors, which were opened ceremoniously by SS guards.

At the door, Goebbels bowed and again kissed Anny's hand, then turned to Max. 'Don't forget what I said. The Führer is counting on you.'

'I'll keep it in mind, Herr Reichsminister, I certainly will.'

Max shook Goebbels' hand, perhaps with a bit more force than necessary. The Reichsminister didn't react, but his smile dissipated. As if remembering, Goebbels resumed his smile, lovingly taking Anny's hand again in his, and kissing it. 'I can't seem to resist you, Frau Schmeling.'

As they were escorted by a young SS officer to a waiting car, Anny wiped the back of her hand on her dress.

CHAPTER 11
HOW TO GET INTO FRANCE

'You catch me at a good time, young Herschel. But how grown-up you look! And still just a boy! I am just returned from a nice holiday in Ostend. Soon I go back to my home in Paris. But while I'm here, maybe I can help.'

Madame Rosenthal was Zaslawsky's sister. She had been immediately taken with the boy's luxuriant hair, his piercing eyes, his charm, even the quaint way he mangled the French language.

'Better in Yiddish. Yes, Herschel? Unless you just want to practise French, which is a good idea, since you will certainly need it where you are going. Also here, of course. Now to the point. We need to find a way for you to cross the border. I shall see what can be arranged.'

Three days later, Madame Rosenthal returned with a plan.

'You may be interested to learn, Herschel, that I have been in contact with your Uncle Abraham in Paris. As you know, he is anxious for you to come as soon as possible to him, where you can stay as long as you like. But how to get there, without papers, without passport?'

'Then it's impossible?'

'Of course not. I found a way. Listen, Herschel, there is

a small town, Quiérvrain, just on this side of the French border. Every day, Belgian men, mostly steelworkers, some in textiles, take the short train ride from Quiérvrain to Valenciennes, just on the other side, where they go to their work, and then they make the return trip in the evening. Nobody ever checks their papers, especially as they carry no luggage, maybe just a small backpack, or a lunch bag. So I think that in this way you can get into France with no passport, no visa, no proof of economic independence.'

'I'll do whatever is necessary.'

—◦—

Autumn was early. On a chilly morning, he and Madame Rosenthal arrived at Quiérvrain's small railway station, recently rebuilt after its destruction in the war. Clumps of workers were milling about on the platform, smoking, laughing. They looked up as the pair arrived, then resumed their conversations. Madame Rosenthal had seen to his clothing. His fine new jacket was carefully rolled up into a worn knapsack. A cloth cap had been found, and his Uncle Wolf had patched up an old jacket which looked appropriate for a worker. As the train approached, Madame Rosenthal handed him an envelope containing five ten-Franc notes. 'You can repay me when you make your fortune.' She brushed his cheek with her lips and left before the train departed.

As predicted, the short journey to Valenciennes was uneventful, but for the boy, it was an ordeal. He felt that everyone was watching him, examining him, unmasking him. It was difficult for him to hide his growing anxiety as the train approached the French border. He also feared that to appear too nervous might alert the police. He slumped down on his seat, tipped his cap forward over his eyes and pretended to sleep. But as Madame Rosenthal had predicted, the stop at the border was brief, French gendarmes waving on the train with cursory glances through the windows. Fifteen minutes later, he was delighted to see the smiling face of his uncle Abraham, whom he recognised immediately. *Such strong resemblance between all the brothers!* He was hugged for a long time.

'Your aunt Chava is preparing a nice welcome meal for you at home. But now we need to hurry, since the Paris train leaves in a few moments. Here is your ticket.'

During the journey, he told his uncle of everything that had happened.

'I'm so looking forward to seeing Paris for the first time. Of course, I'm also looking forward to seeing aunt Chava.'

'Listen, Herschel, I need to explain the situation. My apartment is on the rue des Petites Écuries. You need to remember the address. It is also my shop. The sign on the door says *Maison Albert*. This is to make a distinction from my tailoring business to any Jewish associations, as the French are also sensitive to this. The flat is small, but there is enough room for you. And we are very happy for you to be with us. You father has agreed to send some small money for your upkeep, but you will also need to help me in the business. I hope this will be alright.'

'I'll do whatever you ask me to.'

'Wonderful, Herschel. You can look on me as another father. With us you will at least be safe, especially once we get you proper French documents.'

Two days later, on the payment of 100 Francs, Abraham became the legal guardian of his nephew, and armed with a letter of consent from his brother Zindel, he assumed power of attorney for the boy.

━◄○►━

Over the next months, the boy gradually settled into French life, daily becoming more fluent in the language, saving money for new clothes, or asking his uncle to tailor some new style for him. Abraham was happy to make clothes for his nephew, a surrogate for the son he never had. The fifteen-year-old lad helped his uncle in the shop, carrying bolts of cloth, sweeping up after work, running errands for his aunt. He also enjoyed trying to fix broken sewing machines and treadles.

'You have a real instinct for machinery,' his uncle said. 'Maybe you could learn this as a trade?'

But the boy became increasingly homesick, often anxious and depressed. Simple things could trigger a descent into hopelessness. His depression found its usual outlet in stomach complaints, so much so that his aunt designed a special diet for him, but it didn't help much.

Slowly, he made friends with other German Jews he met at the synagogue. He felt welcome there, attending twice a day. The rabbi, Meyer Goldfarb, was himself a German immigrant, and the boy felt safe speaking in German and Yiddish with him. He was able to share his fears with the rabbi, who listened calmly and sympathetically.

'It's all in God's hands, young Herschel. You must trust in him.'

Why do all rabbis always say this? Is there nothing else that can be done?

He went to the cinema every week, especially with his best friend Nathan Kaufman, another refugee, but with valid papers.

'That Jean Gabin is wonderful, isn't he?' he enthused, 'so strong, quiet, but totally masterful. I think *Zou-Zou* is the best film I've ever seen.'

Nathan said, 'So how many films have you actually seen?'

'Silents, mostly. The Nazis stopped us from going to cinemas, remember?'

'Anyway,' continued Nathan, 'the real star for me is that Josephine Baker. What a woman! I certainly could find a use for her!'

'She's a negress, though.'

'I could make allowances.'

The two friends would often visit the *club sportif Aurore,* a frequent hangout for young Jewish men, mostly secular Zionists from eastern Europe. There they would discuss politics and women in Yiddish, earnestly considering weighty issues over which they were uniquely powerless to have any influence. Still, the group was lively, and introduced new ideas into the boy's sheltered mind, most of which he rejected out of hand. The club was also frequented by some local homosexuals, but he hadn't noticed.

Nathan pointed them out. 'See that group over there?' he whispered. 'Nancy boys.'

The boy looked quizzically at this friend.

'You know, Herschel, queers, *vögels,* little birdies. Usually French, but lately a German – you can tell by his clothes – has been hanging around with them. I think he works at the embassy.'

The German in question looked absently in their direction. The boys averted their gaze. The young man was slight, well dressed, and somewhat pale faced.

'It's nothing to me what they do, and so long as the man isn't a Nazi, he doesn't concern me,' the boy said.

'Of course, you are right, Herschel. This is France, and things are more liberal here.'

Over time, as he grew slightly in stature, the boy became a *flâneur,* sitting in front of cafés with his friends, especially his new favourite, *Tout va Bien*, sipping coffee and gazing at the passers-by. He began to feel comfortable.

But his comfort was subverted by frequent reports from the Yiddish and French press, as well as regular letters from his father, recounting the mounting pressure on Jews in Germany, the ever-growing hostility, and the continuous humiliation of his people. All of this churned in his mind. He became ever more restless to leave Europe, to emigrate to Palestine, and if that were impossible, to the United States. He even wrote a letter to President Roosevelt begging for a visa for himself and his family, but thousands of similar letters arrived at the White House every month, and Congress was hostile to further European immigration, especially of Jews. In France, the growing aversion most French people felt about eastern Jews, resulted in a tightening of immigration rules. His original leave to stay was cancelled. Visas were no longer issued to Jews from Germany, and so the young man became doubly illegal, for entering the country clandestinely, and now without the hope ever of obtaining a residence permit.

PART TWO

CHAPTER 12
PRELUDE: MAY/JUNE 1938

Two months before the Louis rematch, Max returned to New York on the RM *Bremen*. Its staff displayed their usual obsequious veneers – all starch, *heils* and tight smiles. Passengers continually pressed Max's hand, the men asserting their unshakable belief that this upstart savage Joe Louis, even if he were the new champion, was still no match for any German, especially Max. He was used to this. He smiled self-effacingly.

The last day of his voyage had hinted at a multi-fragranced spring awaiting him in New York. As the tugs guided the liner up the Hudson and to the dockside, Max noticed the seagulls, shrieking as they hovered above the ship. *Could the gulls of Hamburg be so noisy? But New Yorkers are very noisy people, if Yussel is anything to go by. So maybe these seagulls are proper New Yorkers.*

The tugboats having tooted off, Max stood at the rail and watched as the ship inched sideways towards the quay, frothy water rushing away, carrying with it flotillas of discarded packs of cigarettes, coke bottles and newspapers.

As he disembarked, offering his customary smiling waves to the thin crowd, he could feel the mood darkening. Even at the top of the gangplank he could hear the protestors on the other side of the barrier. He could just see their placards, their bearers restrained by arm-linked policemen. Shouts and signs exhorted in unison: *Boycott Nazi Schmeling* or *Send the Bum back to Naziland,* or *We don't want no Nazis here.*

The immigration officer looked at his passport, the cover emblazoned with an eagle clutching a swastika. He opened it to Max's photograph and looked up at the boxer.

'What is the purpose of your visit to the United States, Mr. Schmeling?'

'To beat Joe Louis,' he grinned.

The officer remained impassive. 'And when do you intend to depart?'

Max wanted to say, *When I'm champion again,* but said, 'In August. I hope to do some shopping while I'm in New York.'

'Some questions about affiliations, sir, which must be declared. Are you a Communist?'

'Not at all.'

'Are you a Nazi party member, Mr. Schmeling?'

'No. I have never been a party member.'

The officer returned the passport and leant across the desk. 'Just between us, sir, I hope Joe Louis beats the living shit out of you, Nazi.' Then louder, 'Enjoy your stay.'

Yussel met Max in the entrance hall, shouting over the din. 'Hiya, Champ. Welcome back!' He grabbed Max's hand and shook it vigorously, looking in the direction of the press cameras.

Max said, 'I don't think they want me here, Joe. The immigration officer called me a Nazi.'

'Don't aggravate yourself, Max. Most of these people in America actually know that you're a straight-up guy, but everything has gone a bit *mishugga* lately, especially about Germany, and also, you have to remember, there are a lot of Jews in New York. But you still have a good following here and deep down they still like you. As a person. So maybe you should take Dempsey's advice and apply for citizenship. Then everything could be much more pleasant.'

Max furrowed his thick eyebrows. 'You know, Joe, I have thought about this seriously for some time, but you also know, that I am a German and that I will always stay a German, and this is no matter what happens. Anyway, I think that things will become a bit difficult at home for my mother and Anny if I should make such a step, do you understand?'

'Just a suggestion, a thought, an inkling. Of course, you have to do what is right for you. Goes without saying. That's absolutely the main thing. But now, for the newsreels, forget all that and just play it relaxed – show your usual charming self with the press'.

They were waiting for them as they reached the pier's exit. Max wore his most ingratiating smile, but withdrew it when it wasn't reciprocated, even among faces he recognised. Flashbulbs popped, film cameras rolled.

'How was the trip, Max?'

'Good, good, very calm.'

'Do you think you're going to win, Max?'

'Of course. I wouldn't come here just to lose. I want to win back the championship which was so unfairly taken from me in that last Sharkey decision,' Joe nodded energetically, 'and also to show that I am worthy of the honour of being champion.'

'Do you think of yourself as part of a master race, Max?'

'I am no superman in any way.' A slight pang of anxiety crossed his mind as he realised that he had just contradicted the entire philosophy of his country.

'Are you afraid of what will happen to you back home if you lose?'

'Look, I'm a fighter, not a politician. I'm just here to beat Joe Louis.'

'A lot of people say that this is not just a fight between you and Louis, but a battle between the good old USA and Nazi Germany.'

Yussel interjected. 'Look, guys, people are saying all sorts of crazy things nowadays. And others are believing everything they hear. If some numbskull tells them that there is an invasion from Mars going on in New Jersey, a lot of people will believe it and try to run to Texas where maybe even the Martians wouldn't want to go. So I'm just sayin' for you to just give Max a break and let's just talk about the fight.'

They did this for a while, but their hearts weren't in it.

◄о►

During his training, in the camp set up for him in upstate New York, Max kept to his strict routine and tried not to pay attention to the press, most of which was forecasting his defeat. Yussel hid newspapers from him, or cut out the most offending pieces. 'What you don't see, didn't happen so far as you're concerned, in my book anyway. Am I right?'

Max took pleasure in the daily runs, the sparring, and especially the stillness of the rural, star-filled night. Sometimes newsreel photographers would descend upon the camp, asking the same stupid questions, receiving the same patient answers.

'How do you feel about Joe Louis, Max?'

'You know, I have great respect for this man. He has climbed up from deep poverty, and through great talent and hard work, is now the champion. I admire him for this. But still I will beat him again and take the crown back to Germany.'

'You're no spring chicken, Max. Are you in good enough shape for Louis?

'As you can see, he's in great shape,' beamed Yussel.

'I could box even 30 rounds,' Max said. He felt at peace.

◄o►

The weigh-in dumped Max back into reality, into the ugly mood in which the country was swimming. Those who had befriended him before now stood back, offering empty smiles. The officials asked him how he was, but ignored his answers, already knowing his state of health.

Max had already stripped down to his trunks when his adversary arrived, sporting dark glasses, white hat and wearing a light suit with no shirt. Joe Louis slowly removed his sunglasses, hat and suit. The two boxers nodded cordially to each other, but Louis' stare was icy. Max studied his opponent. *This man isn't just a boxer,* he thought, *but an animal, sleek as a cat, his torso emerging from his boxing trunks smooth and hard as if chiselled.*

After their first fight, most newspapers had demeaned Louis viciously, and cartoon caricatures appeared in the sports pages of the New York dailies, copied nationwide. They depicted Louis as a giant thick-lipped gorilla, his name crudely sketched, sometimes on a diaper, sometimes on a jungle necklace. Some cartoons showed him as a grotesquely smashed statue with a victorious Max standing at the base. But to Max this man was no caricature. He understood that he would be going into the ring with a tenacious and merciless predator. He knew this now, just from Louis' stare.

The ceremony itself was innocuous. Louis came in at four pounds heavier than Max. After being weighed, the boxers put on their suit jackets and shook hands mildly, facing the cameras. This relieved Max, who was happy to avoid Louis' gaze. Yussel tried to cheer him up.

'You're looking great, Max, and believe me, I know about these things, just great,' slapping his back while the flashbulbs fizzed and crackled. But Max could only manage a nod.

Joe Louis spoke to the press later that day, just before settling down to a steak and salad followed by a walk along the Harlem river.

'How are you feeling, Joe?' asked one reporter.

'To tell you the truth, I'm a bit scared,' said Joe, his face deadpan.

'Scared, Joe?'

'Yeah, I'm scared I might kill that Nazi tonight.'

CHAPTER 13
THE SECOND FIGHT

All eyes and ears were now focused on Yankee Stadium. The fight was a sellout, all 70,000 seats. The ring was flooded with white light, its glow spreading out from the canvas and the ropes, over the photographers at ringside, their cameras resting on the edge of the ring, over the radio announcers, the celebrities, the movie and radio stars; the glare gradually diluting as it passed the serried seats erected in the dusty infield. The glow didn't extend to the outfield, to the double decker stands or to the distant bleachers. A boundary between the intense and expensive seats at ringside and the geometric rows of gradually more affordable seats beyond could be measured by the intensity of light, the cheaper seats, not all that cheap, steadily becoming engulfed from behind by the blackness of a muggy New York night. Cigarette ends glowed like red fireflies in the noisy, almost liquid darkness. In the upper decks, different people: a few blacks mixed with boiler room mechanics, shop workers and filing clerks, all treating themselves to the sporting event of their lifetimes. The entire stadium smelled of sweat, beer and hot dogs. The noise was constant.

Beyond the stadium, throughout the vast radio-connected continent, seventy million Americans tuned into the broadcast, more than half the population – the biggest radio audience ever. And throughout the broadcast, all social life was interrupted; dances, movies, crap games. The fight was broadcast on loudspeakers everywhere. Streets were almost empty, surprising local cats. In Harlem, the broadcast floated in and out of windows, open to the sultry night, punctuated by the rumble of the uptown IRT train as it pulled itself to the 125th street station.

—◄o►—

In Paris, Aunt Chava had persuaded Uncle Abraham that it would do the boy good to listen to the fight.

'It will distract Herschel from his situation. He worries so much about it.'

'At that hour?' Abraham said. 'Is he not sufficiently distracted by his friends in the café?'

'He worries more at night.'

Abraham relented. He even allowed Nathan Kaufman, Herschel's best friend, to listen to the fight with him. Blankets and pillows, with bolts of cloth for mattresses, had been set up on the floor of the sitting room, which doubled as the boy's bedroom. The two sixteen-year-olds sat next to each other, their faces fixed on the radio dial.

One hundred million people around the world were also tuned into the fight through a telephone link, which was sometimes overcome by static. In Berlin, at 3 am, Arno Helmer, the German announcer, began his passionate report, his pie-round face quivering with emotion.

Even though the Governor of the State of New York, the Jew Herbert Lehman, has involved himself in every type of chicanery to defeat him, our Max Schmeling will not be deterred. For now it is the showdown. Now it is the fight to the bitter end between the animalistic nigger with his Jewish supporters and our Aryan hero, with all of Germany behind him, who – and let us not forget this – has once before proved to the world that a German can defeat any jungle refugee, no matter how brutal his reputation. Discipline, dedication, intelligence, courage and a will of iron must always prevail over brute strength.

The boys stuck out their tongues at the radio.

—◦—

An official opened Joe's dressing room door. Mike Jacobs draped a red and blue dressing gown over the champion's shoulders. It was the same dressing gown he wore the first time he fought Max.

'It's time, Joe,' Mike said quietly, almost like a secret between the two. 'Murder that bum tonight. Don't make an asshole out of me.'

'Don't you worry none, Mike. I ain't goin' back to workin' at Fords and you ain't going back to sellin' hot dogs at Coney Island.'

'OK, champ, I believe you, but just remember to show him some respect. He still has a great right.'

'Don't you even think nothin' 'bout that Max Smellin'. He's gonna need smellin' salts when I finish with him.'

It was a pretty good joke, but there was no smile.

—◦—

Max Schmeling, wearing an old grey dressing gown, walked from his distant dressing room towards the ring, his figure caught in a spotlight which separated him from the inky darkness and hostile faces. He could hear people booing through the rising din. Some nearby threw things at him, banana peels, cigarette packets, Dixie cups not quite emptied of beer or Coca Cola. A few curses and warnings: 'He's really gonna get you this time, you Nazi!' Some mocking raised arms and *Sieg Heils*. Distantly audible were a few organised cheers for him. The German Bund had managed to bring a small detachment of admirers to the fight, but they were far away; a few small swastika flags were waved and then speedily lowered. Max entered the ring first, engulfed in a tide of boos and catcalls.

As Joe Louis and his protective entourage entered the arena, the air seemed to be sucked out of the space and replaced by a Babe Ruth roar. The champion stared ahead, oblivious, ignoring the manic faces of well-wishers. He mounted the steps, passed through the ring ropes, then rocked from heel to toe in his corner, testing the canvas.

A cordon of NY police surrounded the ring, acting as a barrier against excited fans and missiles. Ring announcer Joe Humphreys introduced the obligatory luminaries – New York's Mayor Fiorello LaGuardia, film stars, and former heavyweight champions; James Braddock, Jack Sharkey and Max Baer, all recent victims of Louis' aggression. The boxing celebrities walked to each fighter in turn, shaking their gloved hands, Baer then grinned at the crowd, and raised his own hands in a victory gesture.

He received the laugh he expected, but also some boos which he answered with a clown frown. During this procession, as Max waited nervously in his corner, he stood with his hand down at his sides, shuffling his feet. Across the ring, Joe lightly practised his jabs.

After the celebrities left, Arthur Donovan, the referee, motioned for the boxers and their seconds to join him in the centre of the ring. Yussel, barred from ringside – resulting from a recent silly advertising prank, paced in Max's dressing room, chomping on his dead cigar, gesticulating as if in silent animated conversation. *I should be there with him. What hooey! 'Bringing boxing into disrepute,' what for a beer barrel? Just to show that my kid Tony Galento trained on beer, like he says. Why such a big deal?*

Yussel listened to the proceedings on the radio in the dressing room.

Referee Donovan finished his instructions to the fighters. '…and I don't want anybody from your corners sticking his head through the ropes during this fight. It may cause serious trouble.'

Back in their corners, the bleached centre of the ring now empty, the two fighters waited, concentrating on the moment. Louis rose onto his toes, then returned back onto his heels. He threw a few air-punches, then pulled up his trunks. Schmeling stood absolutely still, staring blankly at Louis. He was unshaven; the harsh light accentuated his stubble and prominent eyebrows. His trainer, Max Machon, almost as short as the missing Yussel, stood on the ring apron, patting Max's arm through the ropes.

'You'll be fine, Max, just fine. Remember, you've beat him before, and you'll nail him again. Just take your time, take your time. Remember what Yussel told you, "you don't need to change anything, not the stance, not the rhythm. Keep your left up and your right cocked".'

He looks like a panther, Max thinks.

The bell. The noise. Schmeling and Louis move quickly to the centre, then circle each other cautiously.

Max sticks out his left, just as he did in their first fight. Louis jabs around it. *Come on, Joe, drop that left*, but Joe's left remains stubbornly high, jab after painful jab. They circle, then Joe lands with a left hook. *Didn't see that coming*. It was like a camera flash going off in his head. They clinch, break, Joe pushing him away, never letting the pace slacken. Schmeling leans back, feels the ropes behind him. Then another painful left hook. *Slow things down. Get into rhythm. Find an opening. You can get him.*

He jabs again at Louis, who shrugs it off then lands a right to Max's face. Another flashbulb. A cheer erupts. They clinch again.

The pattern repeats. From his corner, Machon is shouting, 'Move, Max, move!'

Max lands a stiff right onto the side of Louis' face. *That same punch floored him last time. But now it's nothing to him.* Louis sends a strong right into the side of Max's face, then one to Max's stomach. The relentless power of Louis' attack literally takes Max's breath away and empties his mind of all but instinct. He almost blacks out from the force of another right to the head. Louis is setting him up now. Max backs up, arms flailing, catching the top ring rope with his right hand. He ducks a left, and swings his body away from Louis.

The next punch lands on the side of Max's back. A deep shaft of hot pain spreads through Max's body. His mouth opens into a huge circle and from it emanates a high-pitched scream, a caricature of a woman's hysterics in a gangster film, a scream which travels concentrically throughout the stadium, over the commentary of the radio announcers, into the deep dark of the arena and all across America. Anny can hear it on her radio in Berlin.

And still Louis continues, with a barrage of lefts followed by an overhand right. Schmeling holds onto the rope with both hands, his knees beginning to buckle. *Maybe I should go down, take a count, catch my breath,* but things are moving too fast now. Referee Donovan saves Max for a moment, placing himself between the two fighters and giving Max a standing count, but it stops at 'two'. *Not enough time,* Max thinks, protecting his side with his left arm, as Louis wades into him again. The noise now seems to fill every space, to invade the dressing room, where Yussel interrupts his pacing, sits and lights his cigar.

And then Max goes down from a crisp combination. He falls forward, rolls onto his side. Donovan sends Louis to a neutral corner, but by the time he arrives, Max is back on his feet.

Louis hurries to his work, and drops Max to his knees with a right cross. Max rises again, but too soon. It all seems a blur to him now. Max tries a jab, but Louis swats it away. Then quickly, a left jab to Max's face, another painful right to Max's damaged side, then a left hook followed by a textbook right cross.

Max falls slowly. The stadium erupts, but his world goes silent. He sees a white towel flying gently through the air like a dove of peace, but Donovan throws it back to the corner. The towel lands limply on the middle rope.

Max tries to rise again, Machon screaming 'Stay down! For Chrissake, stay down!' Max gets as far as trying to stand on one leg, but sinks back onto his knees while the count continues. The plug is pulled on the transmission in Germany. Max doesn't make it up to his feet.

The boys can't contain themselves. 'He did it, Herschel, he did it!'

'I hope that Nazi's dead!' the boy shouts.

'Keep quiet in there. You promised,' Abraham shouts from the bedroom.

---◆◇◆---

In all, it was a hundred and twenty-four second execution, the second shortest title fight in history.

In his noisy dressing room, Louis was surrounded by reporters.

'Do you hate Max Schmeling, Joe?'

'No, I don't hate Smellin', I just wanted to win. It was my left jabs that opened him up.'

In the other dressing room Max spoke to the radio audience from a stretcher.

'Ladies and Gentlemen, I have not much to say. I am very sorry, but I won't make any excuse, but I get such a terrible hit, I get in the left kidneys, I was so paralysed I couldn't even move. And then after that it was all over, you know.'

Yussel chimed in. 'Anyway, anyone with eyes can see that it was a foul, that kidney punch, anyone could see it.'

'You wuz robbed again, eh Max?' a reporter asked.

'You said it, pal!' Yussel interjected. 'Now clear a path. This boy needs to get to the hospital. That animal broke his back!'

◄o►

Max was whisked away on a gurney. Yussel rode in the front seat of the ambulance, turned towards Max, talking to him constantly. 'You're going to be fine, Max, nothing to worry about. And you'll get another shot at him, cause you wuz robbed again. Just like with Sharkey.' But Max wasn't listening. He began to doze as soon as the rear door had been shut behind him.

The ambulance snaked its way around Yankee Stadium, through the dispersing crowds making their way to the subway. Some of them banged on the top of the vehicle as it passed, shouting at the unseen Max through the frosted glass.

'You had it coming, Nazi!'

'Who's the master race now, Adolf?'

'Get your broken Nazi ass out of this country, scumbag!'

It was a long drive from the Bronx through Manhattan to the Stuyvesant Polyclinic Hospital, chosen because some of the doctors spoke German; Max wanted to be healed in his native tongue. The ambulance picked up speed as they crossed Macombs Dam Bridge over the Harlem River bridge and then drove down 7th Avenue.

As they approached the centre of Harlem, they were slowed again, this time by a growing mass of cheering people. The ambulance gently pushed its way through the crowd, who were oblivious to the flashing lights and to the passenger inside. Finally, the ambulance continued down 7th Avenue, where the siren was turned on. A few minutes later, Max was wheeled into the hospital building.

As Max was being counted out, Harlem had erupted in joy. A huge, multi-faceted party began, which continued all night and sporadically into the next day. Strangers hugged, dance steps erupted and subsided. Wide grins and joyous laughter burst forth everywhere. An hour later, when Joe Louis appeared among them, the rapture intensified. The noise surrounding their champion was deafening, louder even than at Yankee Stadium. Not even the elevated subway at 125th Street could be heard.

In Berlin, Adolf Hitler sent Anny Ondra a message of sympathy, and Josef Goebbels sent her a large bouquet, which arrived the next morning as she was speaking to Max on the long-distance telephone.

◄o►

Max had few visitors in hospital. Yussel appeared every day, brought grapes and short-crust cookies, in a box with the word *Normandie* printed excitedly all over and secured by a thin pink ribbon tied into a meagre bow. 'Be careful not to shake the box too much,' they advised Yussel as he left the bakery.

'It goes without saying, none of this sugary *dreck* when we're back in training, Max,' Yussel said, wagging his finger in mock chastisement, 'but I think we can take a little exception from all that. The doctor says you will be stiff in a brace for eight weeks, but still, we don't want you to get fat, because that's too much extra work. Next year, though, we'll show them.'

Max smiled and waved the conversation away. He didn't much feel like thinking about cookies, or training. *Maybe I should stop, anyway.*

Two days later he was visited by Hans Dieckhoff, the German Ambassador to the US, carrying a large bunch of flowers which he handed brusquely to the nurse.

'I have come to offer my deep condolences at your disappointment, Herr Schmeling.'

Dieckhoff had the puffed-up look of a provincial bureaucrat, a pinched face, receding hairline and a paunch of self-satisfaction.

'Yes, it is a great disappointment,' Max said. 'Thank you for coming to visit me.'

Yussel said, 'That animal cracked three of Max's vertebrae.'

Dieckhoff frowned at Max's Jewish manager. 'You weren't there for him, were you? Not at the ringside, where you should have been. Even someone like you should know that.'

Max tried to interrupt. Yussel put his hand on Max's arm. 'Why I wasn't there is none of your business. So don't get smart with me, or I'll knock you on your Nazi ass, Ambassador or no Ambassador.'

'Wait, outside, Yussel,' said Max, raising his head from the pillow. Yussel reluctantly agreed. 'Anyway, it was a foul blow. Who could do anything against that, even if I was sitting right there?' he asked no one as he left the room.

'You have to rid yourself of this Jew manager, Herr Schmeling. Especially now, especially after this catastrophe. I spoke with the Führer today and he agrees with this.'

Max sat up slightly. 'Yussel is a great manager, as I have more than once told the Führer himself. He is essential for me, especially if I want to fight in the US. And it makes no difference, his race. Joe Louis' manager, another Jacobs, he is also Jewish.'

Dieckhoff's face reddened. 'The nigger's manager is of no consequence here. A Jew manager for a nigger makes perfect sense to me. But for a German?!'

'Please extend my greetings to the Führer the next time you speak with him. I am honoured by his concern.'

'Very well, Schmeling. But you will need to have a discussion about this when you return to the Reich.' He left the room, ignoring Yussel, who was sitting on a chair just outside the door, chomping on an unlit cigar, which he stuffed into his jacket pocket as he returned to the room.

'Can you believe? Such Nazi arrogance.'

'Forget about it, Joe. It doesn't matter now. Anyway, I'm lying here and wondering if I'll ever box again. I asked the doctor after the x-rays, and he wouldn't be drawn in.'

'They're just cracked, Max. It's painful, but not that

serious. The important thing is to rest. You can start here, in this bed, and then continue next week on the steamship. Have you spoken to Anny?'

'This morning on the telephone. She wanted to come here, but I told her that I will be fine, and that I will be home soon.'

—◄o►—

On the return voyage, no airship this time, Max had asked for meals to be sent to his stateroom, rarely venturing out. Sometimes, during the deep starry nights, he would leave his room, and wheel himself along the promenade in one of the *Bremen*'s complementary wheelchairs, making his way as near the prow as he could. He would sit there, wheels locked, staring at the ocean, watching the waves being rent by the ship, rising up in froth for a few strained moments, then fizzing back into the mass, repeated endlessly, their effervescent sound whispering gently.

'Bad luck, Max.' Someone spoke. He turned to see a figure hunched over the nearby rail, staring out towards a black-pink hint of dawn. The end of a cigarette glowed as the man inhaled.

'Do I know you?' Max asked.

'We met a couple of years ago. I was covering your second fight with Sharkey. There's a lot of crooked money in boxing, Max. Anyway, I was the sports reporter for the *Brooklyn Eagle*. We spoke before the fight.'

'I meet so many reporters,' Max said.

'I'm sure you do. So I won't disturb you. I just want to offer my sympathy. Truthfully, though, I don't think that you or anyone else would have been able to beat Louis that night.'

'I think that you are right about that. My body tells me that you are.'

They looked at the sea together. The reporter brushed some ash from his jacket. Max turned to him.

'Are you covering a fight in Europe? I hadn't heard of anything special going on.'

'No. I'm not on the sports desk anymore. They've moved me to News, which is where I always wanted to be. I'm going to Evian to cover the conference Roosevelt called.'

'I didn't hear about it.'

'Well you've been busy. Roosevelt has persuaded most countries to send representatives to see what can be done for the Jews of Germany and Austria, to see if countries will take them.'

'That's a good idea.'

'From what I hear, nobody wants them, so they'll just talk and nothing will change. Many of the Jews want to go to Palestine, but the British won't hear of it; too much trouble with the Arabs already.'

Max couldn't think of anything to say.

'Actually, I know of one country who said they'd take a large number of Jews, and would settle them onto good farmland. It's the Dominican Republic. Their young President Trujillo told me that he wants more white people to settle in his country, which as you know, is mostly negro or mulatto.'

'That might be an answer.'

'There are plenty of Jews who would jump at it. But the World Zionist Organisation, who is speaking for them, absolutely refuses. They say that if the Jews can't go to Palestine, then they can just stay where they are. It's Palestine or nowhere. They don't think that Jews will be safe anywhere else.'

Max continued to stare at the sea after the reporter had left.

CHAPTER 14

A POSTCARD FROM POLAND

The Grynszpan Family were clearing up after supper, each to their accustomed task; Rivka with her hands in the basin, Zindel drying, Esther putting plates and cutlery into the sideboard, and Mordechai sweeping the floor. They chatted solemnly as they worked.

'The fact is this, Rivka. If Herschel's found out, he'll be deported from France. No doubt about that.'

'Maybe he won't be found out,' Esther said. 'Maybe he can keep under the net.'

Zindel shook his head. 'Sooner or later, they'll find him. He'll make some innocuous mistake, maybe get into an argument. You know him. Sooner or later.'

Rivka looked up at her husband, water from the dinner plate in her hand dripping back into the basin. 'But where will he go? He won't be allowed to come back to Germany, and anyway, he's safer out. But where?'

'Back to Brussels?' suggested Esther, putting the last of the cutlery into the drawer.

'Maybe,' Zindel said, 'but Wolf won't be happy about it.'

'Who's happy about anything?' Mordechai asked nobody.

They hadn't heard the knocking at first; it had been

quite gentle by the standards of the time. The next time it was more insistent.

Zindel opened the door. A fresh-faced Sipo officer stood in front of him, erect in a relaxed way, his leather overcoat partially concealing his uniform, but not his revolver, which rested conspicuously in a brown leather holster at his side.

'Herr Grynszpan? Is this the apartment of the Grynszpan family?'

'It is,' Zindel replied, drying his hands on the dishtowel.

He seemed to Zindel surprisingly polite, smiling, speaking conversationally.

'And is the entire family present?'

'Except my youngest, yes. He is studying in Paris.'

'Good. Very good.'

The officer made four ticks in a small brown notebook.

'I'd be obliged if you all would accompany me to the police station. Nothing to worry about, I can assure you. Merely a clerical matter. You needn't take anything with you, just your passports. I expect you'll be back in an hour or two.'

He looked at each of them, then again at his notebook, then smiled. 'But you should take coats. It's a bit chilly outside.'

They followed him down the stairs, then out into the cold street, still damp and shiny from earlier rain. During the short walk, Zindel and Rivka had difficulty keeping up with the tall officer. Occasionally he would look back and slow down for them. The family exchanged anxious glances as they arrived at the police station.

They were led downstairs into a cavernous room, already occupied by about five hundred people, some sitting on the few available benches, most of them on the floor, and some, predominantly younger men, leaning against the green tiled walls. The Grynszpan family recognised several of their neighbours – they acknowledged each other with small sad nods. Everywhere, whispered fretful conversations.

A door banged opened. Heads turned, conversations stopped. A black-uniformed SS officer mounted a wooden rostrum. He was flanked by a dozen troopers, similarly attired, six on either side, each carrying a clipboard.

'I am authorised,' the officer said, pausing to gain the attention he already had, 'in pursuance of the Police Order of 22 August 1938, to gather you here for the purpose of deportation.' There was an audible reaction, a murmur of pain. 'My officers will process all of you at the long table at the other side of the room.' Heads turned in unison. 'You will form orderly lines, and then sign the papers which are presented to you. Those who do not sign will be punished until they do.'

The officer paused again, to let his words penetrate, somewhat surprised at the muted reaction. 'When this task is completed, you will be taken to the concert hall,' he paused again, playfully wondering if these Jews might be expecting some music, 'until transportation can be arranged to take you to the Polish border. Toilets are to be found through the doors which are situated on either side of the tables. You will not be allowed to return home, except under the most exceptional circumstances.'

In their turn, the Grynszpans signed the deportation orders, as did almost everyone else. But one old man refused. 'I've been here since I was born. I went to school here. I've paid taxes here. I am *German*!' He was made to stand in the corner for twenty-four hours until he relented. He was then sent to Buchenwald, a recently established concentration camp situated on a pleasant hill near Weimar.

Esther said, 'Ever since all of this began, the Nazis, the marches, the edicts, we have expected misfortunes to pile upon us. But this? Ripping us out?'

Rivka clasped her husband's hand. She was quaking. 'And who knows what will happen at the border? The Poles won't let us in because we have been away for too long. Will we be stuck there, not going on, not coming back?' Zindel put his arm around her.

Later that evening, the group was marched to the nearby concert hall which overlooked the river Leine. Lightly guarded, they remained there for all of that night and most of the next day. Although hungry, no one thought to ask for food. They spent the time talking amongst themselves, renewing neighbourhood acquaintances. Sometimes a small laugh would break out, quickly stifled and regretted. Sometimes they dozed. Gentle snoring mixed with supressed sobbing and whispered conversations continued throughout the night and for all of the next day.

The following evening, sleepy and hungry, the deportees were led out of the building. They walked the short distance to the main railway station, their guards chatting among themselves. Jews are not likely to resist, they had been informed. The streets were now crowded with people, many of whom were shouting *Jews out! Go to Palestine!* An organised chant. *If only we could,* Mordechai thought. The five hundred outcasts, now disorientated and demoralised, were taken to the station, and to a waiting train of fourteen coaches, its engine idling, steam gently venting over the platform. Thirty-five passengers were politely and patiently marshalled into each coach, sometimes a few more, in order to accommodate children. Inside were hard wooden benches, designed for third class passengers on short journeys. Many sat on their coats. There was room for everyone; no one had to stand. It was a slow train, stopping often at sidings, so that other trains could hurtle by.

At four the next morning the train arrived at Neu-Bentschen/Zbąszyń on the Polish border. Many other similarly laden trains had arrived that night, from all parts of Germany – Hamburg, Berlin, Magdeburg, Frankfurt – about twelve thousand people in all. They were kept waiting in their carriages until the last train arrived, one from Cologne. There were many children, clutching the hands of their parents who tried to comfort them with kisses and stories. But it was hard.

Heavy rain. Before they were allowed to detrain, SS officers searched everyone, even children, and confiscated their money, everything in excess of ten marks. *You know the rules. Only ten marks can be taken out of Germany. This rule is for everyone, even for you Jews.*

They were then jostled out of the train and ordered to

walk through a leaf-slippery forest that led to the border, two kilometres away, constantly pressed by SS officers with torches, whips and carbines. The rain deepened the pre-dawn darkness. All were wet, all were tired and hungry. They trudged through the gloomy wood, some tripping over hidden roots, falling, leaves gathering on their coats. Those who fell were beaten until helped to their feet by others. Packages were taken from stragglers as they staggered through the forest. *Let me hold this for you until you get through the woods, dear madam. You mustn't be weighed down under such wet and slippery conditions, not so?* It was very dark everywhere, save for the light from the tormentors' torches and a distant glimmer from windows of the Polish border station. Some children wailed, all their Grimm Brothers' nightmares coming true, goblins and witches everywhere in the dark wood.

The Polish border guards were taken completely by surprise, alarmed to see twelve thousand people descending upon them through the rain and darkness. *Are the Germans starting a war?* They grabbed their rifles, rushed outside and fired into the air. The refugees fell to the muddy ground, rigid with fear. One man near the front shouted in Polish, 'Don't shoot! We're Poles!' Then silence, save the noise of the steady rain, as it fell on trampled leaves and the drenched deportees.

A Polish general arrived thirty minutes later. He walked over to the prostrate group and beckoned them to rise. He examined some of their passports. 'All Poles? Jews?' Nods of assent. 'I'll try to do something.'

Three SS officers, who had been standing in the midst

of the dishevelled assemblage, now came forward and entered the border hut. They left a few minutes later, the commander placing a folded paper into his tunic pocket, buttoning it, then patting it down. The German detachment walked back to the main road, where a half-track was waiting to take them to somewhere warm, somewhere there would be coffee and bread, maybe schnapps to warm them up.

An hour later, Polish military lorries arrived. The dripping refugees were helped onto them and then driven along bumpy muddy tracks to Zbąszyń, a small town nearby. Most of the younger men were lodged in stables, the rest in military barracks. A few hours later the refugees had their first food in three days, fresh bread from nearby Poznan. There was coffee too, and milk for the children.

Esther Grynszpan managed to write a postcard to her brother as she sat on her simple frame bunk in the large barrack room. She was relieved that she was still alive. The Poles of Zbąszyń had given her fresh dry clothing, food, and shelter. Best of all, she could express herself freely on this card, now that she was no longer in Germany.

Darling Brother Herschel,
You undoubtedly heard of our misfortune. I will describe to you what happened. On Thursday evening at 9 o'clock a Sipo came to us and told us that we had to go to Police Headquarters. Almost everyone from our entire quarter was already there. We were not told what it was all about, but we saw immediately that everything was finished for us. Each of us had an

extradition order pressed into our hand, and we had to leave Germany immediately. They didn't permit us to return home anymore. I asked to be allowed to go home to get at least a few things. But they refused.

More next time.
Best regards and kisses from all of us.
Esther

He received the postcard four days later. Another, from his mother, arrived the day after.

CHAPTER 15
A BIG FAMILY FIGHT

'Why do you ignore our religion and work on Friday evenings instead of having a meal to honour the arrival of Sabbath? Why also do you work on the Sabbath? We should all go to *shul*.'

'Because, as I have told you so many times, Herschel, I simply can't afford to close the business early on Friday – and also on Saturday to stand around in the synagogue with a book in my hand, swaying and chanting in a language I don't understand with people I hardly know, on the busiest day of the week. If you want to be religious, be my guest, but I can't afford it. The shop makes little enough as it is.'

'But people in Germany are dying for their religion!'

'Don't be so childish. They're being persecuted because they chose their parents carelessly. Religion has nothing to do with it. We can be just as Jewish on Sunday afternoon.'

The boy wasn't mollified. Since being refused a residence permit by the French authorities, he had been living in an attic storeroom nearby, so that his uncle and aunt wouldn't be punished if he were found at their home. He sometimes felt like a prisoner in his small room, but he was able to leave in the evenings. Then, sheltered by the dark, or obscured by the anonymity of café crowds, he could meet his friends.

He arrived at the next Sunday meal after everyone had been seated. In their usual places sat his uncle and aunt; seated next to them, Basila and Jacques Wykhodz, Chava's sister and brother-in-law. This routine weekly gathering was slightly enlarged by the exceptional presence of Nathan Kaufman. It was a typical Grynszpan family meal, consisting of the familiar fare of boiled chicken, boiled potatoes, boiled carrots.

'You see,' said Jacques, 'Chava is the only one who really knows how to prepare potatoes just like we used to have them in Poland.'

'So what's to know? It's just potatoes and boiling water, and not to leave them in the pot either too short or too long,' Chava said.

'Yes, but there's an art to that. Same with the chicken. Perfect.'

'Exactly the same recipe,' said Chava. 'Chicken, water, maybe some herbs. Who needs anything else?'

'Simplicity. That's the secret,' agreed Basila. 'Don't you think so, Herschel? As a man of the world, or so they tell me.'

The boy said nothing, continuing to stare down at his plate. He touched his jacket pocket, felt the postcards. He couldn't put them out of his mind. *How could his parents now survive in Poland, without money, without enough food? What will happen to them? And what would happen to him? Will the French police find him and bundle him in the night to the German border, delivering him to Nazis who would see him dead? And if that happens, what about Aunt Chava and Uncle Abraham? Will they be arrested too?*

He masked his painful ruminations by silence.

Nathan turned to him. 'Listen, Herschel, if you're only going to stare at that chicken leg, give it to me. I can find a use for it.'

Aunt Chava touched her nephew's arm. 'What's wrong with you tonight? Normally I have to hide the food from you.'

He glowered at her and passed his plate to his friend.

Basila Wykhodz continued an earlier line of thought, one which had been interrupted by the boy's arrival. 'So I grant you, it's now even more terrible than ever for Jews in Germany. But the Germans have always hated us, so that's no surprise. Thank God, here in France it's better, especially if you were already born here. But still, not so good as in England where a Jew can get along fine so long as they don't try to act too Jewish, they keep their noses down, make plenty of money and give some of it to the Conservatives. But you can forget about America altogether. They don't want anybody to come in. Of course, in Palestine, that's a different story – in Palestine it's the best of all, truly the land of milk and honey – but…' she shrugged.

He looked up, anger bubbling in his voice. 'The anti-Semitic British won't let anyone into Palestine anymore, because they don't want to aggravate the Arabs, who have no right to the land which was promised by God to *us*. Who now gets entry permits is just a trickle. And even for these few, the Zionists are very picky. They only

123

want the rich, or strong young people who will agree not to speak Yiddish and also to learn to plough fields, or to do plumbing, or carpentry or digging. I tried to find a different way by being a rabbi, and you see what happened.'

He stared at his Uncle Abraham. 'Don't you understand what is happening to my family?'

'Of course I understand it. They're my family too. But your sister writes that they're no longer in immediate danger, so maybe we can look forward with a bit more optimism.'

'How can you say that? Do you not remember what my mother wrote the next day? I've read the postcard over and over, I know it almost by heart. He removed it from his pocket and waved it at his uncle. 'Do you not understand what it says? *The Polish Jews are doing what they can for us, but we are poorly fed, and we sleep on straw sacks – thank God for the barracks and blankets they found for us. Some people who managed to hide some money somehow, lodge in private homes, but the Nazis took all of our money when we got off the train. And we haven't yet received any money from the family.*

'And here's the most important part: *Please tell your aunt and uncle that we are in a very sad situation. We are poor and in misery. We don't get enough to eat. I beg them to think of us. We won't be able to stand this much longer. You mustn't forget us in this situation.*'

The air had become still enough for the sounds of traffic to seep into the room.

'So what do you expect me to do?' asked Abraham, pushing his plate away.

'Send them the money they gave you to look after me. I can look after myself.'

'So how much of that money do you think is left after two years? And do you think that the tailoring actually brings in anything beyond the barest essentials? And even if I sent money to them, who knows if they would ever get it? If the Nazis don't steal it from them, the Poles will. See reason, Herschel.'

'What I see is that you just don't appreciate what's happening to your own family shivering in Poland. And what I can also see is that you don't care for me at all – I certainly can see that.'

'How can you say that? Haven't I done all I can for you? That fine suit you're wearing, who made that?'

The boy rose, his chair pushed back forcefully. 'I'll find some old clothes and return the suit. Now I'm going.' He moved to the door.

Nathan intervened. 'Sit, Herschel, sit. I'm sure your uncle and aunt will find some way to help.'

Aunt Chava looked up at him and held onto his sleeve. 'Sit, child. I promise that we will examine every possibility.' She looked at Abraham for encouragement.

Abraham guardedly nodded assent. The boy slowly relented and sat down, his eyes almost bursting with unshed tears.

Abraham looked at his nephew sadly. 'My dear Herschel, don't you know how much I too am affected by all this misery, how much we all are? Do you think that I have completely forgotten my own brother?'

He thinks that I have been a burden. That I never help

in the shop – how often has he complained about me? That I spend so much time in cafés. But what can he expect? Can he not appreciate my situation? Adrift, no future? How can he say such things to me?

'You could at least answer me,' Abraham said.

'What answer can I give? You make it clear how little you think of me, you make this clear every day.'

'How could you even say such things to me, that I don't care for you after all I've done to help you.' His face hardened. 'In fact, if you genuinely feel that way, maybe you should leave?'

Chava blurted out, 'Abraham!'

Uncle Abraham rose. 'So go if you want. You needn't worry about the suit. It was, after all, a present. Here, you'll need some money.'

Abraham removed 300fr from a drawer in the sideboard and handed it to his nephew, who stuffed it into his coat without looking at it, tears of anger and frustration now making their way down his cheeks. The boy rose again, almost upending his chair. All those months of anger, fear, and frustration now engulfed him. Deaf to his aunt's sobs, he left the flat, slamming the door and clattering down the stairs.

The silence which followed was interrupted by Jacques. 'I'm only an in-law, so you have to forgive me for saying this, Abraham, but maybe you could have handled that better, yes? Just saying.'

Chava shouted at Abraham through her tears. 'How could you say such things to him? Can't you see what he's going through? Is your pride so important, more important than a seventeen-year-old's misery? He's only a child, Abraham. Just a baby, really.'

Abraham spoke quietly. 'He simply doesn't seem to realise the problems we all have here. If he wanders around and is found without a permit, then we'll be prosecuted for harbouring him and not turning him in to the authorities. Nathan, you're his friend, go after him and try to bring him back. Tell him I didn't really mean what I said, but that I am upset as well. Who wouldn't be?'

◄o►

He walked in the direction of *Tout va Bien*, where he hoped to calm himself with a coffee and the conversation of his friends. He walked slowly, gazing absently at the shuttered shops. His mood darkened with every step. *Perhaps I should commit suicide. That would be for the best. But how? It would have to be very public. An unforgettable act. No bathtubs with razors.*

Nathan caught up with him, slightly out of breath.

'I thought you'd be going this way.'

They fell into step together, walked silently for a while.

'They mean well, you know, your aunt and uncle. It's hard for them, but they do care about you.'

'Do they, Nathan, do they? That surprises me, it really does. Because if they really cared about me, he wouldn't speak to me that way, he wouldn't throw me out of the house onto the streets.'

'You wanted to go. You were already getting up to leave.'

'That's not the point. They should have tried harder to stop me. They're all I have here and they have thrown me out into a world where no one cares about me, and where I am in danger. At any moment I could be arrested.' The renewed pressure of tears was pushing behind his eyes and seeping out. Nathan put his arm around his friend.

'Go back to them. They told me to bring you back with me, that it's all been a misunderstanding.'

'It's no misunderstanding. They just don't care if my mother, father, sister and brother all go to their doom for the sake of a few francs. I've made up my mind. I won't go back to that apartment. Better to die like a dog from hunger than to go back on my decision!'

'Maybe you'll change your mind later. Anyway, let's leave the subject and just relax. Look. Is that Sam Schneider over there?'

Approaching them was their friend Sam, another German-Jewish refugee, happily in possession of valid French residency papers. He greeted them effusively.

'Where are you two scoundrels heading? Off drinking again? You know, Herschel, too much coffee will rot your willy.'

The boy couldn't suppress a smile. 'So where are *you* going, then, to the opera?'

'No,' Nathan said, 'to the Aurora Sporting Club. That'll be a healthier option, won't it, even if you just sit in their café. Come with me. We can talk about physical exertion while we have a beer. Of course, Herschel, you can have mineral water.'

Several young people were sitting at a large table when

the trio arrived. Pinky Steinberg stood up and embraced him.

'Herschel! That's some nice coat and suit! Excellent quality material. Who's your tailor? Or did you make it yourself in the shop?'

'Very funny,' he said, with a pretend scowl, but happier now to be amongst friends.

The others smiled at him, greeted Sam and Nathan, pulled up three chairs to the rough wooden table and ordered drinks. Pinky then said, 'As this is a sporting club, we are obliged to talk about sport. It is in the rules, after all. So which sport? That's the pressing problem. Football? Tennis? Wrestling? Better, of course, is that we should actually participate in sport, to become stronger and fitter for when we make *aliyah* to Palestine. What sport should you do, Herschel? Chess? Marbles? Complaining? Especially useful in Palestine, I hear.'

Nathan said, 'Don't forget, for a small *pischer*, Herschel is quite good with his fists. Maybe boxing would be an idea for him. Especially with the mood he's been in lately.'

'This is true,' Pinky conceded, 'but in what division? Flyweight? Featherweight? Gnatweight?'

'He'd be in a classification all on his own,' said Sam.

'And what will your fighting name be? Grynszpan the Great? The Horrible Hun from Hanover?'

'Be careful,' warned Nathan. 'We don't want our champion confused with that loser Schmeling.'

'Good point,' Sam said. 'But didn't we all feel wonderful when that Nazi was completely demolished by Joe Louis in the summer? It gives hope for all of us *untermenschen*.'

'Yes,' said Pinky, 'but it's no comparison between us and that *schwartzer*. No matter how much we hate the Nazis, these Africans are not in the same species as white people. But anyway, he really gave Schmeling such a terrific beating, and in only a couple of minutes it was all over, and then that Nazi was crying on the canvas, so we've that to be thankful for. In fact, it was even a worse beating than Schmeling got from Max Baer, who, for my money, on a good day is even a better fighter than that Joe Louis.'

They all agreed.

'What we now need in France is someone who can beat Louis, preferably a Jew, but I won't be fussy.' The speaker was Chaim Moskowitz, a hitherto unnoticed youth of perhaps twenty, with ginger eyebrows and a flaming red goatee which matched his closely cropped hair.

'What about Cerdan?' Pinky offered.

Herschel looked up at him. 'Are you crazy? Cerdan's a middleweight and Louis is a heavyweight. You know nothing about boxing.'

'About as much as you know about women.'

Sam changed the subject. 'Anyway, aside from your problems making any known boxing weight, how are things with you, Herschel?'

'Oh, the same old thing. Waiting for an entry permit to Palestine, but my French residency has been denied, so I'm a bit in the middle.'

Nathan said, 'I keep telling him that things will certainly improve, but he's just got to have patience, that's the only strategy.'

'Another strategy is to have plenty of money,' Chaim said.

A police van approached the club, its klaxon oscillating menacingly. They all stiffened. Conversation stopped. All relaxed as the vehicle hurried past. 'I know they're not like the Nazis, but the French don't really like us Jews that much either. Why is this?'

'Well, there's the crucifixion,' Chaim said. 'That's good for a start. But they don't hate all Jews, you know. My family has been here for three generations with no problems. You see, it's the immigrants like you they don't like. That and your fancy clothes.'

Everyone laughed. Herschel rose, shook hands all round, and announced, 'It's best for me to be going now, just to keep my head down.'

Nathan rose as well. 'Shall I come with you? Are you going back to your uncle's?'

'Sit, Nathan. I'll find a hotel and think things over.'

Nathan sat reluctantly. 'Don't do anything silly, like picking a fight outside your weight class. I'll see you tomorrow.'

He waved wanly as he left.

--<o>--

Wandering through the city as the evening deepened, he noticed a gun shop. He stared through the slats in the shutters. He could just make out a few pistols, thirty-eights, forty-fives, nine-mm Lugers. These shiny death dispensers fascinated him. Dimly remembered scenes from American films danced through his mind. Cagney,

Raft and Bogart with their Brownings, rods and roscoes, pumping lead into villains. Righting wrongs. Making things better.

He walked over to *Tout va Bien*, happy not to meet anyone. The patron acknowledged him discretely. He ordered a plain omelette and some salad. His stomach had been troubling him again. He ate without attention, staring absently at the posters on the wall, mostly of young men – bullfighters, dancers, movie stars and fashion icons. He paid the bill and wandered off again. On the boulevard de Strasbourg, a few streets from his uncle's apartment, he noticed a small cinema playing *La Bête Humaine*, starring Jean Gabin, but he was too agitated to go in. Next to the cinema: 'Hôtel de Suez, 1ˢᵗ floor.' He walked up a narrow flight of stairs, the muffled sounds from the cinema seeping through the walls.

'It's 22 francs 50 per night, morning coffee included,'

It had been a slow weekend, and Mlle Laurent was bored. She immediately identified the young man as a *métèque*, a foreigner, easily identifiable by his imperfect French. Noticing that he carried no suitcase, Mlle Laurent added, 'Paid in advance.'

He handed the money through the gap below the wire screen and signed the guest card.

'Papers? Can I see your papers, Monsieur?...' The receptionist squinted at the registration card, 'Oh yes, Herr Halter. Is that first name Heinrich? It's difficult to read.'

He nodded. 'Yes. From Hanover. But alas, I have no papers with me. Is that a problem? I'll be off tomorrow.'

'Checkout is at 10 am sharp,' she said as she handed him his key. He ascended the stairs, carpeted only as far as the next landing, climbed another flight, opened the door, took off his coat and flopped onto the spring-squeaky bed. He stared at the ceiling for a long time, wondering what to do, wondering if he should get undressed.

-<o>-

After a long and fractious discussion, a decision was finally taken to find the boy and bring him back.

'You go left, and I'll go right and then maybe we'll find him,' Abraham suggested to Jacques. 'I know that he often goes to the *Tout va Bien*, so I'll look there. Maybe you should try other places that young people go to.'

'What would I know about cafés?' Jacques asked. 'After work I hardly have the energy to go out at night.'

'Well, just look around, that's all I ask. First go to Nathan's flat. Maybe he's there.' Abraham jotted the address onto a torn piece of newspaper and handed it to him.

'And the rest of you stay here, in case he comes back on his own.'

The assembled assented over their thin coffees.

Chava reminded her husband. 'If you do find him, Abraham, be *nice*.'

-<o>-

Nathan had just arrived home when Jacques knocked. He explained that Herschel had left the *Club Sportif* at about 6 pm, and was planning to spend the night in a hotel.

'How can we find him, with so many hotels?' Jacques asked.

'Not possible, you're right,' said Nathan. 'Best to wait and see if he returns. I'm certain he'll be alright. Once he starts missing everybody he'll come back, but after that, someone should tell Abraham to go a bit easy on him, at least for a while.'

◄o►

In the Hôtel de Suez, Herschel had a difficult night. When he finally fell asleep, still in his suit, he was besieged by dreams; of his parents being beaten by gigantic SS men, of being chased himself by brown-shirted thugs, of being grabbed by the throat by a monstrously fat SA man, while Rotweilers growled and snarled. He woke up several times, his eyes snapping open, his heart palpitating. He pressed his hand onto his chest to calm himself, a technique he had once read about in a copy of *Pariser Haynt,* Paris Today, a local Yiddish language newspaper someone had left at the café. To his surprise, this technique worked – until the next dream appeared.

CHAPTER 16
BUYING A GUN

City noises jarred him awake. His immediate thought was that he should start his morning prayers. He looked for his tallis bag, then remembered that he had left it in his uncle's flat. A disappointed shrug. *God will forgive me after all I've been through.* He rang for breakfast. After a few minutes, as he washed his face then smoothed his rumpled clothes as best he could, he heard a soft knock. When he opened the door, he found a tray of food at his feet – croissant, jam, butter, and coffee. He was hungry. Though the croissant was stale and tasteless, he ate it all. His familiar heartburn began immediately. And as usual, this gastric rebellion was accompanied by anxious thoughts, the mantra of worries which accompanied him everywhere, sometimes suppressed by diversions, but always lurking.

He removed a postcard from the inside pocket of his jacket and studied it. On the front, a formal monochrome photograph taken a few months earlier, in a busy, shabby photographer's studio near the Pigalle, much recommended by his friends. Wearing a three-piece suit and tie, he stared straight at the camera, his attitude both serious and haughty, his black hair slicked back, an unlit cigarette resting nonchalantly between two fingers of his left hand, his right arm held behind his back. He thought the result both flattering and lifelike.

He fished the nub of a pencil from his jacket pocket and, sitting on the edge of the bed, wrote on the other side of the card:

My dear family, I couldn't do otherwise. God must forgive me. My heart bleeds when I think of our tragedy. I have to protest in a way that the whole world will hear, and this I intend to do. I beg your forgiveness.

He signed the card and addressed it to his aunt and uncle then placed it in his wallet.

Leaving the hotel quickly, he strode along the Boulevard de Strasbourg, now filling with pedestrians, lorries and buses.

He arrived at *A la Fine Lame*, the gun-shop he had discovered on the previous evening. A middle-aged woman was raising the door shutters, the metallic clatter breaking through the noise of the traffic. He followed her into the shop. She studied him warily. He seemed to her a contradiction; well dressed, wearing expensive clothes, poised – yet unkempt, creased, unshaven.

'Monsieur?' she enquired, her eyebrows betraying her uneasy curiosity.

He needed some time to formulate what he intended to say into the best French he could manage. He looked around the dark shop, crammed with a large display of handguns in glass display-cases, mostly pistols and revolvers. Rifles and shotguns were mounted on the walls behind the counter. Satisfied with his inner rehearsal, he turned to her.

'I need to buy a gun. It is because my father often...'

'If you will excuse me for a moment, Monsieur, I'll call my husband, Monsieur Carpe, who will be happy to advise you.'

Monsieur Carpe arrived before she could fetch him; stocky, sporting a moustache which Herschel thought was slightly too fulsome for his face. His wife went to open the window shutters. Morning light fell onto the wooden floor. He smiled at the young man.

'Why do you need a gun?'

'Well,' he replied, calming himself so that his voice didn't quaver, 'my father is a German merchant who has me to carry large sums of money for him, so I need something to protect myself, things in the world being as they are.'

'What sort of gun are you looking for?'

'I was thinking a 45. Like in the movies.'

Carpe scowled. 'The movies are not real life, Monsieur. A 45 is too heavy. Not for you, my son. What you need is a weapon that a person of your build could handle more easily. Something small, which, by the way, will also not spoil the lines of your jacket.'

He removed a small 'hammerless' pistol from the display case, demonstrating its lightness by passing it nimbly between his hands.

'It holds five rounds, perhaps a bit cumbersome to reload. But I don't expect someone like you will be in any gun battles. It's easy to use and accurate at short range, maybe up to twenty metres, depending, of course, on how well you aim.'

Carpe then explained the safety mechanism. He loaded then unloaded the weapon. He demonstrated the ease of the trigger mechanism, then handed the pistol to Herschel, who pointed the gun at the ceiling and pulled the trigger five times. This all fascinated the boy. The gun seemed simple to him, far less complicated than any sewing machine.

'This particular item costs 210 Fr, plus 35 Fr for a box of 25 bullets.'

He removed the three one-hundred-franc notes from his wallet and pushed them across the counter.

Carpe smiled, pushing the money back. 'Not quite yet, Monsieur. There is no hurry. It's early in the day, not so? First I need to take down your name and address and to see your identity papers.'

He handed Carpe his German passport, and stated his address as 8 rue Martel. After completing the registration form, he passed it to Carpe, who stamped it and handed it back, after writing the details into a ledger.

'You are required by law to take this form to a police station, which as it happens, is just around the next corner. In France, every weapon must be registered.'

'Yes, I understand.'

He handed the three 100 Fr notes to Carpe, and received his change, which Carpe removed from a drawer in a maple bureau behind him, having opened it with a small black key, one among many dangling at the end of a long silver keychain. Carpe wrapped the gun and ammunition in brown paper sheets and secured the packages with string. The boy put the packages into his overcoat pocket and walked to the door, nodding in the direction of Mme Carpe, who was busy dusting display cases.

'You turn left at the next corner. You'll see the police station ahead of you,' Carpe reminded his agitated young customer.

He left the shop, closing the door quietly. He turned left and walked purposefully down the busy street in the direction of the police station. After a few steps, he abruptly changed his course, almost colliding with a surprised pedestrian. He hurried towards *Tout va Bien*. Entering the café quickly, he mutely acknowledged the patron, who was fiddling with an ancient coffee machine. Relieved that none of his friends were there, he walked to the washroom and was instantly assaulted by the acrid smell of recently applied disinfectant. He breathed deeply, entered a cubicle and unpacked the revolver and ammunition. He loaded the handgun – *this isn't as complicated as Mr. Carpe said* – and put it into the left pocket of his suit jacket, smoothing the bulge as best he could. He placed the box of ammunition into his overcoat pocket. As he reached the Metro station, Strasbourg Saint-Denis, he threw the wrapping paper into a bin.

'A return ticket, please,' he asked at the counter.

'It's too early. No return tickets until after 9.30,' he was informed by an already bored cashier.

'A single then.'

139

He rode line 8 to the Madeleine, then changed to line 12 to Solférino.

He arrived at the German Embassy at 9.35. He was unsure about what to do next, but then the gun in his pocket reminded him of his mission.

CHAPTER 17
FIVE FATEFUL SHOTS

'What is the purpose of your visit?' The conspicuously armed officer standing at the gate was neither friendly nor menacing, merely practiced. The boy was churning inside.

'I am here to get a German Visa.'

'This is the wrong building for such requests. You should go to the German Consulate on the rue Huysmans, not here.'

'I went there yesterday. They said to come here.'

The gendarme shrugged and pointed to a door signposted 'Public Entry'.

'You can ask at reception. They will probably tell you the same thing.'

As he approached the building, an expensively dressed man crossed his path, walking purposefully in the opposite direction. Count Johannes von Welczeck, the German Ambassador, had just left his office and was now beginning his habitual morning walk. The ambassador nodded politely as their paths crossed, but the boy didn't respond, not recognising the man. He entered the building, his emotions vacillating between confidence and trepidation.

The first person he encountered was Mme Mathis, the wife of the concierge, briefly deputising for her husband while he changed out of his sooty overalls. He had been working on the erratic boiler in the basement.

Mme Mathis smiled politely at the boy. 'My husband, alas, is currently indisposed. But perhaps I can help you, Monsieur?'

'I require to see an embassy official, Madame,' he said, in mostly adequate French. 'I have important papers to deliver to him.'

'Then Monsieur, you need to go up the stairs to the first floor, and see Herr Nagorka. He may be able to help you.'

Alfred Nagorka was the embassy clerk-receptionist on duty that day. A slim man in his mid-twenties, his black hair was combed back, accentuating the roundness of his face. He looked up as Herschel approached. Nagorka noticed the lad's fine if dishevelled clothing. He also noticed what he surmised were dark Semitic features.

The clatter of typewriters and tintinnabulations of telephones underscored the conversation. Nagorka spoke without smiling.

'Mein Herr? Monsieur?'

He answered in German, and the safety of his mother tongue soothed him. 'I'd like to see one of the embassy secretaries.'

'Have you an appointment?'

'No, but I have very important papers I must deliver.'

'They are very busy people, Herr...?'

He didn't offer his name.

'Very important papers,' he repeated, with more emphasis.

'Perhaps I can deliver the papers for you.'

'As I have said, the papers are extremely important.' He could feel his anxiety rising and tried again to force calm on himself. He unclenched his fists. 'It is absolutely essential that I deliver them personally.'

'Very well, then. I shall see what I can do. If you will kindly follow me.'

He was led downstairs into a quiet waiting room in which several people were sitting on chairs lining the walls. *It's like at the dentist,* he thought. *How I hate the dentist.* He patted his jacket pocket, again reassured to feel the bulge of the gun.

Nagorka reappeared after a few moments. 'If you will follow me, I will take you to a man who might be able to assist you.'

He led him to the small office of the Third Secretary, Ernst Eduard Adolf Max vom Rath, a thirty-one-year-old, fair-skinned, thin lipped young man. Nagorka closed the door quietly. Vom Rath was sitting at his desk, his back to his visitor, facing the window which overlooked the rear courtyard. He was initialling a document. He spoke softly.

'Do please be seated. I'll be with you in a moment.'

The boy seated himself in a leather armchair a few feet from the desk. His gaze was drawn to a framed photograph of Hitler on the wall to his right. *There's the architect of all our misfortunes. I'd give my life to have him in this room!*

Vom Rath turned his chair so that he was facing his

visitor. He smiled in an official way and said. 'Thank you for coming. May I see the documents?' *Have I seen this boy before somewhere?*

The boy's anxiety was now overwhelmed by the rage which had been percolating within him for so many months. His face flushed, and the veins in his neck protruded.

'You're a filthy *Kraut*,' he shouted, 'and in the name of all persecuted Jews, *here* are the documents!'

Vom Rath began to rise as Herschel pulled the revolver from his jacket pocket. Without really aiming, he fired five times, emptying the weapon. Two of the shots pierced vom Rath's body. One entered his torso and lodged in his shoulder. The other perforated his stomach, rupturing his spleen and penetrating his pancreas. Vom Rath staggered to the door, throwing a weak punch at his assailant's face as he passed, shouting for help, holding his stomach as he entered the hallway.

The boy's rage evaporated and he slumped back into the chair, suddenly overcome with weariness. *I hope I've killed him,* he thought. He dropped the revolver onto the floor and waited. In the corridor, the sounds of the typewriters had stopped.

When he had heard the shots, Nagorka pushed his chair away from his desk, rushed along the hallway, and found vom Rath in the doorway.

'I am wounded,' vom Rath gasped, his pain masked by his surprise. Nagorka could see a spreading red stain on vom Rath's shirt. Another embassy colleague, Herr Krüger, quickly approached the pair and together the two men gently lowered vom Rath into a sitting position on the floor, keeping his back resting against the corridor wall. A third embassy attaché arrived to attend to vom Rath, allowing Nagorka and Krüger to turn their attentions to the perpetrator. They grabbed the seated boy, and with a roughness which caused him to cry out, raised him from his chair, pinning his arms forcibly behind his back.

'You needn't be so rough, *meine Herren*,' he shouted, as he was bundled out of the office, 'I have no intention to escape. But all I ask is that you turn me over to the French police.' He managed a quick glance at vom Rath as he passed. 'Too bad he isn't dead,' he added, receiving a punch in the kidneys in response. He was manhandled down the stairs, the two German officials supporting him under his armpits as he stumbled. They rushed him roughly to the main gate, his feet scraping on the ground, then pushed him into the arms of the gendarme who had been his first contact with the embassy only a few moments before.

'This man has just shot an official. Arrest him!' Nagorka shouted.

Herschel was handcuffed.

'Don't worry, monsieur, I will come with you,' he said calmly, relieved to be in the custody of a Frenchman.

Nagorka and Krüger turned away, Krüger loudly muttering 'filthy Jew', as they hurried towards the entrance. When the Germans were out of earshot, the boy shouted after them, '*sales boches!*'

The gendarme signalled for a colleague to replace him at the gate, then turned his captive towards the street. The boy felt limp and hot, his sweat-dampened shirt clinging to his back. The gendarme spoke quietly as they walked, 'What happened?'

'It's a shame he isn't dead,' he repeated, less forcefully this time. 'I have just shot a man in his office. I do not regret it. I did it to avenge my parents who are rotting in a filthy Polish refugee camp – all the work of these filthy Nazis.'

CHAPTER 18
TAKEN TO JAIL

He was led along the road to the nearby precinct headquarters, to the office of M.J. Monneret, the Commissioner of Police for the district. The boy stood handcuffed in front of a large mahogany desk.

'What is your name?' Monneret asked, peering up over half-moon spectacles. His eyes looked tired.

'Herschel Feibel Grynszpan.'

A uniformed officer was sitting at a metal desk behind the commissioner, taking down the details. He interrupted. 'Will you spell those names, please?'

He complied. Monneret continued.

'Date and place of birth?'

'Twenty-eight March 1921, Hanover, Germany.'

'May I see your French papers?'

'Alas, I have no residency permit.'

Monneret nodded. 'Parents' names?'

He spelled those for the officer.

'Please hand me your wallet.'

He removed his wallet from his inside pocket. In it were thirty-eight Francs, and the purchase declaration for the firearm.

'Why did you not register this weapon as required by law?'

'I was about to bring that paper here. Anyway, you have it now.' The wallet also contained three invitations to a dance at the *Club Sportif Aurore*, and three postcards, two from his sister and mother in Poland, and the one he had written the night before and forgotten to post.

Monneret stared sadly at the boy.

'Why did you commit this stupid crime?'

'With the greatest respect, Monsieur Commissioner, it was not stupid. I shot that *sale boche* because it was the only way I could avenge the terrible treatment of my parents in Germany. I could not do otherwise. You must know that in Germany we are all treated like dogs. But I am not a dog. I have a right to live and the Jewish people have a right to exist on this earth. But wherever I go I am chased like an animal.'

'But why him in particular? Why vom Rath? Do you know him?

The boy shrugged. 'Does it matter *which* German?'

He then recounted the details of his movements during the preceding twenty-four hours.

He was photographed after being allowed to comb his dishevelled hair and straighten his clothes. *It is important to have a presentable photograph taken; it wouldn't do to look like a common criminal.*

Commissioner Monneret then arranged for the prisoner and a small team of officers to retrace the events leading up to the crime. They arrived at the Hôtel de Suez in mid-afternoon. Mlle Laurent recounted that there had been nothing particularly distinctive about Herschel's behaviour the previous evening, 'although he did seem somewhat unsettled and of course, he had no papers.' The police team then searched the bedroom, but found nothing. Monneret thanked Mlle Laurent, and escorted the boy back to the police car.

They then proceeded to *A la Fine Lame*, where the owner, Monsieur Carpe, recalled his meeting with the assailant.

'This young man was extremely nervous,' he said, gesturing with his head towards the boy, who was standing between two officers, looking around the shop as if for the first time, 'but once I showed him the weapon, he became more relaxed and very interested. Still, he behaved oddly, and for him to think that he could fire a 45 without the recoil taking his scrawny arm off just beggars belief.'

They arrived at the German embassy twenty minutes later. The boy refused to accompany Monneret into the building. 'I won't ever again willingly enter German territory. I refuse to put myself into their jurisdiction.'

Inside, Herr Nagorka led the police to vom Rath's office: nothing disturbed. Monneret immediately noticed the pistol lying on the floor next to the chair, its price-tag still attached to the trigger guard by a red string. He opened the weapon. Five cartridge cases were in the chamber. A bullet hole was visible in the wall behind the desk; another was found in the coat closet opposite the door. Both shots had been low, about one metre from the floor.

'Thank you, Herr Nagorka. I have all I need now.'

'You will understand that my government in Berlin is taking a very active interest in this incident.'

'That goes without saying,' Monneret responded as he left, returning to the car where his captive was gazing blankly at people passing on the street.

He was escorted into a cell. He sat on the bed, staring at the small barred window. The door clanged and was locked behind him.

Shortly afterwards, Abraham Grynszpan was brought in for questioning.

'When did you last see your nephew?'

'Last evening, sir. He was a dinner guest at my apartment.'

'Did you notice anything strange about his behaviour?'

'He is of course a very excitable boy, he's an adolescent after all, but sometimes he behaves almost like a child. That afternoon we had a fight, it doesn't matter what about because we have many such disturbances. But lately he has been very upset about a postcard which he received from his family who are now refugees in Poland. We disagreed about what to do. As usual, there were shouts and then he left abruptly. I tried to go after him and to calm him down, but I couldn't find him. He wasn't at any of his usual places. But I thought he would come back, so I just waited. The next thing I hear is from you.'

'Did you know that he had no valid papers?'

Abraham averted his gaze. 'Yes, Monsieur Commissioner, I regret to say that I did.'

'Why did you not report this to the police?'

'How can you turn in your own flesh and blood?' Abraham suppressed his tears. 'Especially if it means certain persecution if he is sent back to Germany. Could you do this to your nephew, Monsieur?'

Monneret looked up from his papers and smiled kindly.

'If you want to see your nephew, I can take you to him now. But I must also warn you that you have violated a provision of the French Criminal Code, and that as a result, you may have to appear in court.'

'I understand. Please take me to my nephew.'

The boy rose when Abraham entered the cell. He seemed to his uncle remarkably relaxed. He smiled and hugged his shaken relative.

'What have you done, Herschel? What have you done?'

'I did what was necessary. I did it to avenge my parents, our family.'

'But how will such a deed help? What good can it do? And as a result, we will all be visited by even more of our endless troubles and heartaches. And what about me and your aunt Chava? We may now be arrested, maybe even go to jail, or worse, be deported. Even worse than that, they might think that we were all part of some conspiracy! Didn't you think about this, Herschel?'

His nephew was quiet for a moment. 'It was necessary,' he replied.

At 11 pm Herschel Grynszpan was brought to the Criminal Investigation Department of the Sûreté. Police Inspector Badin, a no-nonsense career officer, questioned him in greater detail. Throughout, the boy seemed almost to be enjoying the attention, all the wonderful theatricality of the drama he himself had brought to life. He saw the situation as a validation of his historic role; to act 'so that the whole world would not ignore it,' as he would recount the next day.

At this interview, he embroidered the story of his encounter with vom Rath. 'Wounded by my bullets, the official put both hands on his abdomen, and he still had the strength to give me a punch in the jaw, calling me at the same time, "dirty Jew, *dreckiges Judenvolk*". Then he made a rush for the door crying "Help!" I wanted to avenge myself further for the insult that he hurled at me, and I tried to throw the weapon at his face but I missed him. Then two other Nazis grabbed me very roughly and pulled me down the stairs. Fortunately, they put me into the hands of a gendarme, or I do not know what would have happened to me.'

It was well after 2 am when he was finally returned to his cell, handed a blanket and abandoned for the night. He fell asleep quickly, after noticing that his stomach wasn't causing him any problems.

CHAPTER 19
DOCTORS

'I am Dr Karl Brandt, and this is my colleague Dr Georg Magnus. The Führer himself sent us to help. We will do whatever is necessary to save this brave German's life.'

Dr Brandt, a thin, stern-faced man, was one of Adolf Hitler's personal physicians. He was dressed in civilian clothes, which he had considered more appropriate for this occasion than his usual SS uniform. The pair of emissaries from the Third Reich solemnly shook hands with the two local doctors who had been treating vom Rath, Dr Baumgartner, a German surgeon resident in Paris, and Dr Jubé, a famous French haematologist.

A nurse waited outside.

Ernst vom Rath was sleeping neatly and peacefully in his narrow bed. A glass-topped wooden table stood to his right; on it, a small water decanter and a vase containing ferns.

'Why was he brought to this Gynaecological clinic?' Dr Brandt asked.

'We intended at first to take him to the American Hospital at Neuilly, as the facilities are far better there,' Dr Baumgartner reported, 'but his wounds were too serious and there was too much loss of blood. I therefore decided

153

to bring him to this clinic and operate immediately. I removed the damaged spleen, sutured the stomach wound and cleared the blood clots. However, the continued bleeding still gives us cause for concern.'

Dr Jubé concurred. 'I have been supervising the blood transfusions. A local French compatriot, decorated in the last war, has graciously offered his blood to help this heroic son of Germany. He is a living proof of the friendship between our two great nations.'

'Which the Jews would wish to destroy, it appears,' said Dr Magnus without emotion as he gently pulled back the covers and examined vom Rath's sutures.

'Neatly done,' he said.

Dr Brandt examined the chart attached to the end of the bed. 'I can see, and will report to the Führer, that everything is being done which possibly could be done. The only sensible treatment now is to continue transfusions and to monitor his condition. Let's hope that the bleeding will come under control. And also let us keep an eye on his temperature.'

'He's very weak,' Baumgartner said. 'His constitution is not strong, not what one might expect from a man of that age. Tubercular history, I am told.'

'We should perhaps give the press a bulletin. Do we agree?' Dr Magnus said.

They all nodded and agreed to meet later in the day. The nurse was called into the room and instructed to contact Drs Brandt and Baumgartner if there were any changes. Dr Jubé proceeded to arrange for further transfusions.

The bulletin read:

*The condition of Secretary of legation vom Rath is
extremely serious, especially because of the damage to
the stomach. The consequences of the considerable loss
of blood, caused by damage to the spleen, can probably
be overcome by further blood transfusions.*

Dr Brandt telephoned Berlin. He asked to speak to Hitler.
'He is expecting to hear from me.'

A short delay. Then the unmistakable voice.

'What have you to report, Brandt?

'Mein Führer, vom Rath is in a stable condition. He has
been sedated. He is very weak, but with proper treatment
he might survive. However…'

'However?'

'Mein Führer, when I looked at his file I found evidence
of anal gonorrhoea. This is from his time in India, I
believe. There is also gastro-intestinal tuberculosis, from
which he is now suffering.'

'And this means?'

'It is possible, Mein Führer, that vom Rath is a
practising homosexual.'

A pause.

'Have you told this to anyone else?'

'Only Dr Magnus, who accompanied me.'

'And he can be trusted?'

'Completely.'

There was a longer pause. Dr Brandt could hear voices
in the clinic corridor, traffic through the windows. After a
few minutes, Hitler came back to the telephone.

'I think it best if you allowed the French doctors to

continue with their own treatment.'

'We should not intervene? We might be able to save him, especially if we can move him to a better hospital and stabilize his intestinal tuberculosis with insulin.'

'No.'

'Vom Rath will probably die in that case.'

'Yes.'

'Thank you, Mein Führer.'

'Good-bye, *Untersturmbahnführer* Brandt.'

—◄o►—

Ernst vom Rath's father arrived at mid-day, accompanied by his younger son. They had taken the train from Cologne and had come directly to the hospital, sending their luggage to the hotel by taxi. They approached the bed, stared painfully at the stricken diplomat for a few moments, then sat in silence.

Gustav thought about how disappointed he had been when his son Ernst joined the Nazi party in 1932, still a student; and how he became more deeply disappointed when Ernst joined the SA, 'this bully-boy brigade,' as Gustav termed them. 'They know nothing but violence and stupid slogans.'

'That's all overstated, father. More important is the camaraderie, the feeling of being part of something bigger, grander. Then there's the outdoor life and the songs when we march. All that communal exercise is helping develop my imperfect physique.'

He smiled at his father. 'Most importantly, the party connections will help with my career. It's not like before.

Now, if you want to get ahead, especially in the civil service, you have to belong to the party.'

But things changed. The revolutionary euphoria of 1933 was followed by the slaughter of leading members of the SA leadership in 1934. This had completely unsettled Ernst, and while he had no particularly strong feelings towards Jews generally, the growing violence towards those who had once been his neighbours began to disturb him.

Early that evening the four doctors arrived and each in turn examined the patient. Another bulletin was issued that evening:

> *The condition of Secretary of Legation vom Rath as of this evening has not improved. The situation is critical. The patient's high temperature remains. There are also initial indications of circulatory problems.*

The next morning Ernst's mother joined her family in the hospital room. She had brought with her one small valise and expressed her intention to remain at her son's bedside until the crisis passed. The three vom Raths sat silently. Ernst's mother had pulled a chair next to the bed and gently held her son's hand. At one point, just after lunch – she had brought some sandwiches and a nurse brought them a pitcher of water – Ernst awoke shallowly, smiled at his mother and tried to speak. His mother squeezed his hand and bent over to kiss her forehead.

'Best not to speak, son. Use all your strength to return back to us.' Ernst's eyes surveyed the room cloudily, and he tried to smile at his family before he returned to sleep.

Drs Magnus and Brandt appeared shortly thereafter. They shook hands solemnly with the vom Rath family. Gustav was pleased that no one offered the Hitler salute.

Dr Magnus announced, 'The Führer has just sent word that he has promoted your son to legation counsellor.' He read from the telegram.

All Germany applauds your heroism and fervently wishes for you to return speedily to full health and to continue to serve the fatherland. I can assure you those responsible for this cowardly atrocity will be punished without mercy. Adolf Hitler.

It was shortly after 3 pm that the newly promoted vom Rath began to descend into a deeper sleep. His breathing became shallower. Over the next hour he gently declined into a coma. After another transfusion, in the presence of his parents and the four doctors, Ernst vom Rath died at 4.25 pm. His family left the room without speaking. They returned to the hotel they hadn't much needed, collected their belongings and boarded the next train for Cologne.

The final communiqué read:

The Legationsrat and party member vom Rath died of the wounds which he received on 7 November. During the course of the morning his condition worsened further. A new blood transfusion was only temporarily effective. Blood circulations reacted insufficiently to medication. The fever remained high. Towards midday the effect of the stomach injury in conjunction with the damage to the spleen became more evident. The loss of the patient's strength could not be arrested; death occurred at 4.30 pm.

Hitler was informed of vom Rath's death that evening in Munich as he was attending the 15th annual commemoration celebrations of his attempted coup of 9 November 1923, known as *The Beer Hall Putsch,* the most sacred day in the Nazi calendar.

CHAPTER 20

A BUTTERFLY'S WINGS

The murder of Ernst vom Rath was an opportunity for Josef Goebbels. Over the last few months, his star had been fading rapidly. He could see it in Hitler's eyes. Where there was once interest and lively friendliness, there was now a blue blandness – the look the Führer gave to functionaries, waiters and chauffeurs. Goebbels' slide from favour had started because of his relationship with an actress.

The affair had begun predictably enough. Goebbels had been in the habit of visiting UFA's Babelsberg film studios for the purpose of scouting young talent for his casting couch. Behind his back, people referred to him as 'the tadpole' or 'the goat of Babelsberg.' He savoured the notoriety. Josef wasn't a handsome man – 'striking' was the kindest way to describe him – frail of build, a thin head, beak-like nose, and with a limp brought about from a 'childhood misfortune', as he termed it. Nonetheless, the combination of his frank eyes, a magnetic personality, a surprising charm, and access to unlimited power, proved an attractive incitement to new actresses, and even to some well-established film divas.

In the summer of 1936, just before the Berlin Olympics,

and just after Max Schmeling defeated Joe Louis, Josef met and was smitten by a Czech actress, Lída Baarová. She was working on a film called *The Hour of Temptation,* co-starring her lover and fiancé, Karl Fröhlich, a famous star in his own right – handsome, suave, tall – everything that Josef was not. The couple had recently bought a house near the Goebbels' estate at Schwanenwerder, and Josef managed to find excuses for regular visits.

It all began in the usual way. At first there were meetings in the Reichsminister's large office, where he would discuss upcoming films and their probable casting. Goebbels suggested that he might put Lída forward for several starring parts. 'A word from me, and any part could be yours.'

She remained reticent at first. Goebbels' usual method with women often involved having his chauffeur drive them to some country house. Inside, a large living room, a wood fire, soft couches, and cognac. But this strategy didn't work with Lída.

'You see, I love Karl Fröhlich, Herr Reichsminister.'

'Of course, you do.' He smiled sympathetically, looking into her eyes. 'Please call me Josef. Yes, Fröhlich is a wonderful fellow, and a splendid actor, it goes without saying. It also goes without saying that likewise I love my wife, Magda. But why, in this day and age, should this stop us from getting to know each other more intimately? No one need know, and I can help you in your film career, and you can delight me with your beauty.'

Lída had heard stories of how those few actresses who had refused his advances had seen film offers evaporate, even those films which were already in production could be cancelled or re-cast without explanation. And so Lída wondered. Perhaps if they really could be discreet... It took her several weeks but she eventually gave in to him.

Then it took hold, tentatively, sporadically. Passionate meetings in his office, sometimes a languorous weekend at a lakeside cabin. He showered her with countless expensive gifts. Gradually, his angular features began to soften, his eloquent voice cloaked itself in velvet, his frail body became tenacious, yet vulnerable and lithe in her arms. Most importantly, she loved being adored by *her* Reichsminister.

Unlike previous affairs, Goebbels now found his lust tempered by a growing tenderness and need. It was Lída's eyes, those brown caverns of excitement and mystery, which had completely ensnared him. He would gaze lovingly at her lustrous hair, her expressive mouth. He loved to stroke her soft knees and satin thighs. And in bed, she moved under him as she had often danced on the screen, with rapturous abandon. To Josef's delight, she spoke to him when they made love, encouraging him, mostly in Czech, and he found the exotic strangeness of that language very exciting. Magda never spoke to him in this way, not even in German. She merely smiled lovingly at him, doing what she was told, seeming to enjoy their couplings.

Despite their precautions, their secret didn't last long. The couple's studied avoidances in public gatherings, furtive looks from corners of a room, badly explained and unpredictable absences, fooled no one. Lída was coy with her friends, with Olga Chekova and Anny Ondra, as they gossiped about Josef over tea; how the Reichsminister tried to get every actress into bed.

'Not me!' said Anny. 'Do you know, he even approached me when Max was being honoured at the Chancellery. I was polite, of course, but I made it perfectly clear that I was not going to be another one of his conquests. No film part is worth having to sleep with that man. Anyway, just let him try. Max would make certain that he never tried it again!'

'Just let him try something like that with me, as well,' said Lída. 'I'll tell him where to go!'

◄○►

Magda Goebbels had heard about her husband's affair with Lída Baarová. She had tolerated previous romances, but feared that this one was serious, a genuine threat to their marriage. At first, Josef tried the subterfuge of partial honesty. He sat with her in their living room, the large glass doors open to the late summer breezes. A small black and gold butterfly flew into the spacious room. For a moment it lighted on Magda's bare arm, opened and closed its wings twice, and then fluttered off.

'You know that I have recently become friendly with the actor Fröhlich and his fiancée Lída Baarová.'

Magda sat, her hands resting patiently on her lap. She smiled but didn't respond. The three children were upstairs with the Nanny, the fourth was moving gently inside her.

'But, darling Magda, I can assure you that there is

nothing going on between this Baarová and me. It is true that she is very beautiful, in a slightly Slavic way, and a good actress, it must be said. To be completely honest, it is hard for me to resist her.' He waited a beat for her reaction. None came. 'But I have resolved to remain loyal to you, especially now, my true beloved Magda, as you are carrying our fourth wonderful child.' He walked over to her and took her hands in his. His eyes were misted over. 'I will ever be faithful to you, my own true Magda.'

She believed him. She told her friends, 'Josef and I are now closer to each other than ever before. It makes me so happy that he is resisting temptation and being true to me.'

Soon afterwards, Josef and Lída travelled to Prague together, on the pretext of a promotional campaign with the Czech film industry. They departed on the day the Goebbels' daughter Hedda was born. When they returned, just as Josef was embracing Lída on the back seat of his chauffeur driven Mercedes, Karl Fröhlich, who was meant to be away working on a film, erupted through the front door of their house, his feet rasping the gravel as he strode towards the car. He pulled his startled fiancée from Goebbels' embrace, yanking her from her seat. She yelped as he slapped her face. Fröhlich walked away quickly, pursued by neither Goebbels nor the chauffeur.

Later that evening, Lída tried to mollify her estranged fiancé.

'What am I to do, Karl?' She was sobbing. 'He controls everything, every film. What can I do? I won't work if he dislikes me.'

'What you are to do, my little whore, is to leave this house. Tonight.'

For the next two years, Magda continued to ignore all evidence of the affair. Then, in the febrile summer of 1938, events in the Goebbels' household came to a head. One hot afternoon, with lake Wansee shimmering in the sunlight, Josef arranged an informal gathering at his lakeside home. The gathered included Lída, and Ello Quant, Magda's sister-in-law from her previous marriage. Anny Ondra was also there, as a favour to Magda.

'It would be wonderful if you could come, dearest Anny,' she had said on the telephone. 'I sometimes feel so isolated in this male world. I need another friendly woman near me. Who better than you?'

The luncheon was simple and pleasant, Josef extending his charm to all the women. After coffee, Josef suggested that they all relocate to his yacht, *Baldur,* to escape the heat.

'Oh, I wish I could come with you, the water seems so lovely and peaceful,' said Anny, 'but Max and I are expected at an art exhibition. Thorak's bronzes of us are on display at the Sportpalast, also the sketches for them. He calls the exhibition, *Champion and Screen-star.* It's part of the build-up to Max's rematch with Joe Louis.'

'I know about it, of course,' Josef said. 'Tomorrow all the papers will be full of pictures of you and your champion. I must say that no bronze can ever do justice to you.'

Anny went over to Magda, leaned in to kiss her on the cheek, and whispered. 'Don't let him get away with it.'

Half an hour later, sporting a white linen suit, round sunglasses and a white wide-brimmed hat, reclining on a deck chair at the prow of the boat, Josef smiled contentedly at the lake and at Lída, who sat by his side. She was wearing a skimpy bathing costume which exposed all of her midriff. Whenever she turned, her modest breasts became demurely visible. She turned often to Josef as they spoke.

On the deck above, Magda chatted with her sister-in-law about the lake, about the occupants of passing sailboats, and about the ruddy health of their fifth child, Hedwig, born just two months before.

'And he still insists on naming every child starting with an H? Has this not gone too far?'

'Perhaps, Ello, but it's too late to change. Since they are all named to honour the Führer, how will the first one who isn't feel? Still more, how will the Führer react? It seemed a good idea at the time, but honestly, I didn't expect to be pregnant so often.'

There was a giggle from below. Josef was whispering into Lída's ear, the edges of his long fingers lazily brushing her midriff, then her thigh. Magda became silent. Ello peered at her. 'But what is it, sweet Magda? You're crying. Tell me.'

'You must promise to tell absolutely no one.'

'You know you can trust me.'

Magda leaned towards her. 'Josef is having an affair,' she whispered. 'With *her.*' She pointed at Lída with her chin. 'It's not like all the others. He's totally besotted. He once looked at me in the same way, so I know that look.'

'Wives are always the last to know,' Ello said, swatting a mosquito which had landed on her arm, and in the same motion brushing away the speck of insect and blood. 'Everyone in Berlin knows about it, they're even becoming tired of talking about it. It's just one of his normal adventures.'

Magda shook her head. 'No. Not this time. A few weeks ago, he brought her home to tea. I didn't make much of it. He had been protesting his faithfulness to me constantly, and more fool me, I believed him. Anyway, after a few minutes of pleasant chit-chat, Josef turned to me and said, "Magda, I have something important to tell you. It is very serious. Lída and I love each other." Baarová looked up at me and said, "yes, it's true".

'You can imagine how I felt. As if the whole world – everything, the children, the house – all were dissolving at my feet. I was too shocked to say anything. And, as usual, Josef filled my silence. "You are naturally the mother of my children and the wife who belongs to me. But after so many years together surely you must realise that I need a lady friend, I mean a steady and serious friend."

'Perhaps Josef took my silence for some sort of consent, I don't know. I just couldn't say a word. But as I rose from my chair to leave, Josef stopped me and put his arms around me. He was crying. "I knew I could rely on you. You are, and will always remain, my good old wife." He said that exactly, Ello, *old*. I am 36! But of course, she is just 24.'

'And how old is Josef?'

'He's 41, but that doesn't seem to matter so much with men, does it?

'But of course you wouldn't agree to such a vile suggestion.'

Magda was silent for a time. She looked at the glistening lake, then at her husband. 'You know, when all is said and done, Josef is really a most remarkable man. Perhaps he deserves more than most men. Maybe he needs, as he calls it, a special friend, maybe a second wife. Such arrangements are common enough in Arabia and India. Maybe she will prevent him from having even more affairs? So I will try to stick it out. To understand him better.'

'You're crazy, Magda. No one should ever put up with that, especially not the wife of this self-proclaimed "genius".' But Magda said nothing and continued to look at the lake.

As the boat turned to make its way back to its mooring, Magda and Lída met in a corridor. Magda was combing her hair in front of a mirror. Lída smiled. 'I love your wonderful silken hair, Frau Goebbels.' Magda did not reply. 'But each woman offers different attractions, don't you agree? For example, Josef loves it when I come into a room wearing a frock like this one with no brassiere.' She turned to admire her profile in the mirror, smoothing down the dress over her taught stomach. 'I guess it's difficult to keep your shape after having so many children. Not so, Frau Goebbels?'

Magda spoke slowly, with a calmness which surprised her. 'You know, Fräulein Baarová, there are better ways to make a career than by sleeping with a minister. For example, you might try working on your acting more.

Merely by looking into the camera as you do at Josef will only get you so far.'

Magda could see Lída's face lose colour. She continued. 'You see, my dear, some day that little crack between your legs will dry up and wear out, and then what will you have?' Magda pushed past her as she left the cabin.

There was a dinner party that evening. Josef had invited Benno von Arendts, the stage director. Josef, Lída and Benno spent the time happily engaged in film and theatre chat. Magda glared at them behind the rictus of a smile. She and Ello were being ignored. Any attempt she made to drift the conversation in her direction was rebuffed.

Josef was discussing the casting of a new film. Various stars were mentioned, including Anny Ondra.

Lída frowned, then forced a smile. 'Of course, Anny is a dear friend of mine, but I think her talents are very limited. In fact, I have struggled to see any talent in her at all. And as for dancing, and capering around on the screen…'

Magda couldn't keep silent. 'Fräulein Baarová, it doesn't become you to speak of Anny Ondra in that way. She has become world famous through her own efforts alone, without any patronage whatsoever. Not even from my husband.' She threw Josef an arch smile. 'Moreover, she is highly respectable, also a versatile and talented woman. She is a good friend of mine, both she and her wonderful husband Max, and I simply can't bear to hear you passing judgement on her in this impertinent and thoughtless way. You're not half the woman she is!'

Lída was about to reply, but Josef put his hand on her arm.

Magda rose slowly from her seat and stared at her husband. Her voice was filled with quiet regret and resignation. 'Josef, I have put up with your betrayals for so many years, maybe out of weakness, maybe from love, I don't know. But this new charade goes too far. I can't stand it any longer, Josef. I want a divorce.' She left the room without looking back.

Josef called after her. 'On this subject you are absolutely right, Magda. It can't go on like this.'

A while later, Goebbels burst into his wife's bedroom, glowing with rage.

'How could you speak to her in that manner? And in front of guests? I will not stand for it. Do you hear?' His voice had been raised to the pitch usually reserved for party rallies. Magda stood silently. She looked at him calmly.

'I want a divorce,' she said.

'You're just being hysterical. Calm down. A divorce is impossible. You'd have to prove adultery.'

'I don't think that would be difficult. All Germany knows what you have been up to. And all the details have been in the foreign press as well. You think you even control the *London Times*?'

'This all may be true, but do you actually think that anyone would testify against me? The chauffeur? The maids?'

'Alright. As I have no other recourse, I shall discuss this matter with the Führer. We will see what he thinks.'

—◦—

Immediately they saw him standing at the top of the stone steps, smiling affectionately at them, opening his arms to them, little Helga and Hildegard Goebbels rushed up to meet Uncle Adolf, their arms splayed in anticipation of a hug. Their little brother, Helmut, remained next to his mother, clasping her hand, his eyes bright with excitement. Hitler descended a few steps to meet the two girls, then lifted them into a brief embrace. His Alsatian bitch, Blondi, panted and wagged her tail maniacally, almost knocking Hildegard over as she was lowered back to the steps. Below, Magda and Josef Goebbels smiled sheepishly at their Führer as they ascended the stairs, Josef's club foot moving more sluggishly than usual.

It was a perfect day at the *Eagle's Nest*, crystal blue skies outlining the jagged Obersalzburg peaks. The air was warm, yet fresh and fragrant with late summer blooms. Magda had always enjoyed being in these mountains, especially now, happy to be away from the summer stench of Berlin. 'We should find a house here, if only for the summer,' she had often suggested, but Josef wouldn't hear of it. He adored his house by the lake, and besides, he didn't want to be separated from the excitement that Berlin offered.

Hitler had arranged for the *Berliner Illustrierte* magazine to take photographs of the Goebbels family, *weekending with the Führer in a relaxed family atmosphere*. These photographs and the article accompanying them were designed to depict the Goebbels' as the ideal German family – happy, fecund and at ease with themselves and with their Führer. After pleasantries on the veranda, Hitler invited the couple to see him, each in turn. Magda was first. Hitler was standing in front of the huge fireplace. He invited her to sit on the over-stuffed settee. He remained standing.

'My dear Frau Goebbels. You have suffered a grave betrayal, as have I,' he began. 'Your husband has lied to both of us.'

Magda looked at him with questioning eyes. *Had Josef lied to the Führer?*

He read her thoughts. 'Oh, yes. This sordid business was mentioned to me some time ago. Your husband has not so many friends in the government as he might suppose. Many are only too happy to tell such tales. In any event, he categorically denied the accusations. And, of course, I believed him. You know, Frau Goebbels, with me, the most important things are loyalty and honour. And your husband has besmirched both.'

Magda shook her head but did not speak. She knew that interruptions were often met with impatience. She could hear the children laughing as they played with Blondi on the patio. Hitler continued.

'However, what I cannot forgive is the way his behaviour has affected his family. How it has affected you, my dear woman, and also, even if they do not know it now, how it has affected your children. And not less important, this infantile behaviour has had a bad influence on his effectiveness as a minister.'

Hitler began to pace the room, his hands clasped behind his back.

'I fully understand that you might wish to be rid of such a husband, and in most circumstances, this would prove no problem. But in this case, things are different.

You have become the model of what a German family should be, and any divorce would be damaging to this ideal. A scandal would also give much pleasure to Germany's enemies. Therefore, for the present, I wish for you to remain married to your husband, at least for outward appearance. I don't care what conditions you make to achieve this, I will support them unreservedly.'

He walked over and took Magda's hands in his. He looked deeply into her eyes. 'I will speak to him. Perhaps after a separation he will see the errors of his ways, and things will eventually return to normal. And also, you need not trouble yourself about that Baarová woman any longer. Of that you can be certain. Rely on me. I will make it right.'

Magda returned to the patio, the children and the dog. She gestured to Josef with a sideways look, indicating that it was his turn. A glacial silence met Goebbels as he entered the room. Hitler stood again in front of the fireplace, his hands clasped tightly in front of him, his face a stone. He did not invite his Propaganda Minister to sit.

'You have disgraced yourself completely with this shameful business.'

Goebbels began to speak, but Hitler silenced him by raising his hand.

'I know everything. Even your adjutant, Hanke, is disgusted with you. Of course, I don't much care about how you spend your time with women. That's your business. But you have taken what might have been a small indiscretion and grown it into a crisis, through your infantile and romantic posturing. And more than that. As a result of all this nonsense, you have been ineffective in office. More than that, you lied to *me*!'

'I am prepared to resign immediately if that is my Führer's wish.'

'That's completely out of the question.'

Hitler began to pace the room in his customary way.

'Now, this is what will happen. You will abandon this silly Czech actress and go back to your wife and family. Fräulein Baarová will be asked to return to Czechoslovakia, and will not work in Germany again. This subject is not open for discussion. It is my unshakable will! Ask your wife to join us now.'

Goebbels walked to the door and beckoned Magda to return. Hitler smiled at her but did not invite her to sit. The two stood before their Führer as children in a head-teacher's office.

'This is what I have decided. For the next year you will be officially together, but you, Doctor, will leave Schwanenwerder for that time. You will only see your children with the permission of your wife. If after that time, you cannot find a way to live together and Frau Goebbels still wants a divorce, I will grant it. She will keep the house. She will have total custody of the children and will be given a large monthly settlement from your salary at the Ministry, for as long as you remain there, of course. The law on this matter is of no consequence. As Führer, if I decree it, it becomes law. Now, let us all go back to the children and see if they might like some nice cakes which Eva has baked especially for them, yes?'

—◄o►—

That evening Lída Baarová was visited by a smartly dressed Gestapo officer who told her that she was to leave Germany within 24 hours. She fainted. Dr Morell, Hitler's personal physician, was summoned. Lída was hysterical.

'I need to see Josef! Please bring him to me!'

'I'm afraid that's impossible, Fräulein Baarová. He's out of the country on official business.'

Morell gave the actress a sedative injection.

She would never see him again.

The Goebbels family slowly began to resume a relatively normal routine and Josef's home visits became more regular. So regular did they become, that Magda fell pregnant again, which cemented their reconciliation.

—◄o►—

But Josef was still in trouble with his Führer. It blew up just after the Munich crisis, when Britain, France, Italy and Germany agreed to partition Czechoslovakia in favour of the German-speaking minority. They had completely caved into Hitler's demands. Goebbels thought that Hitler would be pleased.

'Pleased?! How can I be pleased? I was robbed of the war which was necessary. War with the west now would be far more successful than in a year, when they will have begun to rearm. You stole this war from me, Doctor, by your incompetence!'

Goebbels had never before been at the brunt of such

anger. He was confused and very frightened. He had seen Hitler's rage before, happily watching colleagues cower under the onslaught, but now the storm was directed at him.

'I don't understand, Mein Führer.'

'Because you were so preoccupied with your penis, you missed doing what was necessary. You idiotically portrayed Chamberlain as a well-meaning umbrella-carrying bumbler, and the people followed you in this. As a result, they were completely unprepared for war and I was forced to sign that stupid agreement.'

─◄o►─

On the night that Ernst vom Rath died, Goebbels grabbed his chance. He had accompanied Hitler to Munich for the annual Beer Hall Putsch celebrations. At 9 pm, a messenger delivered a report announcing vom Rath's death. Goebbels walked with Hitler to the back of the hall. He remembered Hitler often saying that in any situation, he preferred people who offered him the most radical solution.

'We can punish the Jews for this, Mein Führer. We can make them all feel the pain of the vom Rath family. We can rise up against them. For once they should get the taste of popular anger!'

'Yes, I believe that something must be done, and quickly, so that the connection is clearly made. But, as I have said on more than one occasion, pogroms are messy. They unsettle the population and inflame international opinion. This then acts against us.'

'Not a pogrom, Mein Führer, a short extraordinary action. One or two days. Burn a few synagogues, destroy some shops, arrest a few thousand. Then we can impose a huge fine on them for all the damage. Goering can arrange that.'

'This action must not, under any circumstances, be led by the police, the SA, or especially the SS. It must seem completely spontaneous.'

'I have such spontaneous groups in readiness across the Reich, Mein Führer.'

'Agreed. But keep everything under tight control at all times. No bloodbath. Afterwards, we'll attack where it hurts them most, in their wallets.'

That evening the curtain rose on the first act of the Holocaust.

PART THREE

CHAPTER 21
ROOM SERVICE

Max walked quickly. It was very late, after 2 am. The air was damp; the sound of shouting and the tumult of fire appliances surrounded him. Everywhere, glass shattering, crunching underfoot, the crackle of fires, shops and synagogues ablaze, lurching gangs of SA troops in mufti, civilians in their wake, bearing mallets and axes, some laughing, some shouting, clattering up many stairs and down again, while policemen in their grey-green uniforms smiled solemnly.

He was overtaken by a group of ten young men trotting by, almost pushing him from the kerb as they passed. They were laughing raucously. One of them stopped and turned to face him, holding a crowbar menacingly in both hands, poised for attack. He then smiled and lowered his weapon.

'Hallo, Max. Want to join us? I can guarantee some excellent punching practice.'

Max recognised the youth – he couldn't have been more than eighteen – as a waiter in one of the cafés on the Friedrichstraße. He knew him to be in the SA.

'Where's the uniform, Karl?'

'Headquarters says we can't wear them tonight. Anyway, blood is hard to clean off, so it's probably a good idea. Why don't you join us?'

Max smiled as best he could. 'Have to hurry back to Anny. She's very worried.'

'Oh, she'll be alright. It's only Jews, you know. But you go to her. Women, eh?'

◄○►

Werner and Henri Lewin were waiting for Max at the entrance of the Excelsior Hotel, shielded from view by an ornamental shrub. They were cold and sleepy; hands in their coat pockets, caps pulled well down, they listened intently to everything, with sharp suspicious ears.

The doorman hurried over to Max as soon as he arrived. 'I was just about to call the police. These two young...' he nodded knowingly at Max, '... lads said that they were waiting for you, but who would believe that?'

'It's quite alright, Herr Meyer. I do know them. I'll make certain they get home safely. Thank you for your patience.' Max handed Meyer a five Reichsmarks coin, and received a salute and suspicious smile in return.

They hurried along the cold street. He led them to an alleyway behind the hotel, arriving at a steel door illuminated by a lightbulb suspended in a cage. Tiny droplets of November mist were spreading downwards, as if emanating from the bulb itself.

'This is the delivery door. It's late, so no one will see us. We'll go quickly to the service lift and then up to my room. You must keep very quiet.'

But the lift itself was noisy with pulleys and rust. The three winced at each squeak. Still, they met no one. They stopped with a clang on the fifth floor. Max opened the door to his apartment, and ushered them in, closing it behind him as silently as falling snow.

'Is Anny Ondra here with you?' asked Henri, who at fifteen, was two years younger than his bother Werner.

'No, Anny's at home at Saarow. She doesn't like the city that much anymore. And she particularly wouldn't like it here tonight. Now lads, I have spoken to your father, and he has agreed that you should stay here with me for a while, at least until things blow over.'

'We were so scared, Max,' Werner said, 'we were frightened to sit at home and also terrified to go out from the apartment. We kept to the shadows, but we were worried what would happen to us if someone saw us.'

'You're safe now, that's all that matters. That's why your father sent you here. But it is important, you will understand, that no one should know you are here, except your family and Anny, of course, so you must never leave the room, never answer the door. I'll put a sign out that I don't want to be disturbed. The Excelsior is very good about such things. We'll have food from room-service, and they will leave the tray outside.

The brothers removed their coats, and Max gestured towards the wardrobe. They took off their caps, exposing small tight curls.

'Now, you two, wash – there are plenty of towels – and get into my bed in the other room. The settee is very comfortable and will suit me fine.'

When he could hear the water running, Max rang David Lewin.

'The boys are fine here with me, Lewin, and I can keep

them safe for a few days at least. It should all die down soon anyway. These thugs become easily bored. Perhaps you can send the boys some clothes, you know, pyjamas, underwear, just essentials. Have a taxi deliver it, and wrap it up so that it looks like nothing special. I'll ring you every day.'

The Lewin brothers returned to the living room, their faces fresh from scrubbing.

'Goodnight Max', they said in unison. He went over and shook each of them by hand with mock solemnity, then hugged them together. This was most un-German, they all thought, but tonight such behaviour seemed appropriate. They relaxed into his soft muscular embrace.

'I'm certain you will sleep well tonight, because it's very late, and also, because we're high up, so there will not be too much noise. Just remember, nothing can happen to you up here with a boxing champion protecting you, can it? Tomorrow, you will awake to a big breakfast – eggs, pancakes, pastries and milk. Good?'

But they were already walking to the bed, and a few moments later, Max could hear them breathing deeply. He rang Anny.

'I was so worried, I couldn't sleep,' she said.

'I couldn't ring you before.'

'Someone rang here for you. Very late. I told them you might be at the Roxy.'

'Yes. I was just about to leave when he rang. David Lewin. You know, that Jewish tailor on the Kurfürstendamm. Where I buy my suits. Anyway, he telephoned me to say that with all of the rioting and smashing of property, he was worried for his two sons who were terrified. They'd taken to hiding under the bed – even though both of them are teenagers. They live near the top of a big apartment house. Apparently, they are the only Jews in the building.

'I told him to send them to me at the hotel. It's quite near where they live, and I didn't think that young lads would be harshly treated, maybe not even noticed in all the commotion. So there they were, after two in the morning, standing in front of the Excelsior, shivering with cold and fear. They probably weren't in much danger, not in front of the hotel. Actually, the expensive coats they were wearing might not have been such a good idea, but what would you expect?

'But what will happen now? What if they are discovered? You could get yourself into trouble as well.'

'My darling, I think it is all probably less serious than it appears. Just a venting of steam. Best the boys stay here until things become quieter. I'll tell the front desk that I have a bad cold and must not be disturbed, no cleaning, visitors, just room service, trays left outside the door with my shoes.'

Anny laughed. 'Can you act a cold? Be careful not to give yourself away.' A familiar mischief entered her voice. 'You're not such a good actor, you know.'

'What about the films I've made?' Max said, with feigned indignation.

'Always playing yourself.'

Max rang off smiling, then wrapped his neck and lower jaw into his scarf. He opened the door quietly and took the main lift to the lobby, where the night desk-clerk greeted him warmly, nodded sagely at Max's request, stifling a wink. A few minutes later, Max lay on the sofa and became dimly aware of the rivers of noise passing below, but he fell asleep before he remembered to take off his shoes.

It was after 10 am when he opened the apartment door to find two silver trays of food at his feet. *Maybe they think I have a secret woman up here,* he thought. *This could be convenient; I could order enough food to feed the boys without arousing further suspicion.* Next to the trays was a parcel. It contained clothes for the boys, packed tightly and carefully by their mother, who inserted a note.

My dear Herr Schmeling. It is such a wonderful and generous thing that you are doing for us. It shows that there are still Germans left who value decency and humanity. We will never forget your kindness. Edith Lewin.

He put the trays on the table in front of the window, looking through the curtains to the street below. Several people were going about their normal business, gingerly negotiating the broken glass and debris which had yet to be swept away. He felt protective of the boys, and pleased with himself for helping them. But he was also worried for them, and their future. He couldn't understand why, Jews having done so many good things for Germany, Hitler insisted on terrorising them. It was like a caldera of madness in the Führer's brain, sometimes erupting into streams of fury and spittle. Those times he had defended

Yussel, he could see the ice form behind Goebbels' eyes, and the glow of hot lava in Hitler's, supressed with difficulty. Worried as Max was, there was no thought of rebellion – they'd crush him and then erase him. No, he would just have to carry on, gradually becoming less conspicuous, fading into everydayness, until things changed.

Max peeked into the bedroom. Werner and Henri Lewin were already awake, whispering to each other in their bed. Max opened the door and smiled at them.

'If I know anything about growing lads – of course, Werner, you are already almost a proper grown man – I know that they are always hungry. Is this not so? Well, there is a big breakfast waiting for you in the next room. So hurry. Wash, brush your teeth and change into the clothes your mother has sent for you.' He tossed the half-opened package to them in a high arc. Werner caught it.

The boys ate slowly but steadily, demolishing croissants spread with butter and plum jam. They had already eaten boiled eggs and cheese. As they were drinking their milk, they could hear new shouts and shatterings below. Henri walked to the window, parted the curtains just far enough to look down.

'What is going on, Max? Why are people doing all this?'

Max thought for a moment. 'You know, I really don't understand it myself.'

He could see that the boys weren't satisfied with that answer.

'You boys know that my life is based on boxing.'

They nodded enthusiastically.

'And in boxing, people try to hurt each other. That's part of it, but not all of it, of course. And sometimes there is anger in the ring, but it never lasts very long. And after the fight, things get back to normal. I've never gone into the ring to hurt anyone, only to win. You know, most boxers I've met are really gentle people.

'But politics can be different. Some politicians like to make people angry so that they will follow them. And when people become angry, especially in a group, they don't think about what they are doing, even if they are really good people at heart.'

'What are they so angry about?'

'It seems a Jewish lad has shot a German diplomat. In Paris. They say he's your age, Werner.'

'Yes, we heard about the shooting, but that was in France and we here had nothing to do with it. Why are they taking it out on Jews? It's not fair, is it?'

'You are right. It's not.'

Their parents had also sent a few books which arrived later that day, wrapped in shirts and shorts. *They can't just sit there and do nothing. At least they can learn something until they get home,* the note said.

'We also keep books in the W.C., so that we shouldn't waste time just sitting,' Werner said. *So very Jewish,* Max thought, and smiled.

◄○►

That day, Wednesday the 10th of November, was more frightening than the night before. The news of vom

187

Rath's death had come too late for any mayhem to be fully organised on that first evening. Many SA men were fast asleep or passed out drunk from the Beer Hall Putsch celebrations. But just after noon, Berlin became embroiled.

Since Hitler had been appointed Chancellor, Jews became accustomed to small and large indignities, from being short-changed in shops, to curses on the street, to being made to walk in the gutter if an SA-man passed. But this day was the beginning of something new, something unexpected. Nothing had prepared the Jews for the calamity which now engulfed them. Many Jewish homes were ransacked, belongings thrown from windows. Only those synagogues which abutted Aryan buildings were not set alight. The rest were smashed and burned, their stained glass carefully shattered, their treasures, the Torahs, candlesticks and goblets, dumped on the pavement and casually looted, against the strongest prohibition by Goebbels. Max, David and Henri saw and heard little of these events. They didn't see the bloody faces, the shattered spectacles, the pleading women and screaming children, as husbands and fathers were dragged from their homes and beaten while passers-by averted their gaze and policemen stared. They didn't see old men being taunted for wetting their pants in fear, their beards tugged and their stomachs punched until they vomited, then cursed and beaten again for dirtying the street. They didn't hear the smash of mirrors thrown from apartments, the ashen Jewish moans, the whistles and shouts, all combining into a fairground of violence, as men were shoved aboard lorries and carried away like sardines, to a place of still greater despair. Werner, Henri and Max experienced none of this. They were safe in Max's hotel room.

Max placed another pair of empty trays in front of his door, careful first to look through the fisheye peephole. The corridor was empty. Newly polished shoes waited patiently in front of bedroom doors. He picked up a complimentary newspaper and glanced at the headlines.

German Hero succumbs to Jewish Treachery.
Dr Goebbels: The Long-held German Patience is finally
at an end.

He folded the paper and put it under a cushion. The telephone rang. The boys looked up.

'Hello, David, how are things with you?' Max turned to the boys. 'It's your father,' he mouthed.

'Well, the tailor shop was completely destroyed last night, but at least Edith and I are safe. For now. Our apartment neighbours are being very civil to us. But who knows for how long? We hear constant banging on doors, Nazis baying in the street, people being rounded up. I don't know what to do, I'm scared out of my wits.'

'How is Edith taking it all?' Max asked calmly, casting a glance at his charges on the sofa.

'She seems to be taking it better than I am. She tries to ignore everything as much as possible by being busy – making plans for us to emigrate as soon as we can. She thinks maybe Shanghai. I'll leave it to her. I can't think straight. Anywhere to be away from all this craziness and horror. At least we are lucky enough to have the means to escape.'

'Yes, I think that women are often stronger than men.'

Max gestured for the boys to come to the telephone. Werner was first.

'Hallo, Papa... Yes, we're fine. Max is taking good care of us... Is Mama alright? ... When can we come home? ... I see ... Alright. Here he is...'

Henri had been leaning impatiently against his brother. 'Hallo, Papa... Yes, we both slept well. You don't get much noise up here, so it was quiet in the night. Anyway, we were *so* tired that we fell straight asleep. Max says that things will calm down soon and then we can come home. Also, we had a giant breakfast, and Max said he'd tell us boxing stories, about how he won the championship and all that ... Alright, *Wiederhören*, Papa.'

For the next hour or so the boys read from their books while Max surveyed the newspaper left at his door.

Put an end to these criminals!!

'I only regret that he didn't die...' said the Jew Herschel Seidel Grünspan, who had been instigated to his treachery by the World Jewish Conspiracy, after he shot the German Embassy official Ernst vom Rath without any reason.

'I've shot him because I am a Jew. I am fully aware of what I have done and I have no regrets...' This was said two years ago by another Jew, David Frankfurter, after he committed exactly the same crime, also without any reason, killing Party Comrade Wilhelm Gustloff in Davos.

'We Jews feel in absolute solidarity with you, dear Frankfurter, and we admire you endlessly…' This was written by the Jewish World League after the murder of Wilhelm Gustloff. At the same time, the same World League made the murderer Frankfurter their honorary president.

Now it is enough!!

For a long time now the German people and their Führer have received daily abuse from the Jewish press all over the world. For a long time now, this Jewish riffraff has been inciting the peoples of the world to instigate war against Germany. The patience with which the Führer, at the head of the greatest people of Europe, has reacted to these insults has been misinterpreted. And now, for a second time, a Jewish murderer has cowardly shot an official of the German nation abroad at the behest of the World Jewish Conspiracy.

Now we will have revenge!

With the entire strength of an honour-loving nation, the German people rose as one when they received news of the latest martyr to the National-Socialist ideal. The German government has now taken appropriate measures against the Jews who are living in Germany, which will warn the World Jewish Conspiracy not to repeat such criminal acts. This is no time for false pity. Those who believe that they themselves know some 'good Jews', Jews who only mind their own business and are loyal to the Reich, should now come awake! There are no 'good Jews'!

With inexorable justice!

Germany will now deliver the consequences. The solidarity and sympathy that the Jewish conspiracy has demonstrated towards this murderer Grynszpan, gives these criminals away. And if, despite of this intolerable deed, the democratic world's conscience continues to trip over itself, continues to plead for 'humanity' and 'pity for the poor Jews', then the whole world will learn this lesson:

Germans are no longer fair game for Jewish criminals!!

Max folded the newspaper and put it back under the cushion. Werner looked up from his book.

'Why do the Germans hate the Jews, Max?'

'I don't know. I think most Germans don't have any bad feelings against Jews at all, but too many now seem infected with this craziness.'

'But why Jews, Max?'

He thought for a moment. 'Perhaps both sides play a part. You know some people feel that the Jews think themselves special, and separate, not wanting to mix with anyone else. This is of course an exaggeration, but many people feel it just the same. And maybe because Jews work hard, study hard, support each other, they have become more prominent in German life, and there is resentment at this, I think.'

'Do you think we Jews are a bad people, Max?'

'Of course not. There are no bad peoples, only bad times.'

'So you don't hate us, Max?'

'Would you be here if I did?'

'What if they come up here?' asked Werner. Both boys looked anxiously at the door.

'That won't happen,' Max replied, his face set into his boxing mask. 'First of all, if they recognise me – and I'm sure they will – they will know that I can handle several of them at one time. So they won't try anything. And anyway, they're bullies, cowards. They don't really like a fair fight. I don't think they'll come up here.'

Relieved, the boys went back to their books. A few moments later Henri asked, 'How did you meet Anny, Max? After all she's a famous actress…'

'Max is famous too, *pischer*. So it's not so surprising. They're a good match. We used to love Anny's films, but of course, we can't go now.

'Even so, I still like to look at the posters in front of the cinemas. Anny always looks so glamorous. And now I can say to myself, I know the man she has married.'

Outside, another angry torrent was flowing, voices rhythmically chanting. *Jews perish. Kick them out. Germany for Germans!*

The boys stiffened. Max tried to divert their reappearing anxiety.

'Are you really interested in how I met Anny?'

'Did she fall in love with you at first sight, like in the movies?' Henri asked, still looking towards the window.

'No, it was the other way around. I was going out with another actress, Olga Chekova, who just happened to have once been married to the nephew of the great Russian writer Anton Chekov.'

'Father told us that we should read *War and Peace*. But it's too long.'

Werner grinned. 'That's Tolstoy, Henri, not Chekov.'

'It doesn't matter for this,' Max continued. 'So anyway, Olga kept the Chekov name. You know, she is very beautiful, but because of Anny she became very angry with me, at least for a while. We were once what was called 'an item' in the press, and people thought that since we played lovers on the screen that we were somehow involved with each other in real life.'

'Were you?'

'Well, perhaps a bit. Anyway. One day Olga suggested that we go to a movie, this was, by the way, in 1932, when Jews could still go to movies, although maybe you two were too young for many films.'

Werner said, 'No, papa took us every week and I remember watching you with Olga in *Love in the Ring*. It was thrilling.'

Henri agreed. 'I liked the boxing scenes best.'

'Me too,' Max admitted. 'Anyway, as I was saying, Olga suggested that we go to a film that her friend Anny Ondra was in, called *The Horrible Girlfriend*. Well, I didn't want to go. I thought I knew all about this Anny Ondra, and that the film title fit her well. She had recently moved into a flat near mine in the Sachsenplatz, and all day I could hear a child screaming from a balcony. It almost drove me crazy. I thought it was her child, since someone told me she was married. And also, to make me even less interested, her chauffeur looked down his nose at me from her big Cadillac, and made me feel like a real nobody in my dirty Lancia.

'But Olga told me that the child wasn't Anny's, but belonged to someone in another flat and that Anny had also been complaining about the racket. So we went to the film. And what happened was that I immediately fell in love with Anny Ondra. She was so small, but so lively and pretty. After the film, I asked Olga if she could introduce me. She got very angry and said, "Do your own courting," and walked off. Later, when she saw how happy we were, she forgave me. We are now good friends with her.'

'Did you go up to Anny's flat and ring her bell?'

'I was too shy for that. So I asked my friend Paul Damski to approach her. He's a fight promoter, by the way, and he is also Jewish, like my manager, Joe Jacobs.'

The boys smiled sympathetically.

'Anyway, I watched from my car as Paul knocked on her door, carrying a large bouquet of flowers I had bought for her. He returned in less than a minute. He said, "I asked her if she would speak to my friend Max Schmeling. But she wants nothing to do with you. 'You must be crazy,' she said. She almost slammed the door in my face. She said that you should give the flowers to Olga.'"

'Two weeks later, I convinced Paul to approach Anny again. He told her that although I was world champion, I was too shy to approach her myself.'

'I can't believe that you're shy, Max.'

'Only with women, Werner. Anyway, Paul told her that it was my birthday the next day – this was actually true – and that my greatest birthday wish was to meet her. Anny had in the meantime asked around about me, and the only one to advise her to leave me alone was Olga Chekova. Finally, she agreed to meet me at Café Corso and we had a nice chat. She must have thought that I was an idiot, because I was looking at her like a star-struck schoolboy, but my mind was already made up.

'She told me after we were married that she had expected to meet a regular Palooka, as they say in America; that I would be uncouth and rude, and maybe even a violent person. But she confessed to me that she was really surprised and even taken aback because I was such a gentleman.'

'Did you get married after that meeting?'

'It doesn't happen like that, squirt. It's not like the movies.'

'Your brother is right, Henri, Anny was playing very hard to get. But little by little, I succeeded. I put flowers on the long bonnet of her pale-blue Cadillac every day. And after several weeks, she allowed me to see her alone. And to shorten the story, we were married a few months later.'

'I'm sorry she isn't here with us,' said Henri.

'Anny loves peace and quiet. That's why we bought our house in the country. She doesn't like the radio on too much, and even her dog is not allowed to bark. Sometimes all this peace and quiet gets on my nerves and makes me homesick for Berlin, so then I stay here. But I really don't like to be away from her for too long.'

'Maybe we can meet her someday.'

'I'm sure she'd like that.'

◄○►

Max approached the front desk early the next morning. He tried to look as if he had a fever. He asked at the desk if there had been any post for him.

'I'll have a look, Herr Schmeling.' The desk clerk turned to a row of mailboxes behind him.

The sound of a large pane of glass shattering punctuated the air outside and entered the lobby. Two young men passed the hotel, dragging, then roughly shoving an old broken Jewish man, grabbing him when he stumbled, then shouting at him. *Can't you walk straight, you Jewish shit swine?* They peered into the hotel as they passed, and recognising Max, they waved and then went off again, kicking the old man for good measure. Max was appalled, but he didn't know what to do. *I really should go outside and flatten those louts. Easy to see them off. But what good would it do? And even if the little Jew escapes from them, he would only be picked up again when he turned the corner. So maybe the best thing now is to keep the Lewin boys safe upstairs and wait until things calm down.*

'No mail, Herr Schmeling', said the desk clerk. 'It's a bad, business, eh, Herr Schmeling?'

'It's a very bad business, Herr Bauer.'

'But not such a bad business as you got from Joe Louis, is it?'

'Yes, that was also a bad business. But at least it was short.'

'He hit you from behind, didn't he? I heard about it. That couldn't have been a fair blow. His manager is a Jew,' he said, as an explanation. Max stifled a great urge to mention his own manager. 'You should make an appeal, Herr Schmeling.'

'No, Herr Bauer. It was a legal punch. I turned away from him just as he was unloading, so he hit me near the spine. Truly a bad business. But that's over now.'

Desk clerk Bauer shook his head sadly. 'Imagine that nigger beating you. I still can't believe it.'

'Well, whatever else he is, Joe Louis is the best fighter in the world, and I should know. The truth is the truth. No one will beat him any time soon, and that I will say for certain.'

Some new shouts outside, accompanied by more running feet.

'You know, Herr Schmeling, maybe this nasty business will all turn out to be a good thing. It's about time we settled with those Jews, to convince them they aren't wanted here and that they should leave. They can't just go about killing innocent Germans. There are plenty of other countries with enough room for them – America, Canada, even Australia – but I hear none of them want Jews either.'

Max returned to the lift, grateful to meet no one on the way up.

◄○►

Over the next two days, a regular rhythm became established in the hotel room. A big room-service breakfast, an ample lunch – the boys really liked Bratwurst, so it was ordered every day – as well as some fruit, bread and cheese for the evening meal. During the day, the boys read from their schoolbooks. Once, when Max opened the door to put out the lunch trays, he noticed a member of the hotel staff looking at him. The young man saluted, smiled and winked, gazing knowingly at the door. He left whistling the theme song from *Love in the Ring*.

There was enough time for Max to recount, in fine detail, all of his fights, round by round, until he noticed the boys' eyes beginning to glaze over. But they were fascinated by his account of the first Louis fight, how he had confounded everyone's expectations, and how he had returned a hero on the Hindenburg. He did not tell them anything about his meeting with Hitler.

Gradually, the violence in the streets subsided. The police resumed their routine duties, fire appliances were returned to their stations, the streets were swept, and Jewish shops were boarded over in advance of their forced Aryanisation.

-◄o►-

At mid-day on the 13th, Max escorted the Lewins, their clothes and books, down the service lift to the basement. The boys were surprised.

'Aren't we meeting papa at the station?' Werner asked. 'Why are we going to the basement?'

'I know a shortcut,' Max said, as he led them through a baggage store to a large steel door through which a tiled tunnel led directly to the Anhalter station.

'This passageway was designed so that guests' luggage could be brought to the hotel without the risk of traffic or weather. A good idea, yes?'

The boys were impressed.

They were dressed as they had been when they arrived,

but they walked less furtively. A hotel porter passed them with an empty trolley. He smiled at Max but ignored the boys.

David Lewin was waiting for his sons under the clock in the main concourse. He gathered them into a hug, then shook Max's hand effusively.

'I'll never forget this, Max,' he said, as the boys gave their champion one last clinch.

'Best to leave quickly,' said Max.

The Lewins disappeared into a taxi. Max wondered if he would ever see them again.

CHAPTER 22
PSYCHIATRISTS

He sat at a rickety wooden table, the surface of which was scored with scratched initials and the misspelt profanities of previous inmates. He was writing a letter to his parents at their transit camp. Lately he had begun to keep a diary, an activity recommended by the prison governor; a small affable man, who took a paternalistic interest in all his charges, especially those in the prison's youth wing. The governor was particularly attentive to his new illustrious inmate, holding regular meetings with him in his office.

Keys rattled. The heavy metal door opened.

'This came for you, Grynszpan.'

My tallis bag! So it seems the governor was true to his word. 'Thank you so much, Monsieur.'

Herschel's politeness amused and charmed his warders, who were more accustomed to sullen silence, grunts, or curses. This particular guard smiled subtly and nodded his head, like a head waiter in a modest provincial hotel.

'By the way, you have visitors, Grynszpan,' said the guard. 'With briefcases.'

The boy regarded himself in the small mirror above his basin, carefully combing his hair and adjusting his tie.

He and the guard strode down the corridor to the

central hub of the prison. He was led into a meeting room, where he found three men waiting. They were seated in high-backed chairs behind a long, battered table – laden with files, notebooks and legal texts.

The roundest and shortest of the trio made the introductions.

'Herr Grynszpan, I am Dr Genil-Perrin – to my left, Dr Heuyer and to my right, Dr Ceillier. We are all experts in the field of psychology and criminology. We are here to interview you.'

'To see if I'm crazy? Psychotic? Messieurs, I can assure you that I am quite sane.'

'No, we are merely here to make an assessment as to your present mental state, and also when you committed the crime. This examination is required in order to inform the court, so that the right conclusion can be reached.'

He sat down to face his interlocutors.

'I am not a criminal, Messieurs.'

'But you have committed a crime, have you not?'

'I acted out of self-defence. For myself and my people. Against an official for the people who would kill me.'

'You do not regret your actions?'

'Unfortunately, the man I shot is dead. I did not want to kill him but only to wound him. I had never fired a pistol before, Messieurs, and my aim was inexact.'

He paused. The doctors did not fill the space.

'By shooting someone at the Embassy, I could make a strong protest. So that the whole world would notice what is happening to my people, who have no one else to fight for them, no one else to be their champion. May

God forgive me for killing someone who was perhaps not guilty. Of course, it is always the poor soldier who is killed; never those who start the war in the first place.'

Dr Heuyer wrote in his notebook. Herschel paused, almost bringing his hand to his mouth to chew any ragged edge of fingernail he could find, but quickly placed both hands on his lap, below the table top so they would not be seen by the panel. Dr Heuyer wrote: *outwardly calm, self-composed, yet exhibits marked anxiety tendencies.*

Dr Genil-Perrin continued.

'Had you ever met vom Rath before?'

'I don't think so.'

Dr Ceillier adjusted his *pince-nez* and looked into the boy's eyes.

'I read in your notes that you have often frequented the Club Sportif.'

'This is true, Monsieur.'

'Why do you choose that particular establishment?'

'They are friendly to me there, and I can meet other men in a similar situation. I can feel relaxed.'

'I have also learned that Herr vom Rath also frequented that establishment. Had you ever seen him there?'

He wanted to chew his fingernails again. 'If he came in, it wasn't when I was there. It's possible, of course. Many people come and go. But most are Jews like me. I can't imagine why a Nazi would go in there.'

Dr Genil-Perrin now made a point of speaking very softly.

'And how do you feel now about shooting Herr vom Rath?'

'I am sad that I have brought misfortune to my aunt and uncle. But I am also happy to see that the whole world is talking about what I have done. Perhaps through my actions things will change.'

'It is said that you are often very anxious,' said Dr Heuyer, 'and that this affects your digestion.'

'This is true, but my digestion has much improved lately.'

'But I see that you still bite your fingernails.'

He looked down at his hands.

'It's a hard habit to break, Messieurs. Since I was a child. Everything was tried – pepper sauce, gloves, telling me off, of course. "You take such care of your clothes, Herschel," they say, "so why are your fingers so disgraceful?" It doesn't matter what they say. However hard I try, nothing seems to work.'

'But you say that you are less anxious now.'

'Because now everything is out of my hands. Whatever I do, nothing will change for me, so I accept my fate, even if it is the guillotine, because I could have acted in no other way. This act was my destiny, and it was my fate to be a champion for my people who are suffering so much at the hands of the Germans.'

The three doctors looked at each other and gathered their papers.

'Thank you Herr Grynszpan. We shall wish to talk with you again. Is there anything else you wish to add to what you have said today?'

'Yes. If there is anything that can be done to bring my family back to France from Poland, that would help me very much. They could testify at my trial – about the hardships they were made to suffer by the Germans, and how hearing about this suffering made me do what I did.'

'We will mention everything you say in the report, of course, but what you ask is really a matter for you and your advocate. Is there anything else you might wish to say on this occasion?'

'You see, never before in all history has a young man of only seventeen years had the courage to carry out a deed such as I have.'

The three psychiatrists looked at him with renewed attention.

'A few weeks ago, the leaders of England and France shook in their shoes before Hitler and gave away Czechoslovakia to him. I alone had the courage to stand up to him. I did this for my people. Now I learn that the day after vom Rath died, Jewish synagogues and homes were burned down and looted. So much trouble, just on my behalf?'

Each of the doctors shook his hand as he left the room.

—◆—

The next interview occurred two days later. The same three psychiatrists were present, wearing the same suits, seated in the same places behind the same table laden with the same files and books.

'Herr Grynszpan,' Dr Genil-Perrin said, 'we'd like you to sit at the table over there.'

A small wooden table and chair had been placed against a bare wall. He looked at Dr Genil-Perrin quizzically.

'Don't worry, Herr Grynszpan. We merely want to conduct a few tests which require you to avoid looking at us.'

Dr Ceillier stood next to Herschel, but slightly behind him.

'Herr Grynszpan, we would like you to look at a few pictures and to tell us what you see in them, or what they remind you of, or anything else which comes into your mind when looking at them.'

He placed the first card onto the desk. It was a rectangle, 24 by 18 centimetres in size. On it was a nondescript shape, each side a mirror of the other, emanating from an invisible central crease.

'Inkblots,' said the boy. 'I saw something about these in *L'Illustration*.'

Dr Ceillier betrayed slight concern. 'Do you know what they are for?'

'I started to read the article in the barber shop, but was called to the chair before I could read it, so I can't say that I remember anything. Just that the inventor had a German name, but he's a Swiss.'

Dr Ceillier smiled with relief. He turned to his colleagues, who were similarly relieved. 'Colleagues, I will present these cards in the order of set six.' They nodded. Dr Ceillier placed the first card on the table. Herschel stared at it for a few moments.

'Looks like a bat,' he decided.

'Could it be anything else?'

'No. It's a bat.'

He looked longer at the second card.

'What do you see?'

'Blood. People fighting and then there comes blood.'

Dr Heuyer, seated at the long table, made notes of all his responses.

'What about this one?'

'A giant. Standing over me. Looking down on me.'

'Is he threatening you?'

'I don't know, but he is very large and looks very strong, and I am just something small beneath his feet.'

Dr Ceillier presented a new card. Unlike the others, which were monochrome or bi-colour reproductions, this one presented a range of washed-out colours; red, green and yellow predominating. He gazed at the new card for about two or three minutes.

'May I turn it around?'

'However you wish.'

He rotated the card, staring at each new view in turn. When it was orientated in its original position, he sat back in his chair and turned to Dr Ceillier.

'Monsieur, I see nothing there.'

'Nothing?'

'Nothing. Even worse than nothing. Chaos. Forces fighting each other without meaning, without shape. Now that I say this, I remember the beginning of the Bible. Before God created the world, everything was in similar chaos, everything without shape, everything was empty. This is what I see, worse than nothing, chaos. I see chaos on this card, and I see chaos everywhere, especially in the lives of my people.'

The three doctors interviewed him on several other occasions. At the end of the last interview, they rose and shook his hand.

'You have been a most cooperative and pleasant young man,' Dr Genil-Perrin said. 'We hope that things go well for you.'

'I have much enjoyed our meetings, Messieurs. I have found them extremely interesting. Thank you for paying attention to me.'

In February 1939, the psychiatrists submitted their 81-page report.

Herschel Grynszpan's passionate idealism and the great influence of the very devout Jewish milieu in which he lived was notable in all conversations with him. He is lively, intelligent and takes an interest in current events, although this interest seems to focus on how these events impact on his smaller world.

The panel finds that Herschel Grynszpan was fully responsible mentally both at the time of the murder and subsequently. We also conclude that his abnormal levels of anxiety were greatly increased by the postcard from his parents which resulted in an overwhelming fear. This fear gradually gave way to a wish for revenge. It is notable that once the act was decided upon he pursued it with diligence and conscientiousness.

After several conversations with Herr Grynszpan, during some of which he offered contradictory explanations for his motives, we have nevertheless come to the conclusion that no credence could be given to his assertion, made in early hearings, that he had intended to commit suicide at the German Embassy in front of Hitler's portrait, or even to shoot at the portrait as a protest.

The panel finds that it is not possible to assume that Grynszpan was in a state of insanity, within the meaning of the penal code, both before, during and after he committed this crime. He is responsible for the act of which he is accused. It is up to the court to decide to what extent Grynszpan's full-blown anxiety as well as his youth could be considered as extenuating factors in his case.

The report was duly delivered to the court, and a copy was sent to Dr Goebbels' office in Berlin.

CHAPTER 23
LAWYERS AND LETTERS

Uncle Solomon paced the visiting room, one hand behind his back, the other stroking his short beard. His eyebrows and lips were in constant motion, as if he were in silent conversation with himself. His nephew, sitting calmly on a wooden chair, stared intently at him, following with his eyes as his uncle moved from left to right, then back again.

Solomon stopped and looked up at the guard, who was sitting blankly in the corner of the room, as if guarding an exhibit in the Louvre.

'May we speak in our own language?'

The guard turned to the older man.

'Do you mean German?'

'No, Yiddish.'

The guard nodded. 'It's all the same to me. But I'm glad it's not German. I hate the Bosch.'

'In this we are agreed, Monsieur.'

Although Solomon Grynszpan lived a few streets from his brother and sister-in-law, the Paris branch of the family did not often meet. The simmering, regularly erupting feud, about money, about their mother, strained fraternal bonds.

Solomon began pacing again, head down, as if speaking to the floor.

'What have you done, Herschel? How can you have done this? A young man has died at your hand.'

'I hoped and prayed that he would live. But God didn't listen to those prayers. So perhaps it was God's will. I didn't mean to kill him, just to wound him, just to make a statement.'

'Some statement. And for this Jews all over Germany and Austria are getting it in the neck. Just because of you. That's some statement.'

Except for the beard, uncle Solomon looks just like my father and my other uncles, he thought. *In fact, the four brothers would confuse an identity parade, so alike they look. All tailors, as well.*

'And now you want me to help you? And now you want me to be the wise king Solomon? What wisdom can I bring to bear here? Your Uncle Abraham and Aunt Chava are bundles of nerves, any day waiting to be arrested. All as a result of this craziness, this *meshigas*. Their meagre lives have been turned upside down and inside out by you, even though they have always tried to do everything for you. They made so many sacrifices for you, Herschel, so many, just like you were their own son. Shame, Herschel.'

He wondered when his uncle would stop. But the men in his family had a habit of arguing relentlessly and at length, even if another person wasn't taking part.

'You've done an idiotic thing, and so now you want me to help you? When you never came to visit me? Only a few streets away? And I should help you?'

He stared at his nephew.

'How can you sit there so calmly? Don't you know what awaits you? Aren't you worried?'

'Do you think it would help if I worried?'

'Very clever. So now you're so brave. But before, you've always been such a nervous little mouse, and now that you have something really to be nervous about, you sit there like a stone.'

'I'm not worried. Because it doesn't matter what they do to me. Even the guillotine.'

At the mention of the word 'guillotine,' which has no Yiddish equivalent, the guard looked over to the pair, then resumed his blank stare.

'A child, a minor, cannot be executed in France. Thank God, in the eyes of the law, you are still a child. Also in my eyes, Herschel.'

'It doesn't matter either way. If I die, it was for the sake of my people, to show the world about how they are being treated. What can it matter, even the guillotine?'

'Let's talk sense, Herschel.' Uncle Solomon sat down and faced the boy. 'Perhaps we can see to it that you serve the minimum sentence, you being so young, and perhaps, if you don't mind me saying so, being so unstable.'

'As you can see, I am now very calm.'

'Alright, I grant you, you act like a proper Buddha now, but maybe being unstable can help you survive this catastrophe. Anyway, there is more than enough evidence for your craziness. The way you shouted at the man before you shot him, the contradictory things you said to the police, all of this points to a certain imbalance.'

He tried to interrupt, but his uncle ignored him.

'So the first thing we need to do is to find you a lawyer, maybe two. I have been asking around, and I have people in mind. They are Jewish, so they are bound to be sympathetic, although they don't speak Yiddish. I'll bring them with me tomorrow.'

—◄o►—

Uncle Solomon appeared the next day accompanied by the two lawyers.

'As promised, here are the advocates who are willing to help you,' Uncle Solomon said. 'Let me first introduce to you Maître Vésinne Larue. You may have heard of him. He defended a woman in a famous trial a few years ago. It was all over the newspapers and magazines, just like you are now. She murdered her parents in order to get money to give to her boyfriend. She was found guilty, but Maître Larue saved her from the guillotine.'

Larue nodded modestly. He was a slight man, wearing a dark brown suit which had been recently and expertly pressed. His light brown hair was thinning noticeably. *Larue looks almost Aryan*, the boy thought, *which maybe is a good thing under the circumstances.*

Larue smiled, a warm and genuine smile, redolent of sympathy.

'And assisting him is Maître Philippe Szwarc.'

Szwarc crossed the room to shake the boy's hand. He was a solidly built young man, noticeably overweight, his stomach battling his waistcoat, buttons straining against the grey gabardine material. His pudgy hand was sweaty and cold. *Look how his eyes stick out from their sockets, and that drooping moustache looks like it was borrowed from someone else's face. Actually, he looks like a carp, my favourite fish.*

'Monsieur Grynszpan,' Larue said, 'if you will permit us to act for you, we will immediately obtain all the relevant documents and statements from the judge and then decide how to proceed in your best interest.'

He didn't reply.

Solomon said, 'Herschel, at least give these gentlemen the courtesy of an answer.'

'I cannot answer because I don't know what to say. But I suppose it wouldn't hurt to make a start, so if Messieurs Larue and Szwarc wish to begin, we can see what happens.'

The two advocates smiled in unison.

Larue said, 'You can count on us to do the best we can for you.' Swarc nodded ardently.

—◆—

The pair of lawyers returned two days later, carrying bundles of papers and folders, which they dumped onto the table. Szwarc was slightly out of breath.

'It's a matter of gaining public sympathy, Monsieur Grynszpan,' Larue said. 'Judge Tesnière has already met with the vom Rath family, showed them every courtesy, and he even invited Friedrich Grimm, that vile lawyer representing the German Reich, to be there as well. We're told that the judge went so far as to ask the interpreter, who is Jewish, to leave the room just as Grimm arrived, using the excuse that vom Rath's French was excellent.

It's also not helpful for us that the newspapers have been reporting vom Rath's story in a positive light, even though the mood in France is generally anti-German. This is because the family have impressed everyone by their dignity. Perhaps you can now understand our task – sympathy, Monsieur Grynszpan. Sympathy is most important for your case. Sympathy not just in France, but throughout the whole world.'

Now breathing normally, Szwarc spoke enthusiastically. 'The two of us – and your uncle – have come up with a suggestion. We think you should write letters, giving your point of view, not just to your family, but also to newspapers, and also to famous people – Roosevelt, Albert Einstein, our President Lebrun, maybe even Hitler, anybody with fame and influence. You could even try sports stars. Who knows?'

―◦―

He began the next day. The first letter was addressed to President Roosevelt.

My Dear Mr President Franklin Delano Roosevelt,
I think that you may have by now heard about me and
what I have done. You will understand, I hope, since I
have heard that you are a wise and sympathetic person,
that my act came up from a deep pain and anger about
how the Jewish people in Germany are being treated.
But I also know that as a result of my action, even more
calamities are now befalling them. I did not intend for
this to happen.

My dear Mr President, can you not use your influence to put some pressure on the British government to allow us, the persecuted, to escape from Germany and immigrate to the land which was promised to us by God over three thousand years ago? Perhaps the Jewish organisations in your country can also put pressure on England, probably financial, to get them to change their mind?

I do not know what will happen to me, perhaps I will be executed. However I do not fear this. Because I know that I have done everything in my power to help my people, even if it costs me my life!

I hope you will respond to my plea.

Yours sincerely

Herschel Grynszpan

After being copied by the prison authorities, the letter was sent to the White House, where President Roosevelt read it and handed it without comment to his son and secretary, James, who filed it away. It never reappeared. The prison copy was sent to the German Embassy, who forwarded it to Josef Goebbels.

He wrote similar letters to Albert Einstein, Charles Lindbergh, and several other prominent people. All of these letters were copied and forwarded to Berlin.

The next letter was to Max Schmeling.

Dear champion Schmeling

I remember when I was a child cheering for you when I heard about your victory over Jack Sharkey on the radio. It did not matter to me that it was a foul which gave you the championship. Anyway, you were far ahead on points, I believe.

As a German, I was so proud and excited at your victory.

But I have to confess that when I saw pictures in the newspapers of you posing with Hitler, and especially after you knocked out Joe Louis, I became less of a fan. Still, none of that matters now.

You will have heard of what I have done, and in Germany it is probable that the news about me is bad.

But I did not act as I did from evil motives, simply to help my people.

I know that you, champion Schmeling, have never been a real Nazi, and even that you have had many Jewish friends, who you visit in Paris. Perhaps the next time you are in Paris you could visit me in Fresnes prison. I could then explain to you why I did what I did, and perhaps you might press your influence onto the German government to help my people. I know that since your recent defeat by Joe Louis, you are less influential than before, yet I still ask you this.

Cordially,

Herschel Grynszpan

The letter was delivered to Schmeling's flat at the Excelsior Hotel. *Poor lad, what a mess he's made. And wanting me to reach out and help. Yet, if I wrote…? He'd probably show it to the newspapers, and then there'd be all sorts of trouble for me and Anny. Anyway, what would a letter from me accomplish?*

Max decided not to respond, or mention the letter to Anny.

The last letter was to Adolf Hitler. It was very difficult to write. *How should I begin the letter? Should I write, 'Mein Führer,' as every other German seems to do? But that would be lying. The last person I would choose to lead me is Hitler, and anyway, Hitler doesn't really want anything to do with Jews, so how could he be our leader? He actually hates Jews and is hated by us in return. I hate him worst of all. Still, I must attempt this. And I mustn't let the hatred in my heart spill onto the page.*

He scratched out many salutations, and rewrote the letter many times. In the end, he sent this.

Your Honour, Reichskanzler Adolf Hitler,
You may be surprised that I am writing to you, especially because of what I have done and because of how you feel about my people. Nevertheless, I write because I believe you to be a man of integrity and resolve, one who perhaps may be persuaded to adopt a mutually beneficial solution to what has been called 'The Jewish Question'.

We Jews have never set out to damage Germany or you personally. Yet the edicts from your government against Jews have reduced us to misery and penury. We agree with you that no German can be a Jew, and also that no Jew can really be a German. This is clear. Our place in is Palestine, and most of us would go there willingly if some way could be found.

I therefore suggest to you that if you remove the most awful restrictions on my people, we will forgive what has happened in the past. We would also make every effort to leave Germany for Palestine. Perhaps you can use your influence on Mr Chamberlain to get him to change his policy towards this problem. American Jews may be willing to finance such a migration, to the advantage of the German economy. All of this is possible.

All that I ask is that you see the reasonableness of my suggestion. I am happy to pay the price for the death of Herr vom Rath, whom I never intended to kill, but only to wound, as a protest. I regret this deeply, but history cannot be undone.

Sincerely
Herschel Grynszpan

The letter was never read by Hitler; it came to Goebbels' attention instead. He ordered the letter to be copied, then forwarded to Gestapo Headquarters for the attention of Heinrich Himmler, who gave instructions for it to be placed in Herschel Grynszpan's bulging file.

—◦—

A few days later, Uncle Solomon reappeared.

'Where are the lawyers?'

'We need to talk about that, Herschel.'

'Have they decided not to help me?'

'No. Let me explain. It seems, Herschel, that there are very many people in America who are interested in your case. One of them is a journalist, a famous one, I am told. Dorothy Thompson. She is always writing in American newspapers and magazines, and even has her own radio programme.'

'That's all very interesting, uncle, but what does it have to do with me?'

'Patience. This Thompson woman, on her radio show, she mentioned you and then asked her audience to send money to help for your defence. She especially asked gentile people to do this as it would look better if Jews weren't included.

'Anyway, to everyone's surprise, people from all walks of American life sent money, and within a few days she had over $40,000! That's one and a half million Francs! So now there's more than enough money to get you a really good advocate.'

'Better than Szwarc and Larue?'

'Maybe keep them on, but yes. I have someone else in mind who might be better. His name is Vincent Moro-Giafferi, with many successful cases. Of course, he is very expensive. But now we can afford him.'

'Wouldn't it be better to have a Jewish advocate?'

'Moro-Giafferi is the best in France. We should at least listen to what he says.'

—◦—

The next day, the famous advocate arrived. He had a room-filling personality, optimistic and ebullient. His body attested to the effects of success and fine dining; he was not so much corpulent as sated. He sported a lavish moustache which added to his air of exuberant demi-respectability.

'Your uncle mentioned that you have been busy writing letters.'

'Yes, on the advice of my lawyers.'

Moro-Giafferi narrowed his eyes. 'I wonder if this is such a good idea. I don't think that anyone will ever answer you, given the political climate in which we live. Perhaps they wouldn't even read your letters at all. Right now in France, people may have some sympathy for you personally, but they also have sympathy for the man you shot.'

'As do I, as I have said many times.'

'As we know. But you see, Monsieur Grynszpan, the French are desperate to avoid another war with Germany at all costs, so they are more likely to believe the German propaganda – that you acted solely to provoke war between this country and Germany. You can see that the prospect of sacrificing countless millions of Frenchmen to avenge a few dead Jews doesn't impress them.'

'Can't they see what has been happening in Germany?'

'The French are not so fond of Jews, especially those from Eastern Europe.'

'*Ostjuden.*'

'Just so. There are two hundred thousand *Ostjuden* living in Paris – there are another hundred thousand or so Jews who were born here. Most are considered by the French to be an alien presence in the body politic, if you will.'

'You think that I am lost, then.'

'Quite the contrary, Monsieur Grynszpan, or may I call you Herschel?'

The boy nodded assent.

'There are many ways open to us, Herschel. The first of course, is to gain sympathy for your family by demonstrating how badly they have been treated. We could start with that approach.'

'Using the postcards from my mother and sister?'

'Yes, that might help. But I have another idea, one which you might feel is unorthodox, but is likely to sway the court in your favour.'

'This is?'

'We could suggest that there was some sort of connection between you and vom Rath which predates the shooting.'

'But we never met before that day.'

'Might you be mistaken?'

He shook his head.

'Let me continue, if you will. Perhaps you met him at the *Club Sportif*, or in *Tout va Bien*. I read in your statement that you often visited there. Perhaps someone would treat you to a sandwich or a coffee. If an elegantly dressed diplomat – and I know of your interest in clothes – if such a person became attracted to a penniless young man, with exotic looks, deep brooding eyes, well dressed, slender. Maybe that made an impression on him.'

'What are you saying?!'

'Hear me out, it's only a suggestion, a viable scenario, a narrative which would certainly help you to escape the guillotine. So perhaps this man invites you afterward to a hotel for an intimate encounter, perhaps at the Hôtel de Suez, or somewhere else near the Gare de Est. In return for such intimacy, the young diplomat agrees to arrange your residency papers, and to acquire permits for your family to settle in France.'

Moro-Giafferi could see the boy's face redden. He continued nonetheless, as if making a summation for a judge.

'Of course the elegant diplomat does nothing to help your parents, does nothing about your residency. And therefore, the shooting was an act of revenge against a sexual predator. And so it becomes merely a *crime passionelle,* and you will escape the guillotine, perhaps even be acquitted.'

Herschel exploded, his eyes bulging and his fists clenched.

'Impossible! You think I am a queer? You think I'm a fairy, a *feigelach*?'

'Nobody is saying that. But if we even mentioned the possibility at your trial, things would go better for you.'

He cradled his shaking head in his hands. 'I could never say such things. Impossible. The shame it would bring to my family.'

'More shame than they have now?'

'They're not ashamed! They are *proud!* Proud because of what I have done for my people.'

'You won't be able to help your people if your head is separated from your body, will you?'

'It's impossible.'

'Very well, it's your neck. We'll go back to the postcards

from your parents.'

Despite the shock of this conversation, the young man decided to engage Maître Moro-Giafferi.

.

CHAPTER 24

THE TRIAL OF ABRAHAM AND CHAVA GRYNSZPAN

Herschel's aunt and uncle were arrested two days after vom Rath's murder. They expected to be summoned, yet the knock on the door still made them jump. Chava dropped a glass she was drying. It fell to the floor and shattered, shards scattering everywhere. Clutching his sleeve, she accompanied Abraham to the door. A gendarme stood before them.

'Abraham Grynszpan? Chava Grynszpan?'

The couple nodded. Chava glanced quickly back towards the kitchen. She could see the glitter of broken glass.

The gendarme smiled with disarming affability. Tall, portly, sporting a proudly waxed moustache, he spoke softly and good-naturedly. The frightened couple recognised him from their neighbourhood. He would often salute them when they passed in the street, fingers raised to his kepi's shiny visor.

'You are possibly aware of why I am here,' he shifted his face muscles into a stern but still friendly arrangement. The couple didn't answer, and Chava looked down at her shoes. The gendarme read from a paper which he removed from inside his cap. His black hair was shiny with grooming oil.

'Under the terms of Article 4 of the Décret sur la Police des étrangers of May 2 1938,' he paused and looked up at them, 'whoever directly or indirectly, assists or attempts to assist the illegal entry and residence of a foreigner will be subject to the punishment of a fine of 100 to 1000 Francs, and imprisonment from 1 month to 1 year.'

A pause. They could hear a noisy clattering of children on the stairs. Then Chava looked up. She was close to tears.

'We didn't know about this new law or that Herschel's papers weren't in order,' she lied.

'Not knowing the law is no excuse, as you should know by now. But if you didn't know about your nephew's papers – well, this may be true, and if it is, I'm certain that you will be returned home very quickly, perhaps after a small fine. But for now, I require you to accompany me to the police station.' He smiled reassuringly.

'Please do not worry. We are after all in France, so you are lucky. I understand that other Jewish people, those arrested in Germany, are not so politely treated, *n'est-ce pas?*'

Chava walked over to the window to see if it was raining. The couple slowly put on their coats and followed the gendarme through the door, then down the creaking stairs.

After being charged, the couple were separated to await their hearing. Chava was taken, unhandcuffed, to La Petite Roquette, a woman's prison in the 11th Arrondissement.

The police van's polished wooden bench was hard and slippery, and she had to hold on to it whenever the van turned a corner.

As Chava was driven through the huge prison gates, she could feel the weight of the gunmetal clouds above, glowering over her, shrinking her further. She was led to a single cell on the fourth floor. The guard tried to comfort her.

'You mustn't worry, Madame. You won't be mistreated here. Do you want some food?'

'Thank you no, monsieur. I have already eaten.'

'I'm sure it was better than what we have here. Perhaps some water? I'll fetch some.'

Then he closed the heavy metal door. He tried to close it gently, yet still it clanged. As the quiet of the cell descended onto her, she became submerged into an overwhelming sadness. She worried mostly about Herschel. Would he face the guillotine? But he's just a child, surely, they'd recognise that. And what would happen to Abraham? She felt empty without him. The cell was cold, much colder than her apartment. After a while the guard brought her another blanket, but the cold soon found its way through that.

Abraham was sent to a different part of the city, to La Santé, a notoriously overcrowded prison, east of Montparnasse. The guard who escorted him to his cell was proud of the prison's history.

'We've had many famous prisoners to lock up here – Verlaine, the poet, also Apollinaire, another writer. Not only writers. Some famous murderers, too.

But all Abraham could think about was the damp, the stink, the noise, and the banal anti-Semitic taunts which assaulted him as he passed through the corridors of cells.

◄o►

The pre-trial examination was conducted by Judge Jean Tesnière. Also involved were the French police and representatives of the German Government. This unusual attempt at cross-border co-operation had been well received in Germany, but the Grynszpan's state-appointed lawyer voiced his disapproval. His objection was waved away with a smile by Tesnière. Chava thought the judge's face kindly, noticing his gentle eyes and his neat King George V beard.

Then the questions.

'What did you know of your nephew's act of violence?'

'Nothing whatsoever, your honour,' Chava said, looking at her husband.

'Did you not argue with him about his plans the night before the assassination?'

'No, we argued about money,' Abraham replied. 'Herschel wanted money to send to his parents in Poland. I said that they probably wouldn't receive it. We parted in anger.'

The chief German representative, Friedrich Grimm, stood up and immediately began to harangue the accused, staring intently first at Abraham, then at Chava, who turned her gaze to her husband. 'Did you not make arrangements in 1936 to travel to Valenciennes to meet your nephew and escort him to Paris?'

'I have never been there, your honour,' Abraham

replied, looking at the judge, 'He arrived at our doorstep on his own.'

Grimm turned to the judge. 'Your honour, there was a similar case in 1936. All too similar. Perpetrated by the Jew Frankfurter. In Davos.'

Grimm then turned to the frightened pair. 'This other assassin was also young, he also had a postcard in his pocket justifying his actions, stating almost word-for-word what your nephew wrote, "I could not have acted otherwise". Is this not part of a pattern?' He looked around the courtroom for the effect he was having on the assembled. Most faces were fixed on the unhappy couple.

'I believe that both Frankfurter and your nephew, and I submit that this was with your collusion, acted in the service of Germany's eternal enemy, the Jew.'

'I never have heard about this Frankfurter man,' Abraham responded, as calmly as he could, given his rising anxiety. 'And I can assure you, that there never was any sign that Herschel was part of anything so complicated. He's a simple lad, really. But too excitable.'

Grimm summed up the German position. 'Learned judge, my conviction, and the firm belief of my government, is that the Jew Herschel Grynszpan's act is not that of a single individual, but part of a larger conspiracy, of which his relatives before you are a part.'

The judge thanked everyone for their testimony and said that he would rule on the matter within a few days. Abraham and Chava were returned to their respective cells and Grimm hurried to his office to cable his report directly to Josef Goebbels.

◄o►

Abraham and Chava Grynszpan's arraignment was quickly brought. The charge did not include any mention of a conspiracy. Grimm's assertion that Abraham and Chava had played a part in the assassination did not appear in the indictment. They were charged with harbouring their 17-year-old nephew even though they knew that he did not have a permit to reside in France.

Judge Tesnière summarised the arguments and delivered his verdict.

'It is clear that neither of the accused can be held responsible for Herschel Grynszpan's actions.'

The public prosecutor, M. Frette-Damicourt, objected.

'I submit, Monsieur Magistrate, that given the present tensions between this country and Germany, and the international repercussions of the accused nephew's actions, that trying the two accused solely on the charge of harbouring an illegal alien would not be well received in Germany.'

The German press corps and legal team mumbled enthusiastically.

'I believe that counsel's fears are groundless,' Tesnière ruled, 'and that Abraham and Chava Grynszpan should be tried on the lesser charge, and that a ruling as to the more serious charge will be delivered at a later date. The trial will commence on 29 November 1938 before the 17th Correctional Chamber of the Department of the Seine.'

Abraham and Chava were returned to their respected prisons, where an identical letter from their nephew was waiting for each of them.

Thank you very much for all you have done for me. I will never forget it. I know that I have brought you great trouble and misfortune by what I have done. I know that you are actually in danger because of me. But I hope that everything will work out well for you. I could not do otherwise than I have done. May God pardon me.

—◦—

The trial of Abraham and Chava Grynszpan took place three weeks later, as scheduled, on a cold rainy day, the sort of day that pushed people indoors.

To make certain that the trial received the minimum of publicity, Judge Tesnière had chosen a small courtroom, since, to his mind, the case was a merely routine matter of the violation of residency and immigration statutes. He didn't want a fuss or a gaggle of reporters and onlookers.

But the Grynszpan's lawyer always drew a crowd. Vincent Moro-Giafferi had decided to defend Abraham and Chava Grynszpan as well as their nephew. The assassin's trial might not take place for several months, and besides, this other case interested him.

The small courtroom was packed, not only with visitors and the press, but also with over twenty lawyers, crammed together to witness what they hoped would be one of Moro-Giafferi's star performances.

In the dock, Abraham admitted that his previous statements to the police had been untrue, and that he did in fact know that his nephew had received his expulsion order but had not left the country.

'When Herschel came to our home, he was in such a state of depression that it was pitiful. He was ill and suffered greatly from trouble in his stomach. How could we have thrown him out? It would have been inhuman, our own flesh and blood, too. Also, we had been given the legal and moral responsibility for him by his parents.'

Then their famous advocate rose. He spoke for over an hour.

'How can the Ministry of Justice apply the law in this case when it had failed to provide, as required, a safe haven for the child?' He always referred to his young client as 'the child'.

'Could no other safe haven been found for him? I suggest that no such attempt was undertaken by the Ministry. As a result, this child had nowhere else to go. And if he were to be deported, to where? He no longer had a valid Polish passport, because that government had cancelled all passports of persons living abroad for more than five years, a measure directed primarily at Jews. After receiving his expulsion order from France, who would renew his papers? And in Hanover, the German authorities had categorically refused the child leave to return. As for other countries, we all see how they continue to refuse asylum to Jews.'

The assembled listened to Moro-Giafferi as if they had one common ear.

'Now let us turn to the boy's aunt, Chava Grynszpan. Surely, she must be found innocent. She had only two choices. The first was to stand with husband and her nephew. The other choice was to report her husband to the police. How could she do that in any conscience?' Moro-Giafferi smiled at Chava, but she was looking down at the floor.

'Now we come to Abraham, the other accused. The regulations clearly state – and this clarity is unusual in such regulations,' a chuckle from the assembled lawyers, 'that in the absence of an alternative domicile for the child, such regulations could not be applied to the person who provides the shelter. It is crystal clear on this issue.

'We need to stress that the accused have been brought to court for shielding a youngster who sought to escape from a country in which he was in danger with no recourse to the German courts. Don't forget, Germany has demonstrated time and again how little respect it has for international law.'

Moro-Giafferi then sat down amidst appreciative murmurs.

The prosecutor rose, but he delivered his argument without much conviction. He agreed that the couple should not be treated with undue severity, but that they should nevertheless receive more than the minimum one-year sentence.

After a short recess, Judge Tesnière announced his verdict.

'Mindful of the prosecutor's suggested tariff of at least one year in prison, the court nevertheless sentences Abraham and Chava Grynszpan to four months imprisonment and a fine of 100 francs each, for having sheltered Herschel after issuance of his expulsion order.'

The German contingent shook their heads in disappointment. Tesnière continued. 'Abraham and Chava Grynszpan are also ordered to be expelled from France, but this order is deferred until the completion of their nephew's trial.'

No one knew when that would begin.

The couple were taken away.

Friedrich Grimm reported to Goebbels at the Ministry of Propaganda. 'Moro used the well-known tactic from the beginning, of wearing down the court, using his exceptional knowledge of the specific provisions of the law in order to unleash, at just the right moment – near the end – his tremendous oratory.'

The next day, a meticulous appeal for the Grynszpans' release was lodged by Moro-Giafferi, but the two remained incarcerated, still being under investigation for having colluded in the assassination of vom Rath. Their fine was paid by the American fund.

─◄o►─

On Christmas Day, 1938, the more serious charge was dropped, and Abraham and Chava were released on bail. As Abraham was escorted to the police car which would take him home, he could hear the familiar taunts echoing through the prison corridors.

'Hey yiddle, it's not too late to buy a small Christmas tree. I can show you where to plant it!'

'Happy Christmas, Christ killer!'

'Trust the French system to release a Jew on Christmas day. Maybe I'll be let out for Passover!'

On 3 January 1939, only ten days after their release, the Appeals court increased Abraham's sentence to six months, and reduced Chava's to three months. They were again incarcerated, but were sent home without fuss after less than a month in prison. Neither the French nor the German press mentioned their release. All attention was now focused on their nephew.

CHAPTER 25
DELAYS

The autumn of 1938, and with it the French fears of war against Germany over Czechoslovakia, dissipated into a winter of ice and ennui. Then, slowly at first, spring insinuated itself on southerly breezes. On chic Parisian boulevards, café owners ordered fresh linen for pavement tables, waiters darted between them with renewed poise and attention. Cars tooted their horns exuberantly, and the pitch of street chatter was raised by several semi-tones. But in Fresnes prison, only an echo of that spring sunshine could be felt; window-bar shadows waxing and waning onto endlessly mopped floors.

◄o►

Uncle Solomon's visits began to irritate the boy. *He never changes his tune. The same old criticisms, the same old complaints, one day about his digestion, the next about his asthma. The same every time. If only Uncle Abraham and Aunt Chava could visit instead, but they are in prison, and all because of me.*

He was frustrated, anxious and bored. He busied himself with his morning prayers, meticulously arranging the *tefillin* around his arm and forehead, the prayer shawl over his shoulders. During the day, he passed the time writing letters or discussing the Old Testament with Chaim Bernstein, the prison rabbi, who visited him regularly and offered him Judaic wisdom.

He was also comforted by the regular appearances by Moro-Giafferi, although the news he brought wasn't always comforting.

'At first, Herschel, we as well as the Germans wanted the trial to proceed without delay. But since this shameful business with Czechoslovakia, the mood in France has shifted in our direction. Now it is the Germans who are moving slowly, not us. There is not much we can do, except wait, and build our case.'

The boy paced his cell. 'What does the judge say? Surely he knows how important this trial is.'

'Tesnière makes no secret of admiring the Germans, Herschel. He has even offered them access to your defence material, a practice which under other circumstances would be considered outrageous.'

'Is he against me, then?'

'Not personally, no. But he wants to avoid upsetting the Bosche. Like many others he abhors the thought of another war. However, his pro-German attitude is an extra hurdle put in our way. But best to be positive. Yes, Herschel?'

The boy stopped pacing and sat on his bunk. Moro-Giafferi, continued, in a more optimistic tone.

'What we must first do, my young friend, is to demonstrate how your parents, and many other Jews, have been so appallingly treated. It is because of this that you committed your act, in a moment of rage, which had been building up for months. Not so?'

He nodded.

'I have here some photographs of your family flat in Hanover, taken just after your parents were deported.

'You can see that the apartment looks a bit untidy, which is hardly surprising since your family were whisked away without warning. We had hoped to get new images which would show a typical German apartment, in a typical German street, inhabited by typical Germans. But by the time the photographer arrived, most of the furniture had been removed, and new people were already moving in.

'The next photograph is of the barracks in Zbąszyń to which your family was taken. The problem here is that the barracks don't look particularly uncomfortable, at least not for a refugee shelter. When I showed this photograph to judge Tesnière, he remarked that he would have been delighted with such accommodation when he was in the army. Now, as you know, your parents have been able to travel to Radomsk, where they have joined your grandmother in the familial home. And now they are safe. However, their testimony could still be instrumental in demonstrating the hardships they endured, and what anguish it caused you. It follows that we need to get them to Paris.'

The boy lit up at the thought. He had that day received a postcard from his father. He removed it from his jacket pocket, now bulging with similar correspondence. He translated it for his advocate.

You must not allow yourself to have gloomy thoughts about us. Things are not so bad. We have enough to eat and drink, and otherwise we lack for practically nothing. We are, thank the Lord, all in reasonable health. Our fervent wish is that we will all soon be happily together once more. Many good wishes and kisses.

Your father

He passed the postcard to Moro-Giafferi, who glanced at it briefly, then handed it back.

'Do you know,' he said, almost to himself, avoiding Moro-Giafferi's eyes, 'if I had received this postcard before, I might never have killed that German.'

A silence fell between them.

Moro-Giafferi scowled. 'This postcard and that thought are not helpful to your case. We must not show the postcard to the judge. If we do, there will be less sympathy for you. And you must never mention that thought to anyone else, not even in Yiddish.'

But Moro-Giafferi knew that this postcard and all other such Grynszpan communications would have been copied, translated and sent to the judge. They would also have been sent to the German Government.

◄○►

He was interrogated by Judge Tesnière a few days later. The meeting took place in the judge's cluttered chambers – a wood-panelled room, smelling of furniture polish and cigars. Tesnière was seated behind a large mahogany desk, Herschel's file open before him. The windows were open, and the bright Paris morning, lavish with spring fragrances and petrol fumes, flowed into the room. The boy stood in front of the desk. A court stenographer sat in the corner.

'Monsieur Grynszpan, there have been so many contradictions in your testimony. Perhaps today we might be able to clarify what you have said, and to discover the truth at long last.'

The boy furrowed his brow, but managed to smile.

'But you know, sir, there has been bad reporting of what I have said before, since my French, as you can see, is not so formidable, and there was never a translator for me.'

'What has been misreported?'

'I assure your honour that I myself did not load the gun. The shopkeeper must have done it in the shop without my knowledge. I thought that it was empty. You see, I only wanted to frighten someone who is German, not to kill or even to wound him.'

'But you still managed to fire five shots.'

'When the gun fired, I panicked.'

'Anything else?'

'As I have said, my first statements about my motives were also reported wrongly, since my bad French. I had never the plan to kill or wound anyone. I am a quiet, peaceful person.'

'Thank you, Herr Grynszpan.' *Why has he called me 'Herr', why not Monsieur as before?*

Tesnière slowly turned over a few pages in the file. He then looked up.

'Over the last weeks, Herr Grynszpan, I have looked at all your statements, as well as depositions from the vom Rath family, from witnesses, and other interested parties. I have also read translations of the letters you have written. In light of this evidence, and of your constantly changing versions of the events, I am forced to reject your current explanation, and to conclude that your first statements were in fact true. I will therefore recommend that you are tried for premeditated murder.'

He had expected as much.

'Whatever my fate, I could not have done other than I have.'

The court stenographer underlined that last sentence. The trial was set for September 1939.

—◦—

During that summer, to the bemusement of Moro-Giafferi, his client continued to write to prominent people, including Paul Marchandeau, the French Minister of Justice. He was convinced that France would come to see that he had acted as a French patriot – if perhaps prematurely.

Dear Monsieur, le Minister Marchandeau,

By now you have heard of me and the case that is pending about me. This procedure is complex and may take a very long time.

I should like to make a proposal to you which could avoid all of this.

In these troubled times, I request that you permit me to enlist in the French Army. In this way, I can redeem

with my own blood, if necessary, the act I committed,
and repair the troubles I have caused the country which
has accorded me its hospitality.
Vive la France!
Herschel Grynszpan

Minister Marchandeau smiled, raised his eyebrows, and absently scratched his nearly bald head. He wrote 'rejected' on the bottom of the letter. Turning to his secretary, he said, 'File this somewhere. You know, at least by killing a German that young Jew has made a good start.'

━◖◗━

Josef Goebbels was beginning to feel more comfortable about his reconciliation with Magda, and was delighted to be reunited with the innocent love of his children. Yet he missed Lída. He missed her smile, her body, her fragrance, her laugh. He missed the way she teased out his gentler side, his artistic side, his guileless side. He wondered, *now that Czechoslovakia is a part of the Reich, could we find some opportunity to see each other again? Perhaps a quiet weekend in the Carpathians. Some pretext could always be invented.* But he quickly put that thought aside, shaking his head, remembering all too vividly the look on Hitler's face at Berchtesgaden, an image which assailed him like iced water. He decided to stiffen his resolve and sharpen his mendacity. He had still to prove himself to his Führer.

His thoughts were interrupted by a knock at the door.

'Herr Reichsminister, Friedrich Grimm is in the anteroom.'

Goebbels rose and stood behind his large desk, fingers spread on the desktop like spider legs.

'Send him in.'

The sharpness of Goebbels' features was accentuated by his mood; his thin nose more prominent, his high forehead accentuated by his swept back hair, his thin lips set firmly, his eyes glaring within deep sockets.

'Why, Grimm, does everything about this case have to be so complicated? It's quite straightforward, is it not? A stupid little Jew murders a hero of the Reich. It is abundantly clear that he was put up to it by the International Jewish Conspiracy. Why is a result so long in coming?'

Friedrich Grimm sighed. He needed desperately to prevaricate, given the hostile public opinion in France. He shuddered at the thought of what would happen if Grynszpan were actually acquitted or even given a light sentence.

'Herr Reichsminister, were this trial taking place in Germany, it would be settled within days. But in France they have their own methods, and like everything else French, they are laborious and slow. For our part, we have built the Grynszpan case methodically. In order to show the nature of the man who has been martyred, we brought back vom Rath's parents to speak to the judge.'

Goebbels frowned. 'Little use they are. Totally unsuitable parents for a hero. The father was never a supporter of the movement; tepid at best. This is why the Führer hardly spoke to the family at the funeral. Of course, immediately afterwards I was able to have a most cordial meeting with the vom Raths, to tell them that it would be in their interests to remind the French that their son was a model National Socialist.'

'And this they did,' said Grimm. 'They returned to France and assured the judge they were ardent supporters of the Führer and the movement, that their son had always been a true National Socialist, and that rumours to the contrary were being put about by the lying Jewish press, or something like that.'

Goebbels sat. Grimm remained standing.

'But the trial will go ahead as scheduled in September, will it not?'

'I fervently hope so, but there is one further complication. The Grynszpans' lawyers want to bring his parents from Poland to testify. Their entire case is based on their belief that since the French public have some sympathy for the little Jew, any first-hand evidence from his parents will help.'

'This must be prevented.'

'Steps have already been taken, Herr Reichsminister. I myself travelled to Warsaw last week, and met with our embassy representatives there. I told the Polish Foreign Minister, Beck, that it would be a shame if the Grynszpan trial were used by the foreign press as propaganda against Poland, accusing them of anti-Semitism in the treatment of refugees. He urged Beck to prevent the Jew Grynszpan's parents from travelling to France.'

'And?'

'Beck said that as Poland was already world famous for anti-Semitism, a little more would be of no consequence.

Still, he agreed to prevent the old Jews' travel. You see, Reichsminister, that despite all, I am doing the best I can.'

'Yes. I can see that, Grimm. Yes. Perhaps we must wait for things to take their course. Perhaps we must wait until that silly little Jew-swine is in our hands. And just between us, we might not have so long to wait.'

—◦—

'No, your parents will not be allowed to travel here. This is a blow, of course. Our case will be weakened without their personal testimony.'

The boy slumped onto his bunk.

'In light of this, I plead with you again, Herschel. Your act, rather than helping the Jewish people, has only served to make Jewish blood flow, by giving the Nazis a pretext. If you could only give a non-political reason for what you did, then the Germans could no longer use it as an excuse to continue this terrible oppression. Also, I should add, it might spare you a long prison term.'

'But I assure you that I never had anything to do with that man before that day.'

'Does that matter so much, under the circumstances? What we need to do is to defend you.'

'What about my honour?'

'Honour?' Moro-Giafferi reddened. 'What does your honour mean? What does your immature sense of honour weigh, in the face of hundreds of thousands of Jews? This is not about honour, child!'

The boy was cowed by his lawyer's outburst. He spoke quietly.

'Do you think that I had relations with that man?'

Moro-Giafferi slowly unclenched his fists and smiled softy.

'Of course not. And whether or not vom Rath was even a homosexual doesn't interest me in the slightest, except insofar as it might help in defending you.'

The boy met his advocate's eyes. 'I just can't do it.'

Moro-Giafferi collected his papers. The guard unlocked the steel door.

'In that case, we will nevertheless prepare the very best defence we can for your trial in September.'

CHAPTER 26
PUTTING ON THE GLOVES AGAIN

Max was shaving. He enjoyed the feeling, especially after a shower. He had returned from New York with two cracked vertebrae and a new safety razor, a gift from Yussel.

'The latest type, Max, thinner blades. *Look sharp, be sharp, shave sharp*, as they say on the radio. Now you can throw away that old cut-throat, so you won't nick yourself. And that's a good thing, especially for photographs, and also – I shouldn't have to mention this to you – in the ring, where these cuts can open up and you can end up losing a fight just from bleeding.'

Max loved the effortless way the blade glided through the shaving cream meringue and peeled away the thick stubble. Lifting his nose with his fingers, he contorted his face in the long-practised ritual, helping the blade find access to hidden bristles. Wrapped in a towel, he stared at his reflection in the wall-length mirror, pleased to see evidence of his returning muscle-tone.

Anny stood at the doorway in a white dressing gown, watching him. Her husband was standing taller, and he was smiling again. They were spending the night before he sailed in the Hotel Deutscher Hof, her favourite in

Hamburg. She particularly liked their restaurant and the old-fashioned four-poster beds.

'When I arrive in New York,' he said, speaking to her reflection. 'I'll look up some old boxing friends, maybe Jack Dempsey. Also, to see Yussel, to see what he thinks. Maybe I'm not so completely washed up. Maybe I could try again.'

'But you just returned two months ago. Your injuries have barely healed. Why go back so soon? To arrange another fight with Louis?'

'No. Too soon, too soon. Maybe better some other matches first.'

'Or to stop altogether?'

Max sighed. 'Prize-fighting is what I do. It's what I *am*, after all. I would go crazy without it. For you, there are more options. You love our little farm and can work all day in it. My interests are not so earthy. Also, you still have your movie work. Although those films nowadays, such nonsense. Some of them are pure evil. Like *Jüd Seuß*. I hope you're not offered a part in it.'

'I told them no. Even before they asked.'

'Do you need to work for them at all? For Goebbels?'

Anny walked over and put her arms around him from behind, her chin resting on his shoulder, looking at their reflection in the mirror, a lovingly serious expression on her face.

'Like you, I too would go crazy without the work. And the only work for me now is in Germany. Where else could I go? England? Hitchcock replaced my voice in the *Blackmail* sound film, because of my accent. So what parts would I get there? Deaf-mutes? Foreign spies? Or should I go back to Prague? But it's no different there, now that Germany runs everything. Where would I go, Max?'

Max smiled at her in the mirror.

'Of course, I'll have to give up the ring someday. This I know. You can't fight the clock. But boxing defines me. Maybe later I could be a referee like Jack Dempsey. Anyway, a few big matches would get us a bit of money for the future.'

'I will be with you whatever you decide, you know that. But you mustn't endanger yourself anymore. We have enough money.'

He turned around and hugged his wife, his towel dropping to expose his muscular buttocks in the mirror.

Anny stood on her toes to kiss his still soapy cheek, grinning when she saw the reflection of shaving cream on her nose. She took his hand. 'Let's go back to bed.'

'But I'll have to shower all over again,' Max said, in feigned seriousness.

'It will be worth it, I think.' Staring down at his penis, she said, 'Part of your fitness programme.'

─◦─

There were fewer passengers on the S.S. *Hamburg* on this crossing; some Americans returning home, a few weary German salesmen going through the motions, grimly anticipating a rougher business climate. Hardly anyone spoke to Max. Some passengers stared.

As he was passing through New York immigration, his

friendly smile met by the officers' indifference, someone within earshot nudged his companion.

'Isn't that Max Schmeling?'

The other man looked up from his newspaper, squinted in Max's direction.

'Big deal. If that guy wants to come all the way over here to get beat up again, it's no skin off my nose.'

—◦—

Yussel's office was in a large room above the gym. As he climbed the stairs Max could hear the comforting sounds of effort; punching bags being pummelled, ropes being skipped, sparring partners bouncing in the ring, gloves banging at muscular torsos and padded helmets. And he could smell and almost hear the sweat, decades of it.

The office door had a sign which read: *Joe Jacobs, Manager of Champions.* Someone had crossed through the last word and wrote *Chimpunzees,* in red crayon. Max knocked.

'Come in!'

Yussel was leaning back in his chair, his feet on the desk, reading a newspaper. Once he would have stood, once he would have walked over to give Max a big hug, careful not to burn Max's jacket with his cigar. Now Yussel just looked up at Max from the sports pages.

'What's up, Champ? Good crossing? Sit down comfy.'

Max sat deeply into a red leather sofa, a recent addition to the otherwise shabby office.

'So what's the score, Max? What brings you downtown?'

'I'm all healed now, Yussel, doing some roadwork near

my home, punching the bag, skipping some rope, you know.'

'Great, Champ. Important to keep in shape.'

'You know, maybe I'm ready to start again. Maybe a few fights. To get rid of the rust before I meet Louis again.'

'You mean fights here?' Yussel asked, staring at the ash on his cigar.

'That's what I was thinking. I could meet Baer again, even Sharkey. I know I could beat them now.'

Yussel put the cigar back in his mouth, took a long slow drag, his eyes following the smoke as it rose thickly above his desk.

'For you, Max, as a German, this isn't such a good time, not now. Most Americans think that Hitler has gone too far, muscling in on the rest of Czechoslovakia last week, after promising not to. Americans might like you personally, Max, but being a *kraut* is not a good idea in this town at the moment. Someone got beat up for ordering the bratwurst special at Mindy's the other day. You know how it is, you read the papers.

'Roosevelt says that he will keep us neutral, but most people, except maybe the wops in little Italy and the goose-steppers in Brownsville, don't think much of your Führer and his henchmen.'

'He's not *my* Führer, Yussel.'

'I know, I know, but those pictures in the papers tell a different story.'

Max frowned.

'Look, Max, let's get you some fights in Europe. Why not Heuser? It'd be no trouble for you to take the

European championship from him. He's a nobody. A pushover. Maybe by then all this Czechoslovakia stuff will blow over.'

'And Joe Louis?'

'Absolutely. You should have, without question, another shot at him. But not now, Max. Later. To be honest, I think that Louis would be more than grateful to fight you again, with all them bums he's had to massacre since you two met. There's really nobody around but you, and after you, there'll be nobody left for him to fight except other *schwarzers*. This whole game is turning black before my eyes. This is just because *schwarzers* are better at fighting. It follows. Because they're really only animals after all. I'll get to work fixing up a Heuser match.'

Max rose to leave.

'Oh, I just remembered, Max. Some guy in a fancy limousine came over to the gym the other day. It turns out the guy works for Coca-Cola, and he must be high up, looking at his suit. I don't touch the stuff myself. Gives me gas. Anyway, he is looking for sporting faces to be part of a new billboard campaign. He's doing the rounds of sports clubs, that sort of thing. OK, so around here, the faces aren't much to look at. But just as he was going, he noticed your ugly mug on that poster on the wall, and remembered you. He mentioned that maybe you should give him a call, because they're expanding their set-up in Germany, and your Aryan puss might be a selling point. He left his card.'

Max took the card, read it hastily, and put it in his pocket.

'Yussel, I've been thinking.'

'Always a good idea, Champ. Shoot.'

'I don't really know how to say this, but did you send me my full share of the Louis fight?'

Yussel's face froze for an instant, then warmed into a fulsome smile.

'Max, Max, you're worried about the cut? Sure, maybe you are. But you're not suggesting that I tried to cheat you, are you? After all we've been through together? Look at it from my side. Do you know how much extra I had to spend on publicity for you, with things the way they are and every newspaper painting a swastika on your ass. It's no picnic being the manager of a German at the moment, Max, let me tell you.'

Yussel rose from his chair, walked over to Max and put his arm around his shoulder.

'Tell you what, Champ. I'll get our accountant Bernie Birnbaum to look into things again and if there's a nickel missing, he'll wire the money straight over to you. It might even get to Germany before you do. Can't say fairer than that Max, am I right?'

Max smiled, hugged Yussel and left the office.

On his way down the stairs, Max thought, *a week across the Atlantic and another back again, for this? No fights, no possible shot at Louis again. And I'll never get a cent of the money he owes me. Better to forget about it. Anny is right, we have enough money. Go back to Germany, Max and stay there, stay with Anny. But first maybe I should see this Coca-Cola man.*

—◦—

On 2 July, 1939, in the Adolf Hitler Stadium, Stuttgart, Max Schmeling faced the reigning European champion, Adolf Heuser, who was favoured to win. Pundits reasoned that Heuser's power and resilience would overwhelm Max, a spent force.

From the opening bell, Heuser charged at Max, throwing a furious barrage of punches. *He's trying to fight me like Louis,* Max thought. But Max had since learned how to absorb and sidestep such attacks. He felt completely in control of his body, his jabs and hooks flowing from a source of renewed energy and rhythm. *Sometimes my punches bounce off an opponent, like they did with Louis last summer, but now they are going right through Heuser.*

As Heuser moved in for another attack, Max landed an uppercut so powerful that it seemed to raise the man off his feet. He fell to the canvas and was counted out, seventy-one seconds after the opening bell. After the count, Max rushed over to his stricken colleague, and helped to carry him to his stool.

Regaining consciousness, Heuser looked up. 'Max, if you'd hit Louis with that punch, you would be world champion now.'

After the ring announcement, followed by the obligatory Nazi salutes, the two men posed for the press, grinning, with their arms over each other's shoulders.

A reporter shouted, 'Max, to what do you ascribe your quick victory?'

'Well, as you know, I had a very good boxing lesson last summer in New York. Also, my wife has put me on a special training regimen.'

—◦—

Walter Neussel, the leading European contender, was next in line to fight Max. A contract was signed for their meeting, to be held in Dortmund in mid-August. Max was keen, and believed that he could defeat his countryman easily. But Anny asked Max to postpone the fight, so that he could help gather the harvest on their farm. Neussel had at first complained, but his manager reminded him of how much emphasis Hitler placed on agricultural issues. It was then agreed that the fight would take place in September.

But September 1939 was a bit too late.

CHAPTER 27
TANKS AND PLANES

It was Anny who woke first. She shook Max gently. He turned to her, smiling, his dark stubble prominent in the moonlight. A late summer breeze carried the sweet aroma of Deutsche Danzig roses into the bedroom.

'Do you hear that noise, Max?'

'What time is it? What noise?'

'It's two am. A low rumble, Max. Listen.'

He shut his eyes to help his ears.

'Maybe it's the boiler,' Max said.

'It's outside.'

Max sat up.

'You're right. We'll go see.'

They rose together and went to the window, he in his pyjama bottoms, she in a thin summer nightdress, her form silhouetted in the moonlight. Max smiled as he looked at her. He was endlessly fascinated by her small, lithe shape.

Then he frowned.

'It sounds like trucks, maybe also tanks.'

Anny leaned against her husband.

'What if it's war, Max? We're so near the border. Should we be worried?

'It might just be another exercise,' he said, unconvincingly. 'Anyway, even if it is war, the Poles won't be coming into Germany, I think, so we're safe in our little home, far away from towns and cities.'

'I'm so worried. I'll never get back to sleep now,' Anny said, looking up at him.

'Let's think of something to do,' Max said as he led her back towards the bed.

'How can you think of such a thing with all this going on?'

'I'll get the jigsaw puzzle instead.'

They fell asleep in each other's arms, sweaty and sated. They were awakened three hours later by swarms of fighters and bombers flying over their home. Anny ran into the living room and switched on the radio.

◄○►

Later that morning, Adolf Hitler addressed the Reichstag in the Kroll Opera House. He began calmly, soothingly, as he often did. He outlined the attempts he had made to secure a lasting peace with Poland. But Poland was unresponsive, he announced, his voice implying more regret than anger.

He then stood more erect, his arms crossed over his chest. He let his voice find its full power.

This night for the first time, Polish regular soldiers fired on our territory. Since 5.45 am. we have been returning the fire, and from now on bombs will be met by bombs. Whoever fights with poison gas will be fought with poison gas. Whoever departs from the rules of humane warfare can only expect that we shall do the same. I will continue this struggle, no matter against whom, until the safety of the Reich and its rights are secured.

There was jubilant cheering in the Kroll Opera House.

The Second World War began. And everything changed.

Between 31 August and 1 September 1939, a heavy black line was drawn onto the calendar, with different worlds on either side.

It took six weeks for Poland to be overwhelmed by a tempest of explosions and steel.

—◦—

'Everything is different now, Herschel.'

'What do you mean?'

Moro-Giafferi stared incredulously at his client. 'Have you not heard? We are at war.'

'I know that. Everyone speaks of nothing else. And of course, I worry for my family, still in Poland.'

'Let us hope they will be safe.'

'I pray to God every day.'

The boy was silent for a moment. Then he frowned.

'But aside from that, *Maître*, what has the war to do with my trial?'

Moro-Giafferi was taken aback. 'You know, young man, it is possible that France has other things on her mind.'

He softened when he saw his client's face.

'Well, Herschel, of course you are right, there is nothing we can do but to press on. We now have a new examining magistrate, since "Captain" Tesnière has joined the army. He has been replaced by Philippe Glorian.'

'Will that make a difference to me?'

'It may slow things down further. Even so, we will immediately push for a quick trial, as no doubt you would walk free the next day. And the Germans can have little to say about it now. Removing Germany from our legal considerations is a relief. Nevertheless, there is still no appetite for this war in France. Even now, the government is looking for another peace treaty. Even now, with tanks and planes killing so many Poles, a peace treaty! Just so we can save our own skins. As a Frenchman, I am ashamed. But at least the English are ready to fight.'

'But we will win the war, no? With England on our side and with the Maginot line protecting us.'

'Let us hope so. Losing doesn't bear thinking about.'

One week later, Herschel was led to Judge Glorian's office. He was a pudgy man; his robes were draped carelessly over his suit, and he spoke whilst smoking a cigarette.

'You say you want to join our armed services, Herr Grynszpan.' He pronounced the name as if it were a foreign object in his mouth.

'That is correct, sir. I can do more for France in the army than I can in jail. If my trial can be quickly brought, I can join up right away. I know that I'm quite small, but I'm strong. Perhaps I could be a German translator in a forward unit, or perhaps I can be used for questioning prisoners. It is also possible that...'

Judge Glorian interrupted the flow.

'Herr Grynszpan, it will take me some days to familiarise myself with all the complexities of your case. It is inevitable, but such are the inconveniences of war, you know.'

The boy deflated.

'But rest assured, Herr Grynszpan, I will bring things to a head as soon as possible.'

—◦—

Autumn came early to Berlin that year. A brisk north wind scoured the Wilhelmstraße while newspapers and hats tumbled along *Unter den Linden.* Everything pointed to a harsh winter.

'It is now even more important to have the trial postponed, Reichsminister. To be frank, we haven't yet found any conclusive evidence of conspiracy.'

Goebbels said, 'This demonstrates what we are dealing with, Grimm. The Jews are so crafty that the very fact that there is no evidence is ample proof of their perfidy.'

'That is of course true, Reichsminister, but also, if the trial were held now, the little Jew would certainly walk free, not because he's a Jew, but because he's a *Pollack.* The propaganda effect on France and the outside world would be immense.'

'This is why we must make better propaganda. I'll give you an example. Hans Bertram has just completed a film celebrating our victory in Poland. It shows how Poland and England planned to invade the Reich, and then the complete destruction of the Polish air force and the rapid advance of our tanks. All of this is very exciting. It also shows the effects of the bombing of Warsaw. Very graphic, to say the least.

'I asked Norbert Schultze to do the music. He's well established, and a good composer. He even wrote *Lily Marleen,* and also, he looks like a model Aryan, which I knew would please our Führer. But when I heard the music, I was shocked. It was very sad, exactly the opposite of what was needed. I called him in and said to him, "This film is about our great victory, so why is your music so funereal?" He said, "I can't help it. When I see scenes of such carnage, I can't think of anything but sad music." That's what he told me.'

'Surely you replaced him.'

'I thought of that at first. But he's a very good composer and the rest of the music is stirring stuff. And then an idea occurred to me. We could make this music work in our favour. So now when everyone sees those bombed Polish towns, and hears Schultze's sad music, they will also hear the following commentary:

You see, Herr Chamberlain, what calamities your stubbornness has created? It is because of you that the Polish people have suffered such a terrible fate. The whole world should now be aware of what your policies mean. And the poor Polish people will now know just who to blame for their misery.

'So now we can feel sorry for the Poles and turn the anger at the British.'

'A very elegant solution, Herr Reichsminister.'

Goebbels rewarded him with a warmer than usual smile. He leaned towards Grimm, as if revealing a confidence in the empty room. 'Now what do we do about the propaganda impact of the Grynszpan business?'

'We should postpone the trial as long as possible, I think, given French public opinion.'

'You are right, Grimm. But rest assured, this business will all be sorted soon, one way or another.'

◄o►

Over the autumn and into the winter, when the German and Soviet dismemberment of Poland was followed by an uneasy calm, Herschel received many letters from the USA and elsewhere; offers of friendship, devotion, even marriage. Most were held back by the prison authorities. 'He already thinks the universe revolves about him. In his eyes, he's even more important than the war. A world celebrity!'

Offers of money arrived as well.

Many, many thanks for the money you have sent, he wrote, but I cannot take it, because I do not deserve it. If you want to do something which I want very much, I ask you to take the money and give it to the thousands of innocent Jews, robbed, exiled and suffering at the Polish border.

His signature was now bolder, larger, and contained calligraphic flourishes.

He seemed unaware that the border no longer existed, did not know that his parents, in the company of most of the other deported Jews, had left the makeshift border camp before the German invasion.

CHAPTER 28
WAR CHANGES EVERYTHING

They had travelled sometimes on buses, sometimes on foot, carrying their meagre belongings; weighed down by the forceful March wind. They had arrived at Radomsk, their original home, the home of the letter-writing paternal grandmother, the home of the relatives and friends they had left behind all those years ago. But after a few months they needed to flee again, away from the Germans who were now devouring Poland from the west, north and south. Herschel's grandmother insisted, beyond the reach of impassioned entreaties, to remain behind in her home.

'I am old. My health couldn't survive a long journey.'

Esther could not be talked out of remaining behind with her grandmother.

'Who else would look after her? Don't worry. What can happen, after all? Anyway, I speak German. So perhaps that will help.'

Rivka, Zindel and Mordechai left without her, trying to make their way east, trying to outpace the Germans.

On 10 September, a German SS 'task force' unit arrived in Radomsk. They emptied every house of any Jewish occupants – some helpful Poles pointed the way – and marched them to the outskirts of town. The people of Radomsk had never encountered these new SS *Einsatzgruppen,* before. They had no idea what to expect. Perhaps they were all being taken away for questioning?

It was a bright sunny day, with just a faint aroma of burning leaves in the air. They walked through a sparse woodland at the edge of the town.

'Esther, darling, are those shoes strong enough you are wearing? We might have to walk a long way.'

'Don't worry, grandmother, they have brought me all the way here from Zbąszyń. They can last many more kilometres.'

They arrived at a large pit. Esther and her grandmother exchanged fearful glances as their worlds disappeared; the colours, sounds, smells, all evaporated into a cloud of fear. Grandmother gripped Esther's hand. All were ordered to descend the steps, roughly cut into the earth. Grandmother lost her footing, but Esther held her and helped her down. Lined in a row with the other Jews, they looked at each other with love and regret. Then they were shot; grandmother, Esther, cousins – every Jew in Radomsk, about one hundred in all. After the first volley, sporadic moaning and crying could be heard. Those Jews were shot again. When all was still, and even the birds watched mutely in the thinning trees, Polish workmen covered the oozing bodies with quicklime. They didn't refill the pit with earth, in case other Jews were found, hiding in barns, in fields, in woods. The SS unit commander wrote the number of Jews killed that day into his notebook, using a short black pencil.

—◄o►—

Anny knew it was bad news the instant she saw the postmark, the ubiquitous spread-eagle clutching a swastika in its talons.

'This came. Only this,' she said, pushing it to him across the breakfast table.

Max opened the letter with his butter knife. He was silent for a moment.

'It seems that I am to report for a physical examination next Thursday. The Wehrmacht district hospital.' He looked up at her worried face.

'It's likely just routine, Anny. Nothing to concern ourselves.' She was not placated.

'What if they take you into the army, Max?'

'They won't. I saw it in the newspaper. Goebbels said that all prominent artists, musicians, actors and sports people are 'indispensable' for the war effort. So, we mustn't worry too much. And also, I'm 35, and I have the scars to prove it!'

—◄o►—

The Wehrmacht district hospital was bulging with queues of men, shuffling along into large waiting rooms. Max was told to sit and wait. He looked around. *So young. I could be their father.*

After four hours, *a taste of the army*, Max thought, someone shouted 'Schmeling'. All faces turned to him as he rose. Most smiled, as if noticing him for the first time. He was directed to a smaller room where he was told to undress. Three doctors sat behind a table, while a junior doctor brusquely carried out the examination. He wore a party badge on the lapel of his white coat.

'Height: 1.85,'

The most senior doctor, Dr Heinrichs, sat in the centre of the group. He smiled broadly. The examination continued.

'Weight: 88 Kg.' A stethoscope was placed on Max's chest.

'Heartbeat: normal. Pulse: 56.'

Doctor Heinrichs asked, 'Is your pulse rate always this low?'

'Only at rest, Major. It's low because I'm an athlete.'

'Yes, we know all about you, Herr Schmeling,' the assistant said curtly, as he reached for Max's scrotum.

'Cough.'

Dr Heinrichs asked, 'What brings you to us, Herr Schmeling?'

Max shrugged.

Heinrichs slapped his thigh. 'Imagine, a world champion, here!'

He rose and walked over to Max, shaking his hand enthusiastically.

Max said, 'You know, Major, I have many sports injuries, not to mention the broken vertebrae, a present from Joe Louis.'

'Yes, that was most unfortunate. He obviously fouled you.'

Max decided not to reply.

'But you see, Herr Schmeling, you are really very fit,

exceptionally so for a man of your age, as fit as any of the younger ones who arrive here. However, you mustn't worry. By the time you're inducted, the war will be over.'

Three weeks later, the induction order fell into the letterbox.

PART FOUR

CHAPTER 29
WELCOME TO THE USSR

Zindel, Rivka and Mordechai Grynszpan agreed: it felt good to be in Swizlocz, even if it was a long way from the family home in Radomsk, not to mention Hanover. Here, in this small *shtetl* near Bialystok, things seemed familiar and homely, as they had been before the family emigrated to Germany. A living memento of their vanished life – the dusty, then muddy, then snowy streets, the ramshackle wooden houses, the old kerchiefed women sitting on rickety porches, peeling potatoes and dropping them into buckets of water. And *Yiddish!* That's all anyone spoke here, except in the small wooden synagogue, where the ancient prayers were murmured rapidly, by men in large felt hats and long beards, in a Hebrew which was barely comprehensible at any speed. But that didn't matter. They felt safer now, snug in their small shack, one abandoned by a family of Jews who had moved further east.

But the German Army soon reached Bialystok, and the *Einsatzgruppen* followed in their wake, arbitrarily shooting Poles and Jews in the streets. Especially Jews. For no other reason. There was no time for a systematic roundup; the Germans knew that they'd soon be handing this part of Poland to the Russians.

As news of this approaching danger reached the Grynszpans, they decided to hide. They couldn't know that they were quite safe in Swizlocz, as the Germans would never actually arrive there. In the company of several other families, they made their way to the Białowieża Forest, pushing food and blankets in an abandoned pram. This forbidding and densely wooded landscape, full of dangers and myths, dripped damp autumn from every branch and stone. Rivka, exhausted, huddled beneath a tattered blanket, sitting on clammy leaves, leaning against a tree. The skies were the colour of ash, with wispy black clouds scudding over the treetops. Mordechai and his father tried, unsuccessfully, to build a small fire from the damp wood. The trees wept softly.

'They say that there are still bears in this forest,' Rivka mentioned, as if in passing. 'Did you hear about that?'

'Bears don't come near people, not if they can help it,' said Mordechai. 'I read about that.'

'Bears or Germans,' Zindel said, 'what a choice! But with God's help, we won't need to choose either one. Besides, with the other families here, we can all look after each other and chase the bears away.'

Several small campfires had been lit nearby. Their crackle and aroma were comforting, as were the sounds of murmuring kindred voices. A man from their village gave Mordechai some dry twigs.

—◄o►—

The Soviet Army arrived two days later, claiming their share of Poland. The treads of their tanks and the din of their loudspeakers could be heard from afar. They called out in Polish and Russian.

Poles! Jews! Come out! We are not Germans! They have left this area! You can all go back to your homes! You are safe! They repeated this over and over.

The exhausted Jews peered suspiciously from behind trees. Word had spread of how the Soviets had sent Jews to Labour camps in Siberia. But on seeing the tanks with their bright red stars, children laughed, ran from cover and climbed onto turrets, their smiling faces open to the Soviets who grinned back at them, tousling hair and pinching cheeks. Lorries were waiting behind the tanks, emptying diesel fumes into the saturated air. The Grynszpans and twenty-two others were helped aboard a canvas-sided truck. They were driven back to their adopted home, shivering with damp and fear.

In Swizlocz, things gradually assumed a new normal. Zindel was able to find some tailoring work, mending trousers and jackets, pulling in seams and waistlines. Rivka helped her neighbours look after a small flock of chickens, chasing after them along the village street. Mordechai helped with building repairs. Both men attended the synagogue every morning and evening, bonding with God and their community. Most evenings were spent in discussions with neighbours. They spoke about the war, about Palestine, about their flickering hopes, about Stalin, about poverty, about despair.

'I don't trust the Russkies,' old Pinkus announced through broken yellow teeth. 'Most of my family are completely displaced after the revolution, sent to Siberia, and wherenot. I never hear from them again.'

'So, you prefer the Nazis?' Rivka stared at Pinkus in disbelief. 'With what they are doing to us?'

Pinkus shrugged, 'Who can choose? But have you seen some of the Soviet soldiers? Straight from the mud of the eastern swamps. Mud-men, that's what I call them. Can't use a fork, don't wash for months, and have never even seen a flushing toilet. And you are happy to live with them?'

Rivka said, 'I'm for anyone who'll help us get to Palestine.'

At first, the village was left to itself. The Soviet Army distributed food, and as the harsh Polish winter approached, blankets.

—◂o▸—

A Soviet officer visited the Grynszpan home one birdsong-bright morning. He spoke to them in Russian. His companion, Junior Sergeant Lidik, stood at loose attention, his broad face a mask of grave vacuity.

'Family Grynszpan, I am Lieutenant Slutsky.' A glimmer of racial recognition passed between them. 'And this is Junior Sergeant Lidik.' Lidik stared straight ahead, thinking of his Siberian sweetheart.

'I need to ask you some questions. Do you speak Russian?'

Zindel answered, 'Yes, Lieutenant. I was born in Russian-speaking Poland, so I speak both languages.'

'Excellent. Are you a communist party member?'

'No, sir. Is that a problem for me?'

'On the contrary. It is your very good fortune. So many

of our German and Polish comrades have diverged greatly from the party line. But you, Grynszpan, are untainted! Of course, you are Jewish, yes?'

Zindel's raised an eyebrow.

'Oh, come now, Comrade Grynszpan, your name, like mine, is Jewish. You have recently arrived from Germany, you are living in squalor, and you are afraid of your own shadow. What else can you be?'

Zindel smiled sadly.

'In the USSR, this is of course not a problem. We do not believe in racism.' He punctuated this assertion with a solemn nod. 'Is this the entire immediate family?'

'No, Comrade Lieutenant, I have a daughter and mother who have remained in Radomsk, and a son, now imprisoned in France.'

'*That* Grynszpan? We have all heard about him. A true revolutionary! But. We will not dwell on this, yes?'

The family were happy not to pursue the subject.

'Anyway, who knows how long our new friendship with the Nazis will last? So, with great foresight, Comrade Stalin has decided quietly to build up our armed forces. Therefore, we are looking for young men to help us defend socialism.' He cast a glance at Mordechai, who stood in mute dread beside his mother.

'More questions.' Slutsky looked at his clipboard. 'Are you trade-unionists? Plutocrats? Polish Generals? Factory owners?'

'I have always worked for myself. Before the revolution I served in the Russian Army, but only as a private soldier, not a general.'

'Then you are a true comrade, Comrade Grynszpan. You have fought for mother Russia, which since the war has been completely transformed – by many of your old army comrades, I might add – into the model of progressive Socialism admired by the entire world. Are you Zionists?'

'We'd like someday to emigrate to Palestine, but we aren't really Zionists.'

'It is wise nowadays not to be a member of a Zionist organisation. At any rate, emigrating to Palestine might take some time, what with things as they are. But what you might not know is that Comrade Stalin has set up a special autonomous Jewish Republic in the east. It is called Birobidzan. And there the language is Yiddish as well as Russian, and any Jew can go there to settle. And the British can't prevent it.'

'We hadn't heard.'

'This is not surprising. Newspapers in the west do not like to print good stories from the USSR. In any event, that is for the future. There's no possibility of sending you there now.'

Zindel, Rivka and Mordechai looked relieved.

'What is your occupation?'

'I am just a humble tailor.'

'A true proletarian. There is much tailoring to do in the USSR.'

Lieutenant Slutsky pointed to Mordechai.

'You, young man, come over here.'

Mordechai, startled, took a few steps forward.

'How old are you?'

'Just turned twenty, sir.'

'Do you speak Russian?'

'Very little, sir.'

'Polish?'

'Better than Russian.'

'Well you can learn Russian if you know some Polish. You are young and your brain is still soft. You will learn many things. Turn around.'

Mordechai complied.

'What do you think, Lidik?'

Junior Sergeant Lidik grinned, exposing tobacco teeth and gaps.

'For you, young Mordechai Grynszpan, there are two choices: labour camp or the army. Staying here is not possible. Have you a trade?'

'I spent two months as a plumber's apprentice.'

'We have plenty of plumbers. We need soldiers.'

Mordechai looked first at his mother, who looked to Zindel, who said, 'Will he learn anything besides killing?'

'Of course. The killing is now over, if one doesn't count the plutocrats who have ruined Poland with their greed. Am I right, Junior Sergeant Lidik?'

Lidik grinned again.

'You will likely join a newly formed Polish unit of the Soviet Army. The training camp is not far from here. Of course, you will be able to write regularly to your parents, and occasionally, you will be allowed to visit them.'

Lieutenant Slutsky then turned to Rivka, who couldn't suppress some silent tears: first her little Herschel, then her daughter, and now her last son was being ripped away from her. They all knew that nothing could change their situation.

'You mustn't worry about your son, Comrade Rivka. He will be well fed, looked after by his comrades like a brother, and will be instructed to write to you every week. From now the future will be better. Is there any trade or skill that you can offer us?'

'I can cook,' Rivka said, 'and I'm strong. Zindel has taught me some tailoring, so I might be able to help him.'

'That's the proper Soviet attitude, Comrade Rivka. Most of the Jews living in this area will be sent east, to labour camps or large industrial sites beyond the Urals. And I came here with that plan in mind for you. Yet, since this family has demonstrated such admirable Soviet virtues, and because your son will be joining the Red Army, you will not be sent to a labour camp. However, we must nevertheless send you both east. A long way east. Comrade Stalin has decided to move as many Jews as possible to the east, over a million! Imagine, so many!'

Lieutenant Slutsky shuffled through his notepad, then assumed a more official posture.

'Comrade Zindel Grynszpan, you will be assigned to a new Tailoring Collective in Astrakhan – Astrakhan, such an exotic name, don't you think? Full of scents and legends of the east. And there the USSR makes all sorts of uniforms – army, navy, air-force – also flags, buntings and parachutes. You and your wife will live there rent free, and there is even a large social club, and plenty of other Jews. You can speak Yiddish there if you like. In the factory, of course, you will speak only Russian.'

'Will we be able to keep kosher? Is there a kosher butcher?'

'Be realistic, comrade Rivka. If meat arrives at all, it's best not to ask how it got there. But you can help raise the tens of thousands of chickens already clucking in the poultry collectives.'

Rivka smiled inwardly, as she liked tending chickens.

─◄o►─

The two-thousand-kilometre trip to Astrakhan took four weeks – by train, by bus, by lorry and by foot.

'Why are we being treated better than the others? Why us? Why not Siberia?' Rivka asked.

'Perhaps he liked our faces, perhaps Mordechai was a ransom, perhaps he got a nice letter from home. God knows why we're now so lucky.'

Finally, as summer bloomed on the Volga, they arrived in their new home.

Darling son,

It is only now that we are able to write you a letter and report that we are completely safe, far from the Germans, far from danger. Your father and I are now in Astrakhan. It's on the Volga river! – who would ever have imagined?! We live in a large block, rent free, with usually friendly neighbours, mostly Poles, some of them Jews like us. The Russians are very sympathetic to us Polish Jews. They have heard of our hardships. When we first got here, people took us from door-to-door and offered us food and household things, just to show their friendship.

Your father works a tailoring collective. It is hard work, and he comes home every day very tired. But we have enough to eat, potatoes, beets – plenty of chicken – a roof over our heads, and especially no Nazis. I work in one of the large collective farms, a short bus-ride away. I am becoming an expert on chickens! And Mordechai is in the Soviet Army! He just wrote to us that he is being well treated and is learning Russian and how to repair trucks. Your sweet sister and grandmother have remained in Radomsk. We haven't heard from them, and every day we pray to God that they are alright. Nothing would gladden our hearts more than to learn something about them, and also to hear from you, darling son. When is the trial? Are you well? Do you get enough fresh air? It's not good to be cooped up inside all the time.

Please write to us. The address is on the envelope. Soon, perhaps you will be free, and our troubles will begin to melt away.

With all our love.

Mother

By the time the letter arrived at Fresnes prison, Herschel was no longer there.

CHAPTER 30
FLIGHT

'Rabbi, I'm scared what will happen. The guards tell me the Germans are all over Paris now, walking around like tourists.'

Rabbi Nachman looked at him with sadness and compassion. 'It seems the war is lost, my son, and we can only pray to God for his mercy and deliverance.'

The boy began to cry. 'The Germans will take me to Berlin, or they will shoot me here. Of this I am certain. For killing that blameless man. Yet I had to do it. I had no choice. You understand, don't you, Rabbi?'

He put his arm around the boy's shoulder. 'Trust in God, Herschel. It is now the time to trust in God.'

The next morning, he stood in the corner of his cell, his prayer shawl draped over his shoulders, the leather bands of the *tefillin* wrapped around his arm, its small black cube of scripture on his forehead. As he stood mumbling into his prayer book, *davening*, rhythmically bending forward and back in the long-established manner, his cell door was opened noisily, waking him from his religious trance. The warden and two officers entered, their brows creased with anxiety.

'You need to leave us, Grynszpan. Here it is no longer

safe. The Germans have set up their headquarters in Paris, even before the war is over. It won't take them long to find you. We are sending all the youth wing prisoners south. While there's still time.'

'Is nobody fighting the Bosche? Has peace begun?'

'Paris has been declared an open city, but it won't be long before the fighting is over, and then they'll do whatever they want with us.'

Shaking, the boy kissed his prayer-book, removed his *yarmulke*, prayer shawl and *tefillin*, and reverently placed them into the blue velvet bag.

'Take just a few things, Grynszpan. It's warm. You won't need much. Officer Broussard will escort you'.

'Where am I going?'

'South. To Bourges.'

Officer Xavier Broussard led him through the warren of corridors, down flights of clanging metal steps and onto the last of three buses idling in the courtyard. Waiting anxiously were fifteen officers and ninety-five other young prisoners. He recognised no one. Broussard handcuffed him to a seat near the front. At a signal from the warden they set off, through the heavy prison gates and into the bleached Paris streets. News of the imminent surrender was being broadcast from loudspeakers throughout the city, echoing through deserted avenues and boulevards.

Citizens of Paris! Lay down your Arms! Our Beloved city has been spared bombs and shells. No one will be harmed. Lay down your Arms! Vive La France!

He stared through the barred window as the prison bus made its way along lifeless neighbourhoods. He had for so long missed the vibrant sights of Paris, the bustle, the chatter, the cafés. *But everything has changed,* Herschel thought. *Nobody on the streets, not even traffic policemen. Abandoned. Like I am.* All the shop-fronts were shuttered; even handles had been removed from doors; café chairs were stacked and chained next to empty tables; thirsty flowers drooped in their hanging baskets; flies hovered over empty fruit barrows; apartment windows remained shuttered against the harsh sunlight and harsher reality. He gazed vacantly at cattle abandoned by farmers on the way to abattoirs, one mooing plaintively in front of the Marie in Étampes.

Just south of the city the convoy became enmeshed in what seemed an endless procession – Parisians, fleeing with what they could carry, pull or push. Over-laden bicycles jostled among wagons, some pulled by horses, some by men and women, all straining and sweating in the rising heat. Motor vehicles were piled precipitously with suitcases and mattresses, cooking pots and chairs. Some, having exhausted their last few drops of petrol at the edge of Paris, were pulled by horses or mules purchased for extravagant prices at suburban stables.

French Army staff cars jostled through, their horns beeping incessantly, officers shouting and gesticulating in their haste to escape. They were booed by the refugees, who were forced to jump aside. 'Cowards! Traitors!'

It's just like in the Bible, Herschel thought, *the flight from Egypt in the book of* Exodus. *But is God delivering us from our enemies or leading us to them?*

With every mile, the prison convoy's progress became slower.

◄o►

He could see them before he could hear them. Small dots in the sky, just above the tree line, approaching quickly from the east. The buses had just crawled through Orléans, where the wretched procession of refugees merged with columns of others, joining the flow, swelling it, slowing it. He stared through the window at the dots, now coming closer. He nudged his seat mate, Pridoux.

'Planes?'

They both stared into the sky, their view sporadically occluded by the branches of taller trees.

Pridoux shouted, 'Hallo, officer Broussard, Look up to your left. Are those planes?'

Broussard turned and squinted. 'They're not ours, that's for certain.' He shouted to the driver. 'Stop the bus!'

Broussard opened the door and ran towards the other buses. He overtook them easily. After short conversations, he ran back.

'Leave the bus! Get behind those trees on the other side of the ditch. Officers, unlock the prisoners.'

Broussard unlocked the front rows of inmates. Officers Mouledous and Brunet released the others, quickly moving along the aisle. Once freed, the prisoners scampered from the bus and into a gulley. Some continued running, moving erratically through the wooded countryside. Near the front of the bus, Herschel dashed out and made for the nearest tree. He squatted behind it, quaking with fear.

Thoughts scurried in his head like mice in a barn. *Should I try to run for it? Others are making their escape, even some guards. I could go as well. No one would care. But where would I run to? I have no money. Where would I go? And what about the trial?*

Above, the first of the Stuka began its dive, rolling gracefully, then pointing its nose downward, hurling itself at the column, emitting its terrifying scream as it descended. At five hundred feet, the pilot released the bomb and pulled out of the dive. The bomb exploded beside the first bus, which rose into the air, then fell on its side into the ditch. It burst into flames as the petrol tank ruptured. There were still eight prisoners aboard.

A second Stuka, which had earlier discharged its bomb during a sortie near Auxerre, came at the convoy along the road, very low and very fast. Its machine guns pocked the road and ripped holes in the buses. Herschel could see bullets punching regular perforations into the roof of his bus, like stitches from a sewing machine. The bullets tore through the last four prisoners and the guards who had not yet managed to leave. Bullets also ripped into his prayer bag, abandoned on his seat during the commotion. The velvet cover, the *yarmulke*, prayer-book, leather *tefillin* and the shawl were shredded.

A third, then a fourth Stuka focused their attention on the remainder of the refugees, many of whom had scattered into the woodland. Machine gun shells ripped into those left in the open, their bodies crumpling, or erupting into fragments of muscle, bone and blood. From exploding heads flew scattered thoughts of children, snatches of Schubert and Piaf, a treasured recipe for Coq au vin, all splattering onto the concrete road.

Then the planes flew off, their receding engine noises uncovering screaming, moaning, shouts.

—◦—

Herschel re-emerged onto the road. Shaking, averting his ears and eyes from the carnage scattered around him, he approached Broussard who was standing with the five remaining prisoners.

'We miserable French,' Broussard snarled, 'even the guards have run away. Like our soldiers.'

'Officer Broussard,' he was still trembling, 'please take me south to Bourges as arranged.'

'Are you mad? This is your chance, all of you. Escape! Join the refugees. Just go!'

The young prisoners made no attempt to move.

'I have no one and I have nothing, Monsieur. No money, no food. If I'm not sent to another prison, I'll surely be captured and shot. I plead with you, officer Broussard.' He began to cry, falling to his knees. 'Officer Broussard, do you not have a duty to take me to prison?'

Broussard removed his pistol from its holster.

'Get up! If you do not run, I will shoot you here.'

A silence.

Broussard stared at the boy. *Is this boy really an idiot? Does he actually want to die here, stupidly, in the middle of a dusty country road?* He raised his revolver and pointed it at Herschel, who tensed in expectation, raising his hands in a pointless attempt to protect his face. Broussard looked at the other prisoners, all now afraid. He put his revolver back into its holster. He shrugged. 'This Jew is as crazy as they say. All right, lads, do you want to continue to Brouges?' Small vacant nods. 'Then we will have to resume our journey on foot. Are you coming, Grynszpan?'

His rage almost overwhelmed his fear. He stood and stared at Broussard, his body clenched. *How dare he call me a crazy Jew, after all I've been through?*

'I'll make my own way.'

'Suit yourself. I'll tell the prison to look out for you.' Herschel watched the group until they disappeared from view, merging into the endless caravan of the displaced. He then set off on his own, leaving behind the wrecked buses, plumes of black smoke, the litter of belongings and body parts.

He was exhausted. He was hungry. But he walked tenaciously, transporting himself through the carnage and chaos which seemed to be everywhere. He quickened his pace, pushing forward, resolute in his wish to continue, determined to reach Bourges and the safety of a French prison.

He overtook other refugees. Some nodded as he passed, some stared at him vacantly, but most looked straight ahead, or down at the road, or spoke among themselves, or comforted children, who remained docile in their terror. The smell of fear and failure was everywhere. *Surely, they must know who I am.*

Later, he noticed two white butterflies pirouetting in the dappled light, flashing bright as they found the sun. *Perhaps they are a sign from God,* he thought, *that through all this misery and death he will lead me to safety.* Then the butterflies vanished behind the trees.

He continued until dusk. The sun, red as a bullet-wound, sank slowly between the tree-trunks. Then the darkness thickened, and the sky was gradually filled with stars. *So many,* he thought.

He found shelter beside a clump of trees abutting the road. A family nearby had already settled in for the night. They were silent – the adults, the children, the dogs. Coffee was brewing over a small fire. An infant slept in the folds of its mother's skirt, its face flickering orange in the fire's glow. Unbidden, one of the men rose, walked over to Herschel, handed him a mug of coffee and a piece of baguette with cheese and ham inside. Not thinking about the dietary implications, he immediately began to eat, smiling gratefully at the man, who nodded and returned to his family. When awakened by a dawn which promised more heat, he saw that the family had left.

◄o►

Xavier Broussard arrived in Bourges the next morning. After only an hour on the road, his prisoners had refused to walk further, and had, with the tacit approval of their jailer, evaporated into woods, fields and villages.

Broussard reported to the warden of the local prison.

'I am sorry to report that the convoy of prisoners which I was instructed to deliver here was attacked by the Germans from the air, and as a result all who survived have escaped. However, one of them informed me that he intends to hand himself in to you, and will probably arrive soon. His name is Grynszpan.'

'Are you mad? Is he mad? If the Germans find him here, he will be executed immediately, and likely me with him.'

'I actually do think Grynszpan is a bit mad, as you say, Monsieur Director,' said Broussard, with a tired smile, as he saluted and walked off into the dusty square.

Herschel arrived just after noon. The prison warden met him at the gate, wiping long rivulets of perspiration from his face with a once white handkerchief.

'Has Officer Broussard arrived yet? He is meant to deliver me here.'

'Broussard has returned to Paris. There is no one to deliver you.'

'What about the Public Prosecutor?'

'I have spoken to Prosecutor Ribeyre today on the telephone. He advises you to disappear. As for me, I want no record of you here.'

Tears of frustration, hunger and fear began to seep from behind the boy's eyes, already red from the dusty road and lack of sleep. He began his familiar lament, and the repetition of the words almost soothed him.

'But where can I go, Monsieur Director? I have nothing, no money, no food…'

The director cut him off. 'I'll give you some bread and cheese for your journey. But you must not under any circumstances remain here.'

'But where, then?'

'Wait here for a moment.'

He returned a few moments later with half a boule and a wedge of brie wrapped in brown paper.

'See here, young man, the Germans have nearly encircled our town. They will arrive within hours. Go south while you still can. Try Châteauroux. Go south. It's the only road still open.'

The director closed the heavy door, walked to his office and crossed himself.

CHAPTER 31
JOURNEY'S END

Friedrich Grimm had bought a new brown suit to celebrate Germany's victory over France. He arrived at Fresnes Prison the day after the first German soldiers entered the city, on the day before the French surrender was signed, on the day Adolf Hitler paid a dawn visit to the city he had vanquished, and on the day Herschel had been bundled with other prisoners and driven south. Accompanying Grimm was the newly appointed chief of security police for occupied France. After showing their papers at the gate to frightened and acquiescent guards, the two Germans found their way to the warden's office and entered without knocking. The warden looked up from his desk, betraying no sign of his surprise or fear.

'Herr Grimm, are we not still at war?'

Grimm smiled. 'Monsieur Warden. This is Chief of Security Police Helmut Knochen. Now that Paris is an open city, we have taken the opportunity to make a rapid start in the Grynszpan business. We have come to remove him and return him to Germany. Please arrange for him to be brought to us. Also, we will require all documents regarding this case to be handed over.'

'Ah, Herr Grimm, the bulk of the documents relating

to this case should be with the Justice Ministry. We only have limited files regarding his incarceration here. Alas, insofar as Grynszpan himself is concerned, I am afraid you are a few hours too late. Along with the other prisoners he has been transported south. For safety.'

Grimm exploded. 'Safety?! Whose safety? And from whom? From us? And what do you think we'd do to your petty criminals? Do you believe all those Jewish horror tales?'

Grimm stared at the warden, as if waiting for a reply. His stare telegraphed malice.

'Where did you send the Jew Grynszpan?'

'To Bourges.'

'This is unconscionable!'

'But I could do no other. In times of imminent danger, prisoners are to be evacuated. It is part of the legal code.'

'You will soon learn to accommodate a different legal code.'

The two Germans left the office abruptly. As they clattered down the stairs Grimm barked an order to Knochen. 'You are to act instantly. Ransack the offices of his attorneys, Moro-Giafferi, as well as the others, the Jewish ones, and anyone in the slightest connected with that little *drecksheiß*. Find anything and everything. And soon! I will take a detachment of SS and follow his trail.'

◄o►

The next day, Grimm interrogated Officer Broussard.

'Oh yes, sir. But they all escaped on the way. After the attack from your planes. But the little Jew said that he would make his own way to the prison. And so he did. A few hours later. Can you believe it? He turned himself in!'

'What, to the prison in Bourges?'

'Yes, sir. But the warden sent him on, after talking to Public Prosecutor Ribeyre.'

Two days later Bourges' public prosecutor was discovered, manhandled, shoved into a van and driven to Cherche-Midi military prison in Paris. He was flung into a cell. For the first few hours of interrogation, he denied all knowledge of Grynszpan or his whereabouts.

'We know that he came to Bourges, we know that you were contacted. Why do you continue with these lies?'

'You are mistaken, Herr Grimm, as I have so often said, Grynszpan never came to Bourges and I have no idea where he might be.'

Grimm placed a pad, pen and his Luger on the table separating them. He turned it so that the muzzle was pointed at Ribeyre. He spoke softly.

'I no longer have time to play this charade with you, Ribeyre. Here is your choice. Either you tell us all that you know or I will give you half an hour to write a final letter to your family, after which time I shall shoot you.'

The Public Prosecutor's face drained of colour and he began to sweat profusely.

'Yes. We sent him south as our city was being encircled. He went on by foot. I don't know where, but it might have been to Châteauroux.'

Grimm slammed the door on his way out of the cell, leaving Ribeyre to stew in his tears and urine. Yet Grimm was worried. How could he explain this shambles to

Goebbels? He rehearsed such a conversation many times in his mind, and each time it turned out badly.

He pictured Goebbels at his desk, his fingers steepled, his face stony cold.

Whatever you might say to me, Grimm, whatever excuses you might weasel out, we both know that you have failed. You have failed on every step of the way. You have failed yourself, you have failed me, you have failed the Führer and the entire Reich at this moment of our greatest triumph. It will not be easy for me to report to the Führer about this matter. As you know, he has been taking an active interest in the Grynszpan affair.

—◦—

Meanwhile, the Gestapo had been making their own enquiries. They interrogated Attorney General Cavarroc in his sumptuous office at the Ministry of Justice.

'You see, Monsieur Attorney General, we lay no blame with you, of course, and it is the Führer's wish that cordial relations between France and the Reich be resumed as soon as possible.'

Carravoc nodded gravely and gratefully. 'As I have said before, I have no knowledge of specific missing persons.'

'Indeed, and that is reasonable enough. Yet, there are still some issues that are not resolved. For example, what has happened to all the documents relating to the impending trial of the Jew Grynszpan? Have they disappeared into thin air? I do not wish to be unpleasant, but it would be necessary to incarcerate you if this question is not resolved.'

'All I know is that they were put into a leather valise for safekeeping, rather a large valise, I think.'

'Do you not know where? This seems hard to believe, Monsieur.'

'I entrusted it to Menegaud, who was meant to report back to me.'

'Bring him here.'

Carravoc pushed a button and a few moments later a tall breathless man appeared in the doorway.

'Menegaud, these German gentlemen wish to know the whereabouts of the Grynszpan material.'

'Of course, Minister. If you gentlemen will follow me…'

He led the two agents through ornate rooms and corridors, then down several flights of steps to more austere surroundings.

'This basement was used as a prison. That was, of course, before the World War,' he explained to men who were not interested.

He came to a cell and unlocked the door. Inside were filing cabinets and cupboards. He opened a drawer and pulled out a brown leather valise, bulging with documents.

'Voila, gentlemen. Inside this satchel are all the papers pertaining to the Grynszpan affair, as well as the official seal of France – which I would oblige you to leave with me.'

The Gestapo men left satisfied. They might not have their man, but they had the next best thing, the files Goebbels wanted, the documents which would be used for the big trial to be held in Germany.

Steadily, sadly, slowly, Herschel continued his long trek, in the company of an army of complete strangers, all moving south. They passed piles of abandoned French helmets, tunics and rifles.

'It's all the Socialists' fault,' muttered one of his companions, 'them and the communists. Never could trust any of them, never will. They corrupted all that was noble in France, so that even the army turned coward. Do you know what? Our army actually outnumbers the Bosche! And still we run from them.'

Darkness fell, colours and shapes merged together. As he settled into a roadside ditch, feeling the night closing around him like a cloak, a man approached.

'Do you recognise me?' Herschel asked.

'No. Should I?'

'Some say that I started all of this by killing the first Bosche.'

'I wouldn't repeat that again, if you want to survive.' The man shook his head sadly. 'My father sent me to offer you some food and coffee.'

'It is very kind of you to help me.'

'It's a normal thing to do, especially at times like these, not so?'

He nodded, biting into the end of a stale baguette.

'Where are you headed?' Herschel asked.

'Away,' an old man said, sipping slowly from a chipped enamel mug.

'South, like you.' A woman's voice.

The old man began to speak again, to no one and everyone. The creases in his unshaven face were accentuated by the flickering light of a small fire. His voice was yellow with age and tobacco.

'We French are ill with pride. And pride always brings catastrophe. But no one listens, do they? Until it's too late. Now we are learning a new truth: freedom is exile. Our exile is complete freedom, a freedom vast and pointless. Have some sausage.'

◄o►

The next morning Herschel arrived at Châteauroux prison, situated in a dusty square, where pigeons warbled and flapped, looking for breakfast crumbs in front of shuttered cafés. A gendarme stared at him through the sentry-box hatch.

'Please Monsieur, I should like to see the warden. I am Herschel Grynszpan, awaiting trial on a charge of murder – a charge, monsieur, which is unjust – and …'

The gendarme glared. 'I know who you are. And we have expected you to come this way. The warden instructed me that if I see you I am not to admit you. Not under any circumstances. He even said that if anyone were to ask after you, I am to deny that I had even seen you. Why do you not escape, idiot?!'

'But you must understand that it is vital that I stand trial, and in France.'

'If you insist on being imprisoned, the warden suggests Toulouse, where, as southerners, they may be crazy enough to accept you.' He then fastened the hatch door.

Through his anger and frustration, Herschel resumed his odyssey. He was exhausted, and still had far to go.

Occasionally he would be given food at a farmhouse, and the offer of a bath before a night in an adjacent barn. Most nights he slept beside the road. Sometimes a lorry or tractor gave him a lift for a few kilometres, never asking him who he was, assuming that he was heading south with the others.

It took him two weeks to arrive at Toulouse. That last night, just a few kilometres from the city, he bedded down near a young family who had accompanied him from Cahors. They had begun their journey in Paris, pushing an indomitable pram, the wife carrying a three-year-old boy who sometimes could be encouraged to walk.

'We are Jews, you see,' said the man. 'Like you, I think. But unlike you, we are also French! So we must travel south, to escape the Bosche until things return to normal. It's all that Blum's fault. I hate him, even though he's a Jew like me. I hate him like poison, the bastard. Him and his Popular Front. All they could do was talk and argue. But that time is now over, I think, Monsieur; the time for talking and discussing is finished. And I hate the English even more. They abandoned us to the Nazis and now they bomb our navy! I am putting my faith in Maréchal Pétain. That old soldier won't let France down.'

Herschel left just after dawn. Entering Toulouse two hours later, he went straight to the prison. He banged on the heavy wooden gate, shouting for assistance. When a sentry appeared, he asked for the warden, who met him ten minutes later.

'Warden, I am Herschel Grynszpan, here to be arrested, so that I can be put on trial.'

The tired, red-eyed man who stood before him sighed, then smiled sadly.

'Young man, your arrival had been long foretold. You are so brave and so strong to have come all the way here from Paris, and I salute you. However, at this moment our prison is full, with other prisoners and also refugees who, like you, have nowhere else to go. They are crammed into every cell. Alas, it might be a day or two before I can accept you.'

The boy collapsed onto his knees. He was crying freely, from exhaustion, fear and gratitude. 'Oh, Monsieur Warden, you are the first person who has spoken to me with kindness. But I am so tired. I have no food, no money, my clothes are rags. I don't think I can last another day.'

The Warden raised him up. 'We'll get the cook to make a basket of food for you. An officer can show you a place to rest, in the park nearby, and then you can come back tomorrow, by which time I will have clothes for you. But Grynszpan, the border is not far from here, and there any many places where you can cross into Spain unnoticed. The Spaniards aren't that fussy about Jews one way or another. Go to Spain. Escape. Nothing good can come to you in France.'

He grabbed the warden's hand. 'Thank you for your kindness, sir. I will gratefully accept your offer of food and I will return tomorrow.'

He was shown to a cell the next morning. *Now I am safe. They will look after me here.*

Unlike the relatively peaceful Young Offenders' wing at Fresnes, Toulouse prison was teeming with aggressive noises – shouts, whistles, epithets, and the clanging of metal cups against doors and bars. Day and night. Unsettled by the clamour around him, he found it impossible to sleep for more than a few minutes at a time. Also, he had no one to speak to, and even worse, he missed his prayer book, *tefillin*, shawl and *yarmulke*, which had been destroyed in the bus. He needed his prayer book to remember what words to say to God.

–◄o►–

Friedrich Grimm wrote a courteous note to the Vichy Government, asking for the whereabouts of Herschel Grynszpan. Unlike the occupied French government in Paris, the new Vichy regime was eager to help. Their ancient leader Maréchal Pétain had made it clear: *The only way to restore France's honour and sovereignty is to co-operate with the Germans. Only in this way will they see that France is a worthy partner in building a new Europe.* After three days of enquiries, the Vichy Minister of Justice, Raphaël Alibert, telephoned Friedrich Grimm to report that Herschel Grynszpan was in Toulouse.

'You know,' Grimm said, hoping that his voice carried a smile, 'the Führer has taken a particular interest in this case, and regards the handing over of the Jew Grynszpan as a demonstration of your new government's goodwill towards the New Order in Europe. Now we can show, through him, that every Jew – man, woman or child – is a deadly enemy of the Reich.'

Grimm set out for Toulouse, but the Gestapo had left the day before.

◄◦►

Herschel's cell door was opened and he was shackled.

'Where are you taking me, Messieurs?

'North. To Vichy. Perhaps Maréchal Pétain will know what to do with you.'

It was a long, uncomfortable journey in a noisy metal van, with no windows, no air, and no one to speak to. He was held for two days in the local prison while arrangements were made for his extradition. He was then put into another van and driven to Moulins, on the border between Vichy and Occupied France. Waiting for him were two guards and SS-Sturmbahnführer Karl Bömelburg, who handed a receipt to the French officers, and in return received the keys to Herschel's manacles. He clicked his heels, gave the Hitler salute, then turned away, followed by his captive and the guards. The boy was guided into the rear seat of a Mercedes saloon. They immediately set off on the long drive to Paris. He was terrified and mystified. *Why is this all happening so calmly? They could just as well shoot me here.* A small comfort was hearing German spoken again, soft trivial things in a language he could understand. Sometimes he dozed. They arrived at Paris-Le Bourget Airport and boarded a Junkers aircraft bound for Berlin. A night flight.

His very first aeroplane journey was a wonder to him, even in the dark. He was guiltily exhilarated by the plane's noisy acceleration and take-off; the airport receding,

300

the lights of Paris occasionally veiled as they climbed through scattered clouds. He stared out of the window for the entire flight, amazed and entranced as the lights of villages and towns shone like electric oases amidst the dark countryside. A sky-full of stars glittered above them, as the plane throbbed effortlessly through the summer-still air. He shifted his gaze to see his reflection in the window. *Not so young anymore,* he thought, but he was satisfied with his appearance. Over Germany, a blackout was in force, but he could still make out moonlit rivers, meandering their way through towns, fields and forests. He was surprised to see the glow of Berlin from afar, but remembered Goering's boast that not a single bomber would make it there. The city soon filled his entire view as they descended to land. On arrival at Tempelhof, he was bundled into an SS staff car and driven through the night-empty streets to Prinz-Albert-Straße 8, Reich Security headquarters. He was led into a small cell, given a blanket and a cup of water. Then the door was slammed shut. He had heard about this place. No one taken there was ever known to have left alive.

Throughout the night he could hear shouting, metal doors opening and clanking shut, stiff boots in the corridor. A symphony of pain played continuously, screams and moans coming from deep inside tortured bodies, piercing the air, reverberating throughout the building. He shivered with fright. *They will torture me, I know it. But what can I tell them that they don't already know?*

Two days later, they came for him. He flinched in the

expectation of rough treatment, but the guards were civil, almost polite. He was escorted to an office illuminated by a single desk-lamp. The walls were padded, the room drained of all natural light and extraneous human sounds. The interrogator sat with his back to him, reading a document. An SS visor cap sat on the corner of the desk, its death's head emblem smiling grimly. Herschel imagined the skull looking deeply into his soul. The interrogator swivelled slowly on his chair. The face which confronted him was angular, stark. *A cold face, a cruel face*, he thought.

'Take a seat, please.'

For a moment, he was surprised, but at first didn't understand why.

'Yes, take a seat,' the man said, pointing to a chair facing him across a desk.

His eyes betrayed his astonishment. The man looked at him with impassive malevolence.

'You are surprised? That I speak Yiddish, your degenerate bastardised language? You think it's a secret, this language, that only Jews can understand it, that Germans are too stupid to learn it? I think my accent rather, good, don't you?' An ironic smile was just perceptible on his thin lips.

Herschel declined to reply. He sat. The interrogator stared at him bleakly.

'But now let us clean our mouths of this sewage. German only. I am SS Sturmbannführer Eichmann. I require you to answer some questions.'

He tapped on the open file on the desk.

'You see, Grynszpan, your case is not merely a judicial

matter, some little Jew killing some little German functionary. If it were, you'd be cold dead by now. No, it is a political matter. Even the Führer himself is interested.'

Herschel smiled inwardly.

'And the length and painfulness of your survival will be determined by what help you give us with our investigation.'

He was beginning to regain his courage. Now able to speak in German, he felt confident that even his enemies would understand what he said. How different from France, where he felt crippled by language. Eichmann's questions were the same ones he had answered in Paris. He gave brief familiar replies. After an hour, Eichmann closed the file, pushed a button, and a guard appeared.

'There will be many more such sessions, my reticent little Jewish swine, and I will get the answers I need. It is up to you how I get them.'

But Herschel wasn't intimidated.

He was driven to Sachsenhausen Concentration Camp, a few kilometres north of Berlin. He was walked to a cell in a small prison block. It was a new building, in a separate part of the camp.

'You are what we call a "high value prisoner", little Jew,' said the guard.

He could tell by his accent that Sergeant Bernhard Schultz was from Hanover.

'And here we have a special part of the camp, built especially just for people like you. You are allowed to read, write, prepare your case at this little table and chair, pencil only, I'm afraid. Food will arrive soon.' Schultz smiled, locked the door and walked down the corridor.

Through his window he could see other prisoners, walking behind the barbed wire fence, all shorn like spring sheep, all in stripes. Yet not he.

After a few days, he was assigned 'work'.

'Grynszpan,' announced Sergeant Schultz, 'as you are eating the same food as the guards, it seems fitting that you should work for us. But such a frail body, such an unlined face would be ruined by the heavy work the other prisoners have to do. So, it has been decided that you are to be my orderly; brushing my uniform and my boots, making my coffee, that sort of thing. I won't ask you to shave me, perhaps you'll want to cut my throat! Ha-Ha. Or miss mine and cut your own! As a special prisoner, you are to have greater freedom than the others, you can move around your area, the courtyard, and up to the entrance of the guards' barracks. This is more freedom than anyone else receives, but frankly, no one expects you to try to escape.' The boy nodded.

'And, since you are so little, with such a baby face, I shall call you "Bubi".'

◄o►

Adolf Hitler was in an expansive mood. France, the first of Germany's arch enemies, lay prostrate and impotent before him. Russia was crumbling on all fronts before the weight of his Wehrmacht, the English were cowering on their small island, and the Americans didn't seem to be interested, despite the machinations of that 'Jew Rosenfeld', as Goebbels renamed the American president.

Hitler had invited the Goebbels family to stay for a few summer days at Berchtesgaden.

Hitler, in a tan uniform, and Goebbels in a brown summer suit, stood side by side, admiring the alpine view, discussing the Grynszpan case.

Goebbels said, 'Of course, by law, he was a child when he shot vom Rath.'

As Hitler turned to face him, Goebbels recognised that familiar glint of disappointment, never far from the surface of his Führer's cold blue eyes.

'The law is what we choose to make it. Never more than that. I decide the law. Instruct the press to print this: *At the time of the offence, the accused had the mental and moral capacity of a person over eighteen years of age, and that the well-being of the nation requires that he be tried and punished as an adult.* In any event, the charges should be changed. Not murder, but high treason. And afterwards, I want a photograph of his severed head published in every newspaper in the Reich and in all the occupied countries.

'Of himself, this little Jew is of no interest to anyone. But the danger of World Jewry is of paramount interest. This trial will explain to the world what we have to do.

'This young bacillus is to be kept presentable for the trial. He must appear healthy and well-fed in the dock, to be shown as he truly is – a malignant pawn in an enormous battle. The shots that killed vom Rath were the first shots in the Jewish war. And now, in the east, we are on the road to settling this war for all time.'

The trial had been scheduled initially for early in 1941,

but Goebbels insisted on delays until the case could be proven beyond doubt in front of the entire world. Yet evidence of the international conspiracy was as hard to find in Germany as it had been in France. Then the invasion of the Soviet Union began to preoccupy everyone's thoughts, and with Hitler's blessing, the trial was postponed.

—◄o►—

Three weeks after his first interrogation, Herschel was driven back to Berlin to be questioned again by Eichmann.

'I have here the results of the examinations you have undergone. Physically, you are slightly underweight, shorter than the average, but quite fit. Psychologically, you are fully aware of what you have done, and it is clear that you were of clear mind when you murdered vom Rath. The psychiatrists also confirm that you are of clear mind today.

'As part of our preparations, we have interrogated many people who have known you, both in Hanover and in France. For example, your teachers. They report that you have a violent nature, that you are mean spirited, ill tempered, sullen, taciturn. And yet, despite this anti-social behaviour, they continued to teach you, and to teach you well. It seems that your grades actually improved after we came to power. Even a little Jew did better under us.'

He banged the desk and Herschel flinched.

'So why attack us? Who made the decisions for you? Did you know David Gustloff?'

'I have already told you this before. I only wanted

to send a message about how my parents were being mistreated.'

'Oh yes, and we all know about your poor unfortunate parents. It seems that their "ill treatment" resulted in the calamity of them being reunited with the rest of your family in Radomsk. Now I learn they are actively helping the Soviets in Russia! Some mistreatment!'

Over the following months, he was interrogated several times, in the same manner, neither beaten nor otherwise punished for his tenacity. In the winter of 1942, he was surprised to see another man in Eichmann's chair. He was told that Eichmann had been called away. He was not told that Eichmann was to be responsible for the organisation of transport for 'the final solution of the Jewish Question' as agreed at Wansee a few weeks before.

'I am agent Jagusch.'

The prisoner nodded courteously.

'You know, Grynszpan, we have been working day and night to prepare the case against you, and we know, and have always known, that your denials are hollow. For example, your former French judge, Tésniere, is now in a prisoner of war camp and has spoken to us at length. He will testify against you. Tésniere had already made up his mind about you in 1938, that you were incapable of committing such a crime on your own.'

'It is irrelevant what he says. As I explained so many times before, I did everything myself. I bought the gun, I went to the Embassy and then I shot that man. No one needed to tell me to do it, such was my fury and despair. No, Herr Jagusch, the deed was all mine, and I am prepared to suffer punishment for it. When will my trial be held?'

Jagusch scowled and shut the file. Herschel was driven back to Sachsenhausen, to his secure and predictable world. The relationship between Sergeant Schultz and 'Bubi' Grynszpan remained cordial, sometimes almost verging on friendship. Over the next few months, Herschel Grynszpan gained a bit of weight.

CHAPTER 32
A BOXER'S WAR

'Another party. For some war charity,' she said.

Anny handed the invitation to Max. He frowned as he read it.

'But I'd like to go, Max. What do you think? All the biggest film people will be there.'

'You know that Goebbels really dislikes me. For you it's no problem, I guess, as you get along well enough with him and Magda, if your frequent visits to Schwanenwerder are anything to go by.'

Practised defensiveness crept into her voice, raising it a few pitches. 'It's work, Max, work. How can we get by if I don't make films? And no matter what you think, without his approval, nobody works. You know that. Anyway, since the Baarová affair, he seems to be keeping his hands to himself, or so I'm told. And he knows that if he tries anything funny with me, I'd go straight to Magda. Not to mention telling you, my protective heavyweight.'

The party was as Max had expected. Anny circulated around the room, smiling and flirting, laughing at terrible jokes. Goebbels stared at Max with polite loathing then sidled over to a group of screen actors. He placed himself behind Heinrich George, the porcine star whose face was ubiquitous in cinemas and posters. The actor leaned forward and whispered conspiratorially. 'Someone told me this one. Do you know the difference between National Socialist Germany and Soviet Russia? No? Well in Russia it is colder.' Laughs were stifled. Goebbels spoke, unsettling George, who had been unaware of his presence.

'It's satisfying to hear this particular joke making the rounds. My ministry has been circulating such witticisms for several months now. They're quite harmless, really, and they help let off some steam. Also, they often lead to less benign sentiments, which we can discover and root out before they spread.' He smiled archly.

In another part of the large living room, Max found himself cornered by boxing enthusiasts. The details of his two Louis fights were raked over. He thought, *only those who have never taken a good punch in the face can speak such rubbish.* The subject then turned to the autobahns.

'This is one of the most important parts of the Führer's genius,' opined a factory owner from Essen. 'He has created work for all those poor unemployed, and at the same time, he has given Germany a road system to be proud of. Also other big projects, bridges, dams.'

'I agree,' said Max. 'In the same way as the American President Roosevelt, who I think is a good man.'

'Have you lost control of your senses, Schmeling? That man is a warmonger!'

'A whisky drinker,' chimed in another.

'And in the pocket of the Jews,' said a third catching the rhythm. Max noticed how the conversation resembled a cabaret patter song.

The conversation stalled. Then a smile from the factory owner. 'Another one of Max's jokes, I think. But seriously, Max, you should be careful saying things like that.'

Max shrugged. His shoulders were patted by many bejewelled hands. They lavished him with winking smiles as they left him on his own, all simultaneously noticing someone they absolutely had to meet.

When Max and Anny arrived home, the telephone was ringing. She picked it up.

'Just a moment. I'll fetch my husband.' She covered the speaker with her hand.

'It's someone called Louis Lochner, from the American Associated Press. He's ringing from New York and says it's urgent.'

'Hard to imagine any urgent business from America nowadays.' He took the telephone from her.

'Schmeling.'

'Lochner, Associated Press.'

'What's so important for you to ring from America?'

'I have sad news to tell you, and I'm sorry that it has to be me. Joe Jacobs died last night.'

'Yussel?' Max felt as if a stiff right cross had connected onto his face.

'Yes. A heart attack. It was very quick.'

'He was only forty-one.'

'Yes. It took everyone by complete surprise. I know it's very sad for you, and also for boxing.'

He put down the telephone. Anny came over and put her arms around him.

Max was surprised at how much pain he was feeling. It

welled over him and through his damp eyes.

'It wasn't the cigars, Anny, or the late nights. Or the lifestyle. It was his temperament. That's what killed him.'

Anny said, 'He used to make me laugh; I remember when I met him in Hamburg. He was so funny. Maybe he didn't realise it. Because whenever I laughed he looked surprised. But I loved hearing his cracking voice, and arms moving around like a broken windmill, and the endless cigars, and how one sentence started even before he finished the last.'

Max couldn't stop the tears. 'He was a wonderful friend to me. Wonderful. Despite all. I would never have got this far without him.' And at this moment, Max finally understood that his old life, full of real friends and courteous excitement, was forever lost to him, and he understood that it had been lost for some time.

◄o►

Another night, another party.

Max was half-listening to Luftwaffe General Dahlmann who was comparing boxing with fighter planes. That same day Max had received an official letter ordering him to report for military assignment.

'Nothing quite like it, an aerial dogfight. I think it comes close to boxing. The manoeuvring, the feinting, the shots, then the kill.'

He stopped abruptly, his face registering a new thought. Max continued to smile pleasantly.

'Listen Schmeling, I hear on the grapevine that you have been ordered to join a military unit. And since the

Wehrmacht does not yet have a combat boxing division, trained to flatten the English with combination punches, why not join the paratroopers? It's better than being a common soldier, especially, if you don't mind me mentioning it, at your age. If you like, I'll contact the paratrooper commander at Stendal. Nothing dangerous for you, maybe just testing the new recruits.'

'That sounds quite dangerous enough to me.'

'Nothing to it. But anyway, I'm certain you won't see combat. You'll merely be used for inspiring the young men and putting them through their paces.'

If it is unavoidable that I must serve, this might be a good option.

Two days later, leaving Anny sobbing at home, Max was driven to the Luftwaffe base. From the moment he arrived, everyone treated him as a celebrity. The soldier at the guardhouse even carried his suitcase. He was welcomed by the base commander, Colonel von Krummer.

'The recruit training programme will be nothing for someone of your physique, Max.'

'But I was told that I would only be testing the new recruits.'

'Absolutely. But to test them, you have to know their experience. Not so? Let me take you to your barracks. No single rooms, I'm afraid, not for enlisted men, but I have found you a billet with only three others. All are great admirers of yours.'

My dearest Anny
The last few days have been very busy and also very

tedious. Learning the rules. Learning how and whom to salute. Learning how to make a bed. And the daily marching. Tedious long treks carrying a heavy backpack, worse than roadwork training, where you can at least change pace, run backwards, even drink from a water flask. The officers insist that I eat in the officers' mess with them, where we only talk about boxing. The other enlisted men don't seem to mind, though.

Being away from you now is very painful. I miss your cheery face and chirpy voice. I miss other things which I can't put into this letter. I even miss how you furrow your brows and pucker your lips just before telling me off. Here, if someone does anything wrong, there are only shouts. Of course, they are much kinder to me than the others, maybe because of my age, but also because to them I'm some sort of hero, still the champion.

I'm sharing a billet with three young men, all in their twenties. They are decent lads. The first, Rüttiger, already has lost most of his thin blond hair. He always carries a chess book with him, and spends every spare minute replaying championship games of the past. The second, Helmut, once worked in Goebbels' ministry. He must have blotted his copybook to be sent here. But he is still spouting all the propaganda learned from his master. But I think that his admiration for me pales against his puppy-love for you, darling. The very mention of your name makes his eyes glow. It's a strange feeling to see your own wife pinned up inside a locker door amongst other beautiful kino divas. It's a flattering picture of you, though, I think a still from The Irresistible Man.

The third of my roommates is from South Africa, the Transvaal, trying to win his country over to National Socialism. He feels that he must first help in what he calls 'Germany's great crusade in Europe'.

More soon. I'm to undergo actual paratrooper training next week. I wonder if I will be scared jumping from a plane?

More love than you can imagine
Max

My dearest darling Anny
Paratrooper training at last. But just as it begins, someone from the Air Force Magazine, The Eagle, comes to take photographs of me. Of course, we have to do the jump again. A bit staged, though, me looking serious while we wait to jump, me at the edge of the open door, my hands ready to push off from the door frame. One of the photographers actually jumped out of the plane before me in order to capture a shot of me in mid-air. I tried to remember not to drop my gun and to keep my legs together (as you must remember when you visit our little friend in Schwanenwerder, ha-ha). I am told that the magazine will appear in May.

But the jump training is worrying for me. I'm always afraid that I will injure the vertebrae so comprehensively seen to by Joe Louis. My boots are very sturdy, though, and I have learned how to roll when I land. But sometimes we need to jump from a lower altitude in case we come in under fire. Which means that we hit the ground harder. So far all of my old bones have held up well enough.

Also, when we have weapons training, the officer always pulls me out for a chat. It seems he boxed a bit when he was younger. When I ask him about this, he says, 'Schmeling, you have nothing to worry about, since you will definitely not be going into combat.' I told him that you would like this news. Once we had an exercise, a real jump under battle conditions. I didn't have a clue what to do when I reached the ground. I just stood there in a field. Then the others began to run in formation, so I copied them, then they threw themselves onto the ground, me as well, then they jumped up, so I followed, then they dug foxholes so out came my spade from my backpack. Pointless. In the evening we sang. I am so looking forward to being with you next week! I want to hear all of your news, normal news, maybe even film news.

I'll save all my love and energy for you now, so I hope we won't jump again before I return to you, darling Anny, my very own film-diva and sweetheart.

Max

Anny looked annoyed when he arrived back home, dressed in his paratrooper uniform.

'You look like a regular soldier now, Max.'

Max grinned. 'I'll look like the same old Max when I take my clothes off. We can talk army later.'

'It's no good, Max. I'm worried sick that you'll be killed somewhere, and then what will be left of my life?'

'They told me that I'm not going into combat, just training other recruits. Anyway, I don't even know how to use a rifle or a grenade. I wasn't trained.'

'I know some people who would be happy to hear that, Max.'

'My darling wife, let's at least spend this time as happily as possible before I'm sent to Greece.'

'Greece!? I thought you said "training".'

'Yes, well training also happens nearer the combat zones.'

'You believe this?'

Max shrugged, sorry that Anny didn't believe him. But he also knew that she was not only beautiful, but very perceptive.

◄o►

The next week, as Max was boarding his transport plane for Greece, Anny was watching a film with the Goebbels' at Schwanenwerder. Throughout the film Josef kept looking at her, then at Magda, then at the children, who were seated cross-legged on the floor, looking up at the screen with consummate rapture.

When the children were packed off to bed, *they have six, I can't even have one now*, Anny thought, remembering the despair of her miscarriage, Josef said, 'A genuine genius. To make those drawings come to life like that, to make us care, even shed a tear for merely an animated young woman, and for the charming racial degenerates around her, and to offer such wonderful colour and music, this is truly exceptional. But of course, Snow White is a German character.'

Anny said, 'I've never seen anything like it.'

Goebbels was still nodding his head in admiration. 'I showed this film to the Führer. You know, he's a big admirer of Mickey Mouse. He said to me, "perhaps when the war is over, we can get Disney to come here and train our own animators". By the way, I might have a film for you, Frau Schmeling.' Magda smiled conspiratorially at Anny.

'It's called *The Gasman*, nothing heavy, just a comedy, in which you, darling lady, excel. The script is quite funny, Karl Fröhlich will direct.'

'Oh, he's very good,' said Anny, her face illuminated by suppressed excitement, 'I love his films.'

'You will be the female lead, playing against Heinz Rühmann.'

Anny clapped with delight, then danced across the room to where Magda was sitting and took her hand.

'Rühmann's just wonderful. His little face always makes me laugh.'

'Good,' said Goebbels. 'It's settled.'

Magda and Anny beamed at each other.

◄०►

Max was surprised, but on reflection, not completely, to find himself on a plane flying low over Crete. There was heavy British anti-aircraft fire and some of the planes exploded before discharging their paratroopers. They jumped at 150 metres, as low as they ever attempted in training. The British sent small arms and machine gun fire at the paratroopers, causing many chutes to tear and sending soldiers plummeting to their deaths. For Max, the sensation of floating beneath a canopy of silk was both exciting and terrifying. He could hear the bullets thunking into suspended bodies drifting near him, he could hear the moans of the injured and dying, and he could see the flak, exploding capriciously into dark blossoms of shrapnel. He was scared that he might be hit, yet also exhilarated. It was a bit like being in the ring – the danger seemed both imminent yet unreal.

A few seconds later Max's boots hit the ground, hard. He wanted to roll, as he was taught, but he had come down into the middle of a vineyard, and there was no space. He felt a sharp pain in his lower spine, and fell onto his back, staring up at unripe grapes. He lay there, sometimes unconscious, for about an hour.

By the time he hobbled to the German lines, the battle was almost over.

'Oh, there you are, Schmeling. We haven't kept you, have we?'

Max grimaced in pain. 'Just fell badly. Aggravated an old boxing injury, nothing more. Painful though.'

'Well, hobble to our forward base at Chiana and bring this sorry looking English prisoner with you. You'll be a fine pair. He's limping as well.'

The lad was very young, no more than twenty, Max thought. He was scared and dirty. Some blood seeping slowly through a bandage on his left thigh, but he could walk, albeit slowly. That suited Max, who decided that they need not hurry. When they were out of sight of the others, they supported each other. The soldier kept looking at Max, sneakily at first, then more boldly.

'You look familiar. Are you a fighter?'

Max nodded gravely, but he was always pleased to be recognised.

'You are! You're Max Schmeling! Well, I never did. My mate Tommy will never believe it was you who captured me.'

'Tommy?'

'Tommy Farr. The Welsh boxer. He's a good friend of mine.'

Max's eyes widened with pleasure. 'He's a very good boxer, that Tommy Farr. Also strong! He went the distance with Louis. That's better than I did the second time.'

'He really likes you, though. Says you're a real gent. Deserve to be champion, you do. Listen, can we sit down for a bit? My leg is killing me.'

They sat in an olive grove, under branches of tiny green buds. There were distant sounds of gunfire. Max handed the lad a cigarette; and was given part of an orange in return. They talked for a long time about boxing.

'What do you think of Joe Louis, Max?'

'I admire him. He dragged himself up from poverty, always worked so hard, and made himself into a champion. Of course, as I can tell you, it's not just hard work. There's a genius there as well. No one will beat him for years. You know, I would love to have met Tommy Farr in the ring. Might have but for the war. I think it would have been a good fight.'

'He told me the same thing.'

The sporadic gunfire intensified around them, but soon died down. The English retreated.

'It seems to be over now. I suppose we should go,' said Max, with real regret in his voice.

'Yes, I guess so.'

They supported each other until Max could see the sentries at the gate of the German base.

As he handed the lad over to the guard, he said, 'Mention me to Tommy Farr. Sorry we never met in the ring. You're lucky, you know, since for you the war is probably finished.'

'The war will be finished when I am home,' the soldier said, as he limped off into the German camp. *They won't be so friendly with him as I have been.* Max thought, as he slowly made his way back to his unit.

—◦—

Goebbels was laughing scornfully, looking at the front page of *The New York Times*.

'Do you see, Anny? Do you see how they lie, this Jew infested American Press? *German Boxer Max Schmeling killed in Crete,* they crow. But we know better.'

Anny's face turned ashen. 'I didn't even know he was there. I thought it was Greece. Is he injured? Where is he now? Can I go to see him?'

Goebbels smiled and raised his hand, walking over to calm her. 'He's fine. No wounds. Just a little bruising from the parachute drop, which was heavy, I have been told. He's in hospital, but not for any wound, but because he has contracted a mild dysentery. He's recovering very well, and will be home in a week or two. In the meantime, I will arrange for these same lying American newspapers to interview our champion, so he can tell the real story!'

Anny was awash with the simultaneous feelings of anger, fear, disgust and gratitude.

‒◦‒

Max's hospital bed was constantly surrounded by well-wishers. He had lost a bit of weight – *I'll need to beef myself up if I want to fight again.* Near the end of his convalescence he was visited by the American journalist, Bill Flannery, of the International News Service.

'Hi Max, how're you doing?'

'Fine, Bill, as you can see. But I'm looking forward to going home.'

'Did you do much fighting after you landed?'

'There weren't many of our unit left on the ground, but we did our part.'

'Some people are saying that the English ignored the proper conventions of war, Max. They report that some German soldiers were shot after surrendering, and some even mutilated.'

'I don't think that could have happened, Bill. The English may have put German flags on the wrong ground to decoy paratroopers, but during the actual fighting, they fought fairly and bravely.'

'What about excessive cruelty towards the Germans, Max? There have been reports.'

'I never heard of it. Maybe some local Greeks who had their homes and farms destroyed in the action, they may have taken it out on some of our soldiers, but I don't think it was the English who did that.'

'Do you think that there will be war between Germany and the USA?'

'That would be a great tragedy. I have always seen America as my second home.'

Josef Goebbels was incandescent, his bony face turning red, engorged veins protruding and pulsing on his neck and forehead. He crumpled the newspaper in his hands then tore it with such violence that strips flew around the room.

'I'll have that traitor in front of the People's Court! I'll make certain that he's shot! That ingrate!'

Magda tried to calm him. 'You know, Josef, he's just a simple and honest man. It's only that he doesn't think about what such an interview might mean.'

'He's not so simple, Magda, don't be fooled. He's been playing us a merry game for years, keeping his Jewish manager, visiting his Jewish friends in Paris. But now there needs to be a reckoning with him.'

'Best to let him be, Josef. What will a trial achieve? Only to bring all this up again, and do you need that? Is this the sort of publicity we need just now?'

A minute of silence elapsed and Josef calmed visibly. He smiled at his wife.

'You are always a rock of serenity and sense, my love. Of course, you are right. But Schmeling mustn't escape punishment entirely. It would have been best if he'd actually been killed on Crete as reported.'

He walked to the telephone.

'Get me Max Amman in the Press office.' He turned to Magda. 'I have an idea.'

'Amman? Josef... Schmeling has really done it this time...You read it? ... So you see. Alright, tell all the newspapers, from now on not one mention of Max Schmeling shall ever appear in any publication throughout the Reich. It goes without saying that the scandalous interview he gave to the Americans will never be reprinted here. I'll tell Hadamovsky at Radio... See to it.'

—◄○►—

The day of his medical discharge, Max was visited by Major General Süßmann, the commander of his army group.

'Don't rise, Schmeling.'

Max smiled weakly. He had not planned to stand.

'It's clear that your earlier boxing injuries have been aggravated by your parachute landing, and that there is no other option for you, or for the Wehrmacht, than for you to be listed as unfit for frontline duty.'

'I don't want to seem a coward, General, but I'm happy to hear this news.'

'Cowardice doesn't come into the question. You fought bravely.'

'Will I be sent back home?'

'Yes, but you will still be required for duty.'

'In an office?'

'I have an idea which might be better suited to your talents. The army has been trying to establish more cordial and fraternal relations with Waffen SS units. This is not always so easy, by the way. After discussing this with the respected leaders, including Reichsführer Himmler and Field Marshal Keitel, the army thinks that the best way to use your services is for you to visit the troops, recount your famous matches, instil into them the German fighting spirit you exemplify. We also think that it would be good to have you involved through sporting competitions, especially boxing, which will bring out the aggressive and also the more chivalrous natures of our troops. No one is better suited to be at the forefront of this endeavour than you, Schmeling. I hope that you will find it agreeable. You will be able to live at home, but will need to travel regularly to army and SS posts. Some of these posts are in occupied territories, France, Poland, later elsewhere. It goes without saying that there is a promotion involved. What do you say?'

'May I think about it?'

'Until tomorrow, when your plane leaves for Berlin.'

CHAPTER 33
FIGHTIN' FOR UNCLE SAM

People were so crushed together that it was hard to move. Newspaper reporters, cameramen and army brass all jostled to get a glimpse of the US Army's latest and most famous recruit.

'This way, Joe. Smile.'

Flashbulbs popped and fell, still smoking.

'How do you like the Army, Joe?'

'I've only seen this room. It ain't so bad this far.'

'Are you going to do basic training?'

'They say I have to, but I guess it won't be so hard, compared to all my normal boxing training.'

'What does your wife Marva think of you as a soldier, Joe?'

'Well, she thinks I'm doin' a good thing by enlistin'. And you know, for her army life won't be so different, me bein' away, since I've been often away at trainin' camps and all. So it won't be so bad. Unless they send me to the Pacific.'

'Are you the "champion of Democracy, Joe", like President Roosevelt said?'

'Well, I don't know about that, but I'm here to help my country.'

'That's great, Joe.' More flashbulbs.

'And another thing.' Everyone looked up, surprised that Joe had something else to say. 'Maybe my next fight will be against that Max Smellin' in no-man's-land. I won't be pullin' any punches when we meet there, that's for sure.'

'That's fine, Joe.' But only the Harlem newspapers used that quote.

—◦—

The day he finished basic training, Joe was summoned by a general.

'Private Barrow, you won't be going overseas with the others, not into combat, at least. You're much more valuable to us as a symbol, Joe,' said the man with two stars on each shoulder. 'You'll be visiting the troops, giving boxing exhibitions, that sort of thing. Show everyone what America stands for. We'll make you a sergeant, of course.'

'Will I visit white units or negro ones?'

'Both, Joe. You're popular everywhere.'

'Pity they have to be separate, though.'

'The President is working on that.'

'Hmmm.'

—◦—

Two months later, relaxed and happy, the champion was sitting on a big sofa in his Harlem apartment with Mike Jacobs and John Roxborough.

'You settlin' in as a soldier, champ??'

'The Army ain't so bad, Mike. All I do is boxing training, visit other camps, pose for photographs, lookin' like a soldier, that sort of thing. But it feels kinda' bad, fightin' for the USA when negroes can't have a normal American life. Roosevelt says fine things about helpin' us, and about us all pullin' together, but he ain't in no hurry to do much for us folks. Willkie promised an anti-lynching bill if he got to be President and that's why I voted for him in '40. Anyway, all this publicity is a good deal for me and the Army too, I guess. I can be their pin-up boy and they're lettin' me stay in the ring and defend my title.'

'Which is why I told you to fight Billy Conn.'

'You were right, Mike. But that guy really surprised me. He could'a won it. I underestimated him. He wasn't in the "bum of the month" club like all the others. He has style, and he's strong. I thought he'd won it. He had me on points for sure. But then he came over all cocky and stupid in the 12th, so I could nail him.'

'You were real lucky, Joe,' said John Roxborough.

'Uh-huh. You know what he said after the fight? "Why couldn't you lend the title to me for a while, just for a lousy six months? I'd'a given it back." And I said, "Well, I lent it to you for twelve rounds and you didn't know what to do with it." We're friends now.'

'Like I said, you were lucky, Joe.'

'I ain't always been lucky, Mike, but I guess I'm lucky now.'

'But you're going to get really unlucky if you don't change some things.'

'Such as what?'

'Money, for one thing.'

'I got plenty of that stuff, Mike. More coming' in every

day. Even the $78 a month from the Army.' John laughed. Mike didn't.

'Yes, but you spend it and waste it faster than you make it. You're in hock to me for 75 Gs, and you owe the taxman even more.'

'Yeah, but that was a mean thing, to expect taxes from purses I donated to the Navy and Army.'

'I told you to be careful, Joe.'

'I just don't seem to get it with money. In the mornin' I could have $500.00 in my pocket, and then by that night I have to get some more.'

'Where does it all go?'

'There's always people needin' stuff, and you know how I like clothes, and other fine things. And I like to tip well, especially to coloured waiters. And I like a bet, especially when I play golf – you know, Mike, I'm gettin' pretty good at it – but I still lose. And then there's Marva, she needs fine things, too.'

'She just wants *you*, Joe. That's all she wants. She wants her champion to stay at home. To plan a future together. Maybe have a baby. Not to go off without a word for weeks at a time, usually with some other woman. Like that Lena Horne. I argued with Marva for hours until she finally agreed not to file for a divorce. But if you keep carrying on like this, mark my words, she will. Try hard to get her back, Joe.'

'I can't help the way I am, Mike. Women's like whisky for me. I just get drunk with all those beautiful, excitin' women. I mean Marva is pretty and all, but she don't hold a candle to Lena.'

329

'Too much bad publicity about you and that woman,' said John, shaking his head slowly.

'But I can't stop seein' her. She seems so sweet and nice when she sings, and in the movies too, but in bed, oh, brother. Such a filthy mouth. She's an animal. The only thing animal about Marva is the fur coat I buy her last Christmas.'

CHAPTER 34
SNOWY WARSAW

Hans Frank's receding hair was slicked back, his uniform was sharply pressed, flattering his growing girth. His nails were manicured to a mirror shine, and his smile, ubiquitous for those he wished to charm, vanished completely when dealing with his 'inferiors'.

'You know, Governor General, I have visited Belvedere Palace several times before, but still I marvel at its beauty,' Max said, taking his place at one end of a baroque table set for luncheon. He smiled at Frau Brigitte Frank on his left, and nodded to a slim dapper man seated opposite. The man smiled.

'Call me Hans,' the Governor General said. 'You're among friends here, Schmeling.'

'I am honoured to be considered one of your friends, Hans.'

Hans Frank smiled.

'In fact, the Governor General indeed has very many friends,' the man opposite said, with an Italian accent. 'By the way, permit me to introduce myself, as Hans seems to have temporarily forgotten my name. I am Curzio Malaparte, an Italian journalist, covering the eastern front for *Corriere Della Sera*.'

Max was intrigued. 'That's an interesting name, if you don't mind me saying.'

'Of course not. I chose it specifically for its interest. An inversion of Buonaparte, you see. In truth, I was born and baptised as Kurt Suckert, a far less interesting name despite its Germanic sound, don't you think? Changed it when I joined the Fascist Party. Of which I was then, and am now, immensely proud, since it brought to Italy order out of anarchy.'

Max smiled, hoping not to exhibit too much enthusiasm for fascism.

A giant artificial wisteria, arranged to look as lifelike as possible, climbed the walls on all sides, culminating in pink rayon blooms which dangled from the ceiling. Max's eyes were drawn upwards. He recalled a previous visit, when a fresco, 'The Triumph of Venus' had adorned the ceiling.

'Wonderful effect,' Max said.

Brigitte Frank laid her hand on his arm, as if to reveal a secret.

'You're possibly wondering what happened to the fresco, Herr Schmeling? Hans and I had it carefully removed, and we managed to retrieve most of it. It is now being restored in Florence, where it will be displayed. But it was totally wrong for this room, you see, especially now. I thought that something which represents thrusting life, culminating in ethereal beauty, would be more suitable. And as my husband doesn't much care about such things, he let me design this room.'

Max noticed the furniture, all heavy, overdressed,

Germanic, much like Frau Frank herself – stout with success, her black hair lustrous with dye and oils. A lace blouse, adorned with a double set of pearls and a Nazi party pin, covered her ample bosom.

'It certainly makes its effect,' Max said.

Malaparte smirked. 'Very National Socialist, don't you agree?'

Hans Frank laughed. 'Our Italian friend's sole purpose in life is to offend authority. He does this through his eccentric sense of humour. Does Mussolini enjoy a good joke, Curzio?'

'Oh, indeed he does, Hans. Sufficiently to arrest and imprison me several times, yet still have me serve as an officer in the military and as reporter on our flagship newspaper. That's very *droll*, isn't it?'

'He must like you then,' Max said.

'Well, at least he has a sense of humour, if only among close associates. He makes a show of being hard, but it's all theatre, really. We Italians love opera, and he's our lead tenor now.'

Hans Frank clinked a spoon against his wine glass. It released a pure crystalline note which reverberated around the room, dying slowly. 'Czech,' he said, admiringly. 'The factory is now Aryanised, of course. The Poles, on the other hand, can't make anything. No art, no craft, terrible music. The only thing they can reliably produce is Catholics.'

A liveried waiter filled glasses with Riesling.

'Thank you, Isaac,' Brigitte said.

'He's a Jew, of course,' Hans said. 'I plucked him from

the ghetto, as I have most of my servants. They work harder and are less insolent than the Poles, whom you have to watch every minute, or they'll steal from you, or spit in your food.'

Max said, 'Yesterday, when I was preparing the boxing ring for tomorrow's exhibition, a little Pole, no more than five feet tall, maybe fifty years of age, was spreading sawdust onto the canvas. He crossed himself when I entered the room. He then said – in German, by the way – "if our Lord Jesus had possessed a couple of fists like yours, he never would have died on the cross". Then he crossed himself again and left.'

Frank, laughed. 'If Christ had your fists, Schmeling, and had used them, the world would be a better place.' He raised his glass, and the others responded. 'To my gathered friends, to our Führer, to the Reich, and...' he looked at Malaparte, 'to Benito Mussolini.'

They drank.

Frank continued his thread. 'The Poles are convinced that Christ is always on their side, even in political matters, and that He prefers them to any other people, even to the Germans, if you can imagine. In this, they are just like the Jews, who think that the God of the Universe is Jewish and is interested in them alone. Of course, for all I know and care, He could be. Serve them right.'

A starter of duck liver pâté and thin toast was served.

'This fellow was quacking just this morning. Now he makes us happy,' Frank said, spreading some pâté on his toast. He stopped abruptly, then focused a cold glance at Max.

'Do you think I could fight you, Schmeling?'

'Best not. I think I could knock you out with just one punch, even, with respect, a stiff jab. Your head is frail, you see.'

Frank's smile inverted for a moment, but then he laughed. 'Well, it is not my intention to test your theory.'

'I am relieved to hear it.'

After the meal, Hans Frank announced, 'It's such a beautiful winter's day, why don't we go for a drive?'

There were murmurs of reluctant assent.

Powdery snow was falling sporadically. Coats, hats and scarves appeared.

'It will be just like a country sleigh-ride from my childhood,' Brigitte said.

The guests were escorted to two waiting Mercedes. Hans Frank, his driver and Malaparte rode in the first, Max, a second driver and Brigitte Frank in the other. The tops of both cars had been lowered despite the cold, and blankets were found to cover knees and laps. Brigitte pulled the collar of her fur coat so that it covered her ears. Flakes of snow settled on her hair. She stuck out her tongue and caught one, giggling. 'You'd think I've had enough of snow, living here, but it always amuses me, especially at first.'

As they travelled into the centre of Warsaw, Max could see the results of the Luftwaffe bombing. Not much had been repaired, even after two years; many rubble sites, empty spaces between barely standing buildings, others hollowed out like rotten teeth.

They arrived at the entrance to the Ghetto. Guards in

steel battle helmets stood in front of a wire-mesh gate; rifles slung over their backs, pistols in their shiny holsters.

Brigitte turned to Max. 'He likes to bring people here. I don't know why, since I find it upsetting. But it seems to give him energy. I always tell myself not to come, but each time I go anyway.'

A silent movie of dread flickered through Max's thoughts. *My God. What if I meet someone I know, one of my many Jewish friends from before? What would I say? 'How are you doing Goldberg?' 'Oh, not too bad under the circumstances, Max, and you? How's Anny? By the way, can you get me out of here?'*

Hans Frank broke into Max's rumination. 'See this high brick wall?' He gestured expansively. 'No concrete, no watchtowers, just two SS sentries at the gate. It's nothing like the Americans report it. And inside? Complete freedom. The Jews can do whatever they like, I persecute no one. They even have their own police!'

On the Governor General's command, the gates were opened and the group walked through, to the salute of the guards. The visitors continued down the street, their feet crunching on the snow. Frozen silence. Thinly clothed people shuffled about. The stench was overwhelming. Malaparte covered his nose with his silk scarf.

Frank said, 'one gets used to the smell. They're filthy people, Jews, so what can be done? Of course, it's worse in the summer.'

Max turned to Malaparte. 'They look very hungry.'

Frank had overheard.

'You see, Max, in Poland we have a system. Germans

here receive about 2,600 calories a day, Poles 900. In the Ghetto, of course, they need less, about 150.'

'Don't many starve?'

'Unfortunately, yes, but there is a war on. Should we feed our enemies better than ourselves? Of course, those who work well for us, they sometimes might get a bit more. This is especially true for those who work in the factories and workshops we have established for them. Some of these Jews are very good tailors, you know.'

Brigitte almost stumbled over a corpse, buried in new snow. A wagon pulled by two emaciated men had been making their way to collect the body, their thin wobbly wheels tracing erratic black lines in the snow.

'Quickly, will you?!' Frank bellowed.

Max could see the men trying to pull the wagon faster, avoiding the eyes of the Governor-General, his wife and guests. They undressed the body and threw it unceremoniously onto the wagon, on top of five other naked corpses. They put the clothing into a bulging sack of rags.

The visitors gradually encountered more people as they approached the ghetto's centre. Everyone had waxy, paper-thin skin – on almost every face death waited just below the surface. But their eyes were alert, constantly darting about, looking for danger, scraps of food, a discarded shoe. The men avoided Hans Frank's gaze, but some women looked straight at him, holding their stare longer, hostility glistening in their eyes. Everywhere there was filth, the reek of wet clothing, the stench of misery.

Two naked Jewish men crossed their path, escorted by SS officers.

'Why have they no clothes?'

'It's normal. Before their execution, people will normally strip naked and distribute their clothes to others.'

'The devil has laid an egg, and here, in this place, it is hatched,' Malaparte whispered to Max.

Frank pointed at one man who was walking on the other side of the road. The man averted his eyes from the group, having recognised Hans Frank. He began to move more quickly.

'You. Jew.'

The man stopped, terrified.

'Come over here!'

The man complied, looking steadily at the ground.

'You're new here, aren't you?'

Max asked, 'How could you tell that?'

'He's not very skinny yet. Jew, where are you going? Are you on holiday?'

'No, your Excellency. I am making my way to the tailoring shop for my evening shift. I make German uniforms.'

'So, there still is a use for you scum after all. Off with you, then.'

They all watched Abraham Grynszpan shuffle away.

'I find this quite amusing, don't you? This little rodent is now working for us, and more than happy to do it. Very gratifying. But Himmler wants the ghetto liquidated. I asked him why? The Jews are useful, I told him, they help in the war effort, and the irony of their situation is wonderful. But Himmler has no sense of humour.'

Brigitte said, 'Hans, can we go back now? I'm absolutely

freezing out here. Tell the drivers to put the tops back on the cars.'

'I have already anticipated your wishes, Oh Queen of Poland, and the engines are already running to put warmth on your feet.'

Brigitte eyed him acerbically.

Frank shrugged. 'You see, no matter how high you climb, there is always someone higher telling you what to do. All right *liebling*, let us return our guests to their hotels. Max, you ride with me this time.'

Max was reeling from what he had seen. *Is this what I have been fighting for? What will happen to these wretched people? Who knows about this? Does Hitler? Surely if he did, he'd stop it.*

'So, what is the boxing plan tomorrow, Max? I'm looking forward to it.'

Max took a moment to answer, settling himself. 'The usual, at different weights, three rounds between SS and Wehrmacht units. It is designed to foster camaraderie between these two branches. We have been quite successful recently, in Leipzig, Prague, Paris, Bruges.'

'And after tomorrow?'

'Next week, Sachsenhausen. Then Dachau, then Mauthausen. To cheer up the camp guards.'

Hans Frank shook his head. 'They have it easy in Sachsenhausen compared to what goes on with us here. It's just the same in all the other German camps. Too easy. Not like here in Poland, that's for certain. You should see for yourself at Auschwitz, or Maidanek, or Treblinka. We have others too. The guards there are often quite tense, and need diversion even more than elsewhere.'

Frank looked intently at Max for a few seconds, then changed the subject.

'By the way, Max, are you not tempted to put the gloves on yourself, to teach these young pups a lesson in real boxing?'

'So far, I have avoided this temptation.'

—◄o►—

The portable seating in the newly built SS sports hall was completely full, and many people had to stand in the balconies. There were several matches, all of which passed good-naturedly, with little blood and no knockouts. Max enjoyed refereeing. He noticed that as a rule the SS boxers were better taught, but the Wehrmacht fighters took more risks. The final and deciding bout was to be between heavyweights.

Unteroffizier Erik Landsmann entered the ring for the Wehrmacht. His farming roots seemed obvious to Max, the flat Saxon face, the large muscular arms and hands, the thick neck. He was thick about the midriff as well, Max thought, and probably between the ears. Landsmann was a lumbering, popular man, immensely strong. Wearing green shorts and a white vest, he was loudly cheered by his comrades. He wore a continual smile of polite idiocy.

SS-Obersturmführer Helmut Eisenborn was waiting in the other corner. He was of an entirely different type. Tightly muscular, crisply dressed, wearing grey-black shorts and a white vest on which was emblazoned the familiar SS double lightning logo.

Max beckoned the boxers to the centre of the ring and explained the rules. The SS man glared menacingly at his opponent, who smiled back pleasantly.

At the bell, the Wehrmacht's Landsmann approached cautiously, pawing with an extended left arm, trying to gauge the distance for his famous left hook. SS Eisenborn jabbed twice, unsettling his opponent, then threw a right cross, which landed squarely on his adversary's jaw. Landsmann blinked and staggered, but quickly regained his composure. The SS man repeated the pattern – two hard jabs, flowed by a right cross. Each flurry had a similar effect, but Landsmann seemed not to see the pattern. Then Landsmann lunged at his assailant, throwing a wild arcing right which Eisenborn ducked. The SS man moved inside quickly, throwing a strong left uppercut. Landsmann staggered back, Eisenborn in pursuit. Two more crashing lefts and a straight right put Landsmann onto the canvas. Max started the count, taking a bit longer than he might, but Landsmann was unconscious. He was carried from the ring by his seconds and was revived on his stool. Eisenborn raised his hands with a thin-lipped smile of triumph, to the cheers of the SS contingent.

Hans Frank entered the ring. 'Today we have seen what young German manhood can become under the leadership of our Führer – strong, courageous and merciless. Congratulations to all boxers, and especially to SS-Obersturmführer Eisenborn, whose boxing skill is an inspiration to us all. I wonder, however, how he would fare if he met a genuine champion. How about it Max?'

Max waved his refusal.

'I can't believe that a world champion would be scared of a young SS pup.'

SS-Obersturmführer Eisenborn stared at Max, his eyes signalling malice and contempt.

'Ex-champion,' Eisenborn corrected. 'Beaten by a nigger and a Jew.'

Max put on Landsmann's gloves. Frank agreed to referee.

The bell sounded. Eisenborn walked briskly up to Max in the centre of the ring, threw two jabs, but Max sidestepped the predictable right cross. Max then threw a left hook which caught Landsmann on the jaw. His eyes rolled upwards as he fell backwards onto the canvas, to be revived five minutes later.

The Wehrmacht contingent cheered loudly, their SS opponents clapped unenthusiastically. Max smiled. He couldn't wait to tell Anny about it.

CHAPTER 35
BOOTS IN THE COURTYARD

The interview room at Prinzalbertstraße-8 was very cold, the heating having been suspended for want of coal after an allied bombing raid. As he was escorted into the room, Herschel was surprised to encounter Adolf Eichmann again, facing him, sitting behind the small metal desk, wearing a thick SS coat and gloves. Herschel huddled himself inside his jacket, a thin affair given him on arrival at Sachsenhausen. He missed the warmth of the coat his uncle Abraham had made for him in Paris, the same one he wore to the German Embassy, in what seemed centuries before.

Eichmann pointed to the chair. Herschel sat. He looked into his interrogator's face. *I can almost see your soul in your eyes,* he thought, *a soul dark and corrosive.*

'You are here for one last occasion, that I may describe the trial we have arranged for you.' His words were accompanied by plumes of freezing breath. 'And to offer you one last chance to help your situation.'

He looked up at Herschel, who stared at him blankly.

'The trial will take seven days. I will now outline the procedure for you.'

Eichmann's gloves were too thick for him to open the

folder. He removed one glove, blew on his hand, opened the folder, then replaced his glove.

'Day one. On this day, the People's Court will hear the undisputed facts concerning the assassination. There will be a witness appearance by Embassy Official Nagorka, who led you to vom Rath and then helped to restrain you when you tried to run away.'

'I was not running. I remained seated in the chair,' he said calmly.

'That will be decided by the court. We will also hear evidence from the receptionist at the Hôtel Suez and from the gun dealer, Monsieur Carpe, as to your state of mind at the time. Also, Judge Tesnière will give evidence as to the unreliability of your statements.' He looked up at Herschel who stared back at him, his hands stuffed into his pockets.

'On the second day, the Red Cross will testify that those Jews, including your family, who had been taken to the Polish border...' looking at the dossier, he mumbled the next phrase, then more clearly, '...and in every case were treated well, with all possible care and courtesy. It was this alleged ill-treatment of your parents that you have consistently contended was the motivation for your terrorist act. This will be contradicted.'

'My parents would not have written lies to me in their postcards.'

'We have read these postcards. We believe them to be complete exaggeration, typical of Jewish women, who are prone more than others to such hysteria.'

Herschel prevented himself from making further comment, clenching his hidden fists.

'We also suspect that your parents' writing might contain some sort of Kabbalistic code, a signal to begin the uprising against the German Reich. Our best cryptographers are now studying this matter. It seems that the spaces between words might hold some clues.'

Is Eichmann playing a game, or is he just stupid?

'Also on that second day we will hear character references relating to Ernst vom Rath, as well as testimony from your victim's father.' He continued without looking up.

'Then for the next three days we will hear irrefutable testimony from Dr Grimm and others, as to how every attempt to develop friendly relations between the Reich and France have been frustrated by concerted Jewish efforts to spread enmity between our two proud nations. We will unmask those who stand behind the scenes, this vile International Jewish Conspiracy. And it is here that there is still a chance for you to contribute, and thereby, mitigate your situation.'

He stared back at Eichmann, who then continued reading from the file.

'On day six, the final arguments will be presented. And on the seventh and last day, the judgement will be delivered and the punishment decided.' He closed the file and stared directly at Herschel with the merest inclination of a smile.

Eichmann placed his gloved hands on the desk. 'We are now at the end of your particular journey. But you can make the outcome somewhat better for yourself, less severe, if you tell me the truth, if you name those who put you up to the deed. It can then be argued that you were just a pawn in this larger cabal. That argument, especially since you were legally a child when you committed the murder, will weigh in your favour.'

Eichmann looked at his prisoner more intently, as if willing him to answer. *What a thin beak of a nose he has. I wonder how he will react when I tell him what no one wants to hear?* Eichmann was just about to close the file and order the SS guard to return Herschel to Sachsenhausen.

'I do have a confession.'

Eichmann raised an expectant eyebrow. He tried as best he could to smile paternally. 'Tell me, Herschel. Who are these people that made you do this terrible thing?'

'Not that. There were no others, no conspiracy. Just as I have said from the beginning. But the truth is that I knew Ernst vom Rath before that day. I had met him a few times at the *La Renaissance* bar in Montmartre. Near the *Sacre Coeur*. He had been smuggling money for Jewish refugees out of Germany and into France in order to help them, or so he said. Ernst told me that he could help me as well. He would bring my parents to France from Poland, and also, he would get for me official residence papers so that I could remain. In return, he required me to perform various sexual acts with him.'

Eichmann's half-benign smile melted.

'I did this because I was desperate,' he continued, 'and I felt very ashamed. I still do. Later when he told me that he could not in fact help me or my parents, I vowed to take my revenge. The rest follows. And that is the entire story.'

Eichmann retreated behind his SS mask. He closed the

file and gestured to the guards. Herschel was returned to Sachsenhausen.

Back in his office, Eichmann telephoned Goebbels to make his report. He could feel Goebbels' displeasure through the telephone wires. When he finished, Goebbels said, without emotion, 'Thank you, Obersturmbannführer Eichmann. I will make this report to the Führer. You may now return to your more important duties, that of helping to cleanse Europe of its Jewish pestilence.'

Goebbels met Hitler the following week at Berchtesgaden.

The day before, Hitler had received a report from the acting Minister of Justice, Roland Freisler.

The Jew Grynszpan has admitted, in an encrypted note to his family, that his claims of homosexual relations with vom Rath were untrue. However, he insinuates the suspicion that the murder victim had homosexual relations with others. In this connection, it is of interest that a brother of the murdered vom Rath, a First Lieutenant and commander of a cavalry squadron, was sentenced to one year's imprisonment and loss of rank by the Field Court-martial of Division 428, Special Mission, for sexual offences with men.

Hitler sat in his favourite armchair and listened impassively to Goebbels' news, staring at the late snow on the top of the Obersalzburg, and at a glimmering of spring in the valley below. When he had finished, Goebbels sat on the edge of an armchair, his hands clasped in front of him.

'What to do,' Goebbels half asked, half mused.

Hitler made a small movement with his left hand, as if shooing a fly from a strudel.

—◄o►—

That same day in Astrakhan, a Sunday, Zindel and Rivka Grynszpan enjoyed a day off, a walk in the thin spring sunshine. As they strolled beside the Volga, they were shocked to notice bodies floating down the wide river, first in ones and twos, then in dozens. Russian and German corpses, now unlocked from the ice, their greatcoats faded into similarity, were being transported on the current from the hell of Stalingrad to the calm of the Caspian Sea. The Grynszpans did not know that the huge battle which had produced these corpses had saved their lives. They did not know that this monumental German defeat in the snow was in fact merely a side show, that the real target of the summer offensive had been their new home, Astrakhan. Capturing it would have allowed the Germans access to great quantities of oil, and more importantly, would have prevented the Russians using it. But Hitler was, as usual, fanatically driven. He insisted that the army should first secure a victory over the city which bore his arch-enemy's name, the psychological impact of which, as he told his despairing generals, was worth twenty infantry divisions.

—◄o►—

Herschel was pleased with the shine he had managed to achieve on Sergeant Schultz's boots. He could see his face in the toecaps; even the shafts were gleaming. He was carrying them into the courtyard when he stood as still as he could. A group of officers, SS and Wehrmacht, were making their way across the courtyard, smiling, patting backs, laughing in that masculine way which signals bonding rather than pleasure. In the middle of the throng, and dwarfing them by several centimetres, walked Max Schmeling, his Wehrmacht uniform recently adorned with new Sergeant's insignia. SS Sturmbannführer Hans Lorinz, the camp's commandant, noticed Herschel and gestured angrily for him to go back inside.

Herschel was transfixed. *Schmeling is actually here! Here in Sachsenhausen. Max Schmeling, the German champion, flesh and blood and here.* Then, as if responding to his thoughts, Max looked over to him, and offered him an apologetic smile, before being jostled away by the entourage. Herschel was mesmerised. *He saw me and smiled! Max Schmeling!*

After the group had passed, he walked across the courtyard towards the SS barracks carrying Sergeant Schultz's boots under his arm. He could see Schultz through the barracks window, talking on the phone, standing at attention. Immediately Schultz noticed Herschel's approach he put down the phone. He came outside, smiling affably.

'That was Max Schmeling, wasn't it Sergeant?'

'Yes, I think so. Someone mentioned a boxing tournament, maybe that's why.'

'He smiled at me.'

'And I am smiling at you as well. Now, leave the boots by the door, Bubi, and come and see something with me.'

'I hope that you will notice the fine shine I have produced for you, Sergeant.'

Schultz gave the boots a cursory glance. 'Very good, Bubi, the best yet. But now I need you to come with me to the back of the barracks. Leave the boots and come with me.'

'What is it?'

'Someone has written something about you on the wall, which you should see.'

Herschel was bemused.

As they walked, an emaciated inmate in a striped uniform approached them. He bowed extravagantly at Herschel, in the manner of a circus ringmaster, an invisible top-hat sweeping the ground in an exaggerated arc.

Herschel scowled at the man. 'I did it for *you*, you know. For all of you.'

'Indeed,' said the inmate, 'and you can see, just by looking at me, how much you have helped us.'

Schultz shooed the inmate away. Herschel wondered what might be written about him on a concentration camp wall.

'It's something good that is written, I'm sure you will think,' said Sergeant Schultz, resuming the conversation. 'But it's written very small, so you'll have to get close.'

They approached the brick wall, Schultz now two paces behind.

'The writing is just in the centre, at about your height.'

Herschel continued, squinting as they approached, trying to see the writing. At about ten metres from the wall

Sergeant Schultz quietly unclipped his holster, removed his Luger and shot Herschel in the back of the head. Blood and brain spattered onto the wall. Herschel fell, first onto his knees, then onto his face, blood seeping into the gravel. Schultz re-holstered his pistol, then walked to the main camp and detailed some prisoners, the circus ringmaster among them, to cart Herschel Grynszpan's body to the newly constructed crematorium.

CHAPTER 36
LOOSE ENDS

1961

Picture this. An NBC television programme, Sunday at 10.30 pm. Theme music, then the monochrome familiarity of Ralph Edwards, who welcomes his audience to another episode of *This is Your Life*. The camera follows him to a banquet being held at the New York Hotel Astor, where various sporting notables are assembled, the men bedecked in dinner suits and bow ties. Among the faces caught on camera – Floyd Patterson, the heavyweight boxing champion, Jack Dempsey, various football and baseball stars. They have finished their dinners and are relaxing into alcohol and bonhomie.

A spotlight signals Edwards' appearance. He is carrying a large book. He teases the audience and the viewers. Who will it be tonight? Sugar Ray Robinson? Phil Rizzuto? He moves among the notables, finally stopping behind the seat of a heavy-set black man. 'Joe Louis, *This is your Life!*' Cheers and smiles from the sportsmen, loud applause from the studio audience, a shy smile from the genuinely surprised ex-champion. A quick encouraging comment from Jack Dempsey, seated next to him, then Louis is shepherded behind the curtain, and somehow immediately appears in the television studio. A fake boxing ring has been built as part of the studio set, with a stool in the corner. 'Don't know if I'll be able to get up again,' Louis quips as he sits, to the audience's delight.

The procession begins. Most of Joe's large family are brought on, grinning. Brothers, sisters; anecdotes about his childhood. His siblings admit that they didn't know he'd be a champion. 'He couldn't lick any of us. He could run fast, though.' His sister mentions that even she could 'whup him easily when he was a boy.' Joe says, 'I bet you still can.' More comforting laughter.

Then the family leaves and are replaced by Joe's managers, John Roxborough and Jack Blackburn, talking about how hard Joe trained, how clean he lived. They exit stage left.

Then Max Schmeling is announced, 'Coming all the way from Germany!' Appreciative applause from the audience. He strides quickly across the stage, a grin set wide across his face, his black hair Brylcreemed back. He pumps Louis' hand, then they both hug. Louis looks surprised and delighted to see him. Some banter about their two fights. Then Max disappears stage left.

◄○►

In fact, informal contact between the two men had begun years before. Max had done very well after the war. He had convinced the allied powers that he had never been a genuine Nazi. 'I refused so many times to join the party, and even defended my Jewish manager, Joe Jacobs.' Max prospered. He was invited to buy the German concession for Coca Cola, and was granted rights to distribute the sugary concoction throughout his homeland. He and Anny lived quietly and comfortably on their farm. They raised chickens and minks. For them, even without the children for which they had hoped, life was very good. Anny worked occasionally in film and television, but was not much in demand. In fact, after *The Gasman,* and Goebbels' displeasure at Max's adventures on Crete, Anny's career declined. She made only one subsequent film during the Nazi period, a comedy, which sunk without a trace.

But the Schmelings took part in West-Germany's buoyant optimism. The *Wirtschaftswunder,* the 'economic miracle', spearheaded by Volkswagen, Siemens, Beyer pharmaceuticals and other similarly de-Nazified companies, raised Germans' standard of living beyond expectations.

America was also booming, but Joe Louis was not doing so well. He still owed serious money to the government in back taxes. After being beaten unconscious in his 'comeback' bout with Rocky Marciano, who visited Joe's dressing room afterwards with tears in his eyes, Joe tried to make ends meet by acting as a 'greeter' in Las Vegas, and embarrassing himself in the wrestling ring. Sports headlines read: *Say it ain't so, Joe.* He appeared anywhere a former champion's aura could be of monetary value. Learning of Louis' difficulties, Max decided to send Joe regular donations.

Max's largesse continued until Joe's death in 1981. Schmeling was a pall bearer at the funeral; he had paid for much of it. Several days later, he asked Henri Lewin, one of the two brothers he had sheltered in the Hotel Excelsior during *Kristalnacht,* and now a prominent Las Vegas hotelier, to deliver an envelope with $5,000 in it to Louis' wife. Max stipulated that the payment must be paid directly to her, and in cash, so that it wouldn't get into the hands of the government.

In 1989, Lewin invited Max to a dinner at the Sands Hotel in Las Vegas to celebrate his career. In the audience were boxing stars of the past and present, Mike Tyson, Sugar Ray Robinson, others.

When Henri Lewin rose to his feet to speak, he surprised everyone, especially Max. Often in tears, he recounted how Max had saved him and his brother on that November night in 1938. No one except Anny had ever heard this story before. He reminded his audience that what Max did was an act of complete and utter treason to the Nazi regime. 'He risked his life to save me and my brother for no reason whatsoever, other than he knew my father.'

Max rose to speak. He was very moved, and spoke quietly and slowly, his English now clumsy from lack of practise. 'What I did on this night was only simply the duty of any man.'

No one mentioned Herschel Grynszpan.

◄о►

After Anny's death in 1987, Max spent the remainder of his lonely retirement at their home, with his memories, Anny's films and occasional visits from his ageing friends.

A housekeeper looked after him. Sometimes he would be interviewed. He enjoyed being interviewed, but only about boxing, or Anny, or Coca-Cola.

Maximilian Adolph Otto Siegfried Schmeling, boxer, born on 28 September 1905, died on 2 February 2005 at the age of 99. At his request, he was buried privately and simply beside Anny, his wife for 54 years.

◄o►

Magda Goebbels had three previous surnames. She was born Ritschel, but changed her name in honour of her stepfather, a Jew named Richard Friedländer, whom she adored, then again on her marriage to Günther Quandt. During her time as Magda Friedländer, she was involved in a passionate affair with Chaim Arlosoroff. This young man was an ardent Zionist, and there was talk of the two of them emigrating to Palestine together. At this time, Magda could be seen wearing a gold chain with a star-of-David pendant. The affair ended before Magda's marriage to Quandt.

Arlosoroff, having emigrated to Palestine, became very active politically, and was soon to become the *de facto* Zionist Foreign Minister. To this end, he travelled to Berlin only weeks after Hitler came to power, with a view to arranging the removal of Jewish assets to Palestine through the auspices of the Nazi government, later to become formalised in the Ha'avarah agreement. On this visit, he tried to contact his old flame Magda, now the wife of the Propaganda Minister, with a view to enlisting her husband's support in the scheme. She warned him off, telling him that a meeting would put them both in danger, and she demanded that he disappear. A few weeks later, while taking an evening stroll with his wife on the beach in Tel-Aviv, he was approached by two men, one of whom shot him in the head. His funeral was the most lavish ever seen in Palestine.

On 1 May 1945, shortly after Magda Goebbels had poisoned her six children, she and her husband Josef committed suicide in the rubble-filled courtyard above Hitler's bunker. Josef first shot his wife, then turned the pistol on himself. Their bodies were only partially cremated, as most of the available kerosene had been used to incinerate Hitler and Eva Braun some hours before.

◄o►

After a lengthy de-Nazification process, Friedrich Grimm resumed his law practice in West Germany, primarily to defend old party comrades. He died in 1959.

◄o►

Ten months after David Frankfurter assassinated Wilhelm Gustloff in Davos, Hitler and Gustloff's widow officiated at the launch of a *Strength Through Joy* steamship, on which German workers could take inexpensive holidays, named after the slain Party Comrade. During the war, the ship was assigned to the navy, first as a hospital ship and later as a troop transport.

On 30 January 1945, the twelfth anniversary of Hitler's coming to power, the RM Wilhelm Gustloff was transporting women and children from Danzig, escaping the inexorable Russian advance. The ship was crammed with over 10,000 people, almost all of whom were civilians, when it was torpedoed and sunk by a Russian submarine. All but a handful were lost in the icy Baltic, making this the greatest maritime disaster ever recorded.

Six months later, David Frankfurter was released from prison. He emigrated to Palestine and was later commissioned as an officer in the Israeli Defence Forces, joining in the struggle to liberate that country from its indigenous population. He died in 1982.

◄o►

What happened to the Grynszpans?

After the war, Herschel's father Zindel, his mother, Rivka, and brother Mordechai, recently released from active service in the Red Army, obtained permission to emigrate from the Soviet Union to the new State of Israel. Zindel testified as a prosecution witness against Adolf Eichmann, staring into the bland eyes of his son's interrogator, confirming that he had heard nothing from or about Herschel from the time he was taken into German custody. He spoke of the family's forcible removal to Poland in 1938, and how enraged his son had become, this rage leading to the murder of Ernst vom Rath. None of this had much to do with Adolf Eichmann, but the trial was less about that man than about the murderous regime he served and now unwillingly represented. For the first time, a large global audience became aware of the true horrors of the Nazi empire. This was the real intention of the trial, made explicit by the Israeli Prime

Minister, David Ben-Gurion. Zindel told people that he was pleased when Eichmann was executed.

In 1942, Zindel's brother Abraham was transported from Toulouse to the Warsaw ghetto and then to Auschwitz, where he died. Abraham's wife Chava was sent to Gurs, a camp originally designed to shelter Republican refugees escaping the war in Spain. Chava managed to survive the war. In 1945, she returned to Paris, married another tailor and re-opened her shop, renaming it *Maison du Tailleur*.

Herschel's mother, Rivka, died in Israel in 1963. I have found no record of his uncles Solomon or Wolf after the beginning of the war.

◄○►

Herschel's fate

In 2016 a photograph appeared in British newspapers purporting to be of Herschel Grynszpan. It was taken in 1946, at an anti-British demonstration against the UK's policies restricting immigration into Palestine. Facial recognition experts testified to a significant likelihood that the photograph was indeed of Herschel. Yet, if so, many questions would have to be answered.

What would have prevented Herschel from making his survival known? Would he not have tried to contact relatives? Would he not have welcomed some renewed press interest in himself? Would he not have wished to tell his story? After all, he had throughout craved publicity and acceptance.

In truth, no one really knows exactly what happened

to him. The Nazis, usually punctilious about record keeping, seem to have been less so regarding Herschel, especially after 1942. His trial was never cancelled, merely postponed indefinitely. Early post-war reports of his survival included accounts of him working in a garage in Lyon under a new name, or moving to the south of France. These sightings have persisted, but have never been verified. It seems reasonable to assume that Herschel Grynszpan was executed when the trial against him collapsed. In the aftermath of Stalingrad, and the immense military reverses which followed, the German government had other things to worry about. Herschel was declared officially dead by a German court in 1960, the date of his death being listed as 8 May 1945, the day the war in Europe ended. Many other untraced deaths were similarly dated.

Despite his deed, he is not much celebrated today, except in Israel. No street is named after him, no statue erected. He is less well known than Max Schmeling, certainly less well known than Joe Louis, who was perhaps the most genuine champion of the three.

The deep tragedy which surrounds this story still resonates. Anti-Semitism continues, as does its sister, Islamophobia. The widespread conflation of fact and fiction feeds nationalist delusions, bringing about division, enmity and violence. A swelling river of refugees from hunger, war, torture, and genocide flows as a reminder of that time, and perhaps as a harbinger of darker times looming ahead.

AUTHOR'S NOTE

A particular date in German history

Before the destruction of New York's World Trade Center, most Europeans would have abbreviated 11th September as Eleven-Nine; the sensible habit of arranging dates from the smallest unit to the largest being common on the Eastern shores of the Atlantic. The other Nine-Eleven, 9 November, is also a thought-provoking date, especially in German history. Of course one could reasonably argue that any particular date is equally connected to interesting events, since one three-hundred-sixty-fifth of everything that has ever happened would have occurred on any particular day (you will note here that I ignore the 29 February, on which date nothing has ever happened except by mistake, being intended for 1 March).

It was in Germany in the 20th Century that the 9th of November regularly collided with history. In 1918 the Kaiser abdicated; five years later the failed Munich Beer Hall Putsch brought Adolf Hitler to the attention of his countrymen (although he was actually Austrian at the time); and in 1989 the Berlin Wall came down. But the hinge of this particular story is the 9 November 1938, in Berlin, where the first chapter of this novel began.

◄o►

A novel, even one which is based on real people and real events – a 'non-fiction novel', as Truman Capote referred to his *In Cold Blood* – has nevertheless to filter actual events to accommodate the needs of the narrative. In many cases, this can be achieved by compression, or by inconsequential alterations to the chronology of events, or by conflating several characters into one. In *Champion*, almost everything depicted actually happened, especially the events which seem most improbable. It is much more difficult to discover what characters may have said at dinner, what they ate, or how they filled the relentless everyday repetitions of their lives.

The needs of a novel sometime demand jettisoning events and characters that are less important to the story, whose inclusion would distract the reader from its core trajectory. There are several examples of such exclusions in *Champion*. I have conflated the roles of Herschel's antagonists into one person, Josef Goebbels, aided and supported by another, Friedrich Grimm. These two did play an important role in Herschel's history, but there were many others. For example, Herschel's extradition to Germany was accomplished not by Grimm, but by the German Foreign Office, headed by Joachim von Ribbentrop. Adding him to the cast of characters would have served no dramatic purpose. Another example: the Gestapo made regular reports about Grynszpan to Reinhard Heydrich, head of the Security Service, as well as to Josef Goebbels. However, including such reports here would have cluttered the tale. Similarly, Herschel's French defence team included other lawyers, too many to be mentioned without confusion. Their roles have been compressed into the efforts of Herschel's chief defender, Vincent Moro-Giafferi, aided by two Jewish lawyers.

The parts of the story which concern Max Schmeling and Joe Louis are treated similarly. Joe Louis had three principal managers/trainers in his corner, but I have focused primarily on Mike Jacobs, the promoter, and to a lesser extent, John Roxborough, Joe's trainer. Very little mention has been made of Jack Blackburn in my novel, as it would not have made much difference to the story (but I admit that this omission might disappoint those who know more about Louis than I do), and would create a crowd in the corner.

Here are some other fluctuations:

Max Schmeling had actually met Adolf Hitler several times before his victory over Joe Louis, but the novel urged me to focus on the meeting following Max's triumphal homecoming. Recounting any previous meetings, while more truthful historically, would have diluted Max's excitement;

Schmeling's wartime activity of promoting boxing competitions between the Wehrmacht and SS is nowhere documented in detail. The single source of this information comes from Curzio Malaparte's novel-shaped account of his own wartime journalistic experiences, *Kaputt*. There may be some supportive or contradictory accounts in German sources (if there are, I have not found them), and Hans Frank's diaries allude to such a meeting, but Malaparte's disclosure helped me to bring the novel together;

Herschel was sometimes moved from Sachsenhausen to other prison locations in Germany, but such moves are not particularly germane to the thrust of the story. It is known that he was interrogated by Eichmann at least once, but not whether Eichmann interrogated him at the end. Similarly, my account of his death is plausible, but conjectural. His relationship with SS-Sergeant Schultz is representative of several accounts of Jewish prisoners being treated as 'pets' by their jailers;

The Soviets did indeed move many Jews from Eastern Poland to the USSR in 1939–40. It is reported that by doing so, Stalin capriciously managed to save over one million lives. However, most were not as fortunate as Zindel and Rivka Grynszpan. The bulk were sent to labour camps, where many died. However, many more Jews survived this relocation than those who remained in Poland to face the Nazi *Einsatzgruppen* and the death camps;

We know very little about the death of Uncle Abraham Grynszpan, other than that it occurred in Auschwitz-Birkenau. For the purposes of this novel, I have placed him in Warsaw between his arrest in Paris and his transportation to Auschwitz. I am reliably informed that this is feasible, if fairly uncommon; that most Parisian *ostjuden* had been sent directly to Auschwitz. It was important for the story for Max to see him, and for him to see Max, but that neither recognise the other. That Max visited the Warsaw ghetto with Hans Frank and Malaparte is documented in *Kaputt*.

There are several similar changes or elisions throughout.

I hope that notwithstanding these omissions, compressions and assumptions, I have told this remarkable story honestly, and have done little violence to what actually happened.

SOURCES

There are several reputable histories and biographies of the characters, agreeing in some respects, diverging in others. The main sources for material about Herschel came from Gerald Schwab's 1990 book *The Day the Holocaust Began,* Jonathan Kirsch's *The Short Strange Life of Herschel Grynszpan* (2013), and Armin Fuhrer's *Herschel,* published in German (also in 2013).

Less material is available about Max Schmeling, beyond boxing histories and sports books. The two principal sources were Max's own (rather sketchy) *Max Schmeling, An Autobiography,* published in English in 1998, from a denser German version published in 1977. In neither is there any mention of Max's role in the lives of the Lewin children. However, this episode is well document on web-based sources, especially those covering the death of Henri Lewin in 2008. Dorothea Friedrich's 2001 book, *Max Schmeling und Anny Ondra* was also consulted.

There is much written about Joe Louis and the two fights he had with Max. Patrick Myler's *Ring of Hate* (2005), offers much background to the two fights and discusses both boxers in the context of their times. Randy Roberts' *Joe Louis* (2010) fills in much of the story. Both fights can be viewed on YouTube.

Curzio Malaparte's *Kaputt* (2005), is a valuable source of information about Hans Frank and his meeting with Schmeling.

ACKNOWLEDGEMENTS

I am grateful for the invaluable encouragement and advice I received from Dominic Power. He helped me find a consistent tone of voice.

Lucie Skilton has done a wonderful job as Editor. Her insight, advice and expertise helped me to develop this book in subtle and less subtle ways, enriching it.

I am also beholden to Angelica Kroeger, who helped me with German translations.

For all those who read early drafts, I am ever grateful.

Stephen Deutsch